The Original's Return

DAVID WATKINS

Copyright © 2014 David Watkins
All Rights Reserved
No part of this novel or any of its contents may be reproduced, copied, modified or adapted, without the prior written consent of the author. Any similarity to persons, either living or deceased, is entirely coincidental.

ISBN: 1499280297
ISBN-13: 978-1499280296

For Tinú

Part One: Devon

Monday

Chapter 1

1

What the hell is that noise?

Jack stopped running and took out one headphone. He looked around, his head torch picking out trees and shrubs around him. The night was beginning to give way to a murky dawn, but it was taking its time. The noise came again: a high pitched whining.

Where's the dog?

Jack looked around. Rain landed on his face, cold and hard. The wind made him shiver; this really wasn't the best start to a day he'd ever had. He bent his leg behind him, stretching his muscles as he stood looking for Ginny. In his left ear, Bruce Springsteen sang about better times with a girl called Mary on the banks of a river. No other sound reached him.

The whining resumed suddenly, followed by lots of barking. Jack swivelled, until he was facing some bushes. Slowly, he walked forward pushing the branches out of the way. He started to call for the dog, but something made him stop: they had been running together in the woods for nearly three years now – surely nothing would spook her?

Light from the head torch appeared weaker now, a tiny white circle in the gloom. The branches swished back into place, covering his tracks. He was in a large clearing, trees dotted around the circumference like soldiers on parade. Jack snorted; he ran alongside this clearing every day and had not paid it any attention. If he had run on another fifty yards, he wouldn't have had to come through the bushes.

There she was, lying on her belly on the other side of the clearing, looking straight at him. She whined again when she saw him, a noise he'd not heard her make before. Even at this distance, he could see the fur raised on the back of her head. He stepped forward and she immediately stood and started barking hysterically at him.

He stopped. She growled.

"Ginny?"

She wagged her tail once then resumed growling.

"Okay, girl, it's alright." The rain came harder then, cold needle pricks on his face. Bruce had moved on to singing about a crush, a song he had always hated.

"Come on, girl."

She growled at him again.

"Gins, come on." He reached into his pocket for her lead, but it wasn't there. *Left it in the car.* "Ginny, come here girl." Jack whistled, two notes, the second longer and lower pitched than the first. Ginny didn't move. Jack looked at his watch.

6:45 a.m.

For God's sake. He had to leave for work in half an hour.

Jack started to run across the clearing. Ginny immediately started barking again, far more aggressively than he had ever heard her before. He ran a little faster, hoping to either force her to move, or to catch her before she did. He wasn't too bothered either way.

He was halfway across the clearing when he saw the hole. *Rabbits?* The thought was half formed in his head when the ground started to sag under his feet. He didn't even have time to swear before the earth gave way and he was falling into darkness.

2

Jack opened his eyes and blinked as rain water hit him. He turned his head slightly and tried to think. He could move his head so that had to be a good sign. High above he could see the hole he had fallen through and he could faintly hear Ginny doing the barking and whining combination. He could also hear the faint strains of music from his mp3 player.

He moved his left hand towards his pocket, surprised at the fact that the movement was not only possible but didn't hurt at all. He slipped his phone out and reached up to dial. The phone case was cracked all down one side, the screen smashed beyond repair and the keypad clung on by just one wire.

What now?

His phone had been an extravagant birthday present to himself just a month ago. It was the latest smartphone with all sorts of bells and whistles but now it was incapable of doing the thing he *really* needed it to do. His considerably cheaper mp3 player – he preferred the sound from that over the sound from the phone - still worked though, which was no comfort whatsoever.

He was contemplating the unfairness of all this when his mind registered the huge spear sticking through the middle of his chest.

3

There was no pain. As he stared at the thing sticking out of his chest, he kept thinking *it doesn't hurt.* He looked more closely at the spear, taking in details: red top with a streak running down it; a small lump of tissue balancing precariously on the tip; lumps of dirt scattered all over it in a way that would make Jackson Pollock proud, and a dull white reflecting the torchlight. He breathed a sigh of relief that the torch still worked – it would be very, very dark in here without it.

Not a spear then.

A bone.

Jack shuddered and retched to the side. *Impaled by a bone, but no pain.* He guessed that the bone had a diameter of around two inches and arched to a height of about a foot above him. If it was arched then it had to be a rib.

He felt his chest where the bone was sticking out and lifted his hands. The torch light showed him what he was beginning to suspect: no blood. He reached underneath him, arching his back and felt the base of the bone. It definitely was sticking through him. *Jesus.*

Whining from above forced him to concentrate. Ginny was up there alone. How much time had gone by? Was he being missed yet? Katie worried if he was five minutes late home from work so she'd be terrified by now. He lifted an earphone and heard Bruce still going strong. *Not that long then.*

He raised his head a little and tried to look around. As he turned his head, faint torchlight bounced off the walls. He could make out mud, rock and what looked like a tunnel running off approximately twenty feet to his left.

He pushed his hand underneath him and lifted tentatively. His torso raised easily and the bone came with him. Jack lay back down, took a deep breath and sat up. His legs fell away from him and he realised he was sitting on a ledge of some kind. The floor lay four, maybe five feet below him. The bone was still sticking through him and without thinking, he pulled it forward. It came through him with a wet squelch.

No pain.

He looked at it for a second and threw it to one side. Bile rose in his throat and he threw up over the cave floor. Still perched on the ledge he looked down at the hole in his chest. His clothes were ripped in an almost perfect circle and they were stained with blood, but his skin shone pale in the torchlight.

Skin.

No cut in his chest, no hole, no wound.

No pain.

Jack was sick again: shock was beginning to make it through his weird calm. He looked up at the hole in the cave roof. Ginny was still there, still barking, still whining. *What could she smell? What the hell was this place?*

Jack jumped off the ledge and landed lightly on his feet beside a slab of stone roughly eight foot long by five wide. It was in the exact centre of the cave. On the top were more bones, most crushed where Jack had fallen on them. If he had run a little further before the floor gave way, he would have missed it completely.

And I would be dead.

Jack knew that with utter certainty: something weird was going on in this cave, but it was good weird because he was still alive. *Alive doesn't quite cover it though – I'm not hurt.*

At all.

He shuddered, a cold chill running down his back. He looked at the bones again, but could tell nothing from them. What sort of creature had it once been? He had no idea, beyond that it had been enormous. There didn't appear to be a skull, unless he had crushed it when he landed. The other ribs had fallen away from the spine when he landed, saving him from multiple piercings. He could feel bile rising again and swallowed it down. He couldn't process what had happened, couldn't dwell on *how* he was still alive. *There are more pressing problems here Jack, like how the hell am I going to get out of here?*

He explored the cave further. It was a large round space with a smooth stone floor. The walls were also stone up to a few feet but it varied around the room and ran to mud the rest of the way to the ceiling. Piles of rubble lined the perimeter of the room.

Something was bugging Jack, but he couldn't put his finger on it. He looked around the walls again, but it kept eluding him. He stopped, facing the black hole of the tunnel again. *One more step closer, go on, I dare you.* The torchlight didn't make a dent in the dark. Another shiver went down his spine.

Jack turned back towards the stone slab. Something in his peripheral vision caught his attention and he walked closer. Hunching down, he scraped some mud away from the base of the slab and saw carvings in the stone. He scraped more vigorously and then fell back quickly.

The carving in front of him was of a man sitting cross-legged. In one hand he was brandishing a horned snake and in the other, he held a large ornate ring with a similar ring around his neck. Huge horns protruded from each side of his head.

4

Jack stood staring at the carving, shaking. He was struggling with what he was looking at, every rational fibre of his being screaming to get away. Was Ginny barking and so nervous because he had found an underground lair of someone who worshipped the Devil? The very idea was nonsense, wasn't it?

But you are alive when you should be dead.

"Hello, anyone there? You alright?"

The shout made him jump, literally, in the air. He looked up. A figure was silhouetted against the brightening sky.

"Hello?" Jack shouted back, adding an unnecessary: "I'm down here!"

"You alright?" The voice shouted again. *Who is this idiot?* Something in the timbre sounded familiar though.

"Terry? Is that you?"

"Yep. Who's that?"

Terry was an old man who ran his four dogs round the woods at least three times a day. Jack had no idea how old he was, but the rumour in the village was that he was in his seventies despite looking far younger.

"It's Jack, Terry. I'm stuck." *Understatement of the year.*

"How did you get down there?"

"I fell, but I think I'm alright – I can't get out though. Can you help? Ring someone on your mobile."

Even as he said it, Jack knew he was being optimistic.

"I ain't got one of they, Jack. I'll go get someone for you though. I'll take your dog wi' me."

Without another word, he was gone. *Jesus, don't leave me.* He looked at the altar again. The grinning horned figure smiled directly at him and Jack felt goose bumps rise on his arms. He backed away slowly, keeping the figure in sight all the way.

The room suddenly got darker and Jack realised that he was walking into the tunnel backwards. He spun quickly and light finally penetrated the gloom. Cobwebs hung from every conceivable angle and wall and stretched back as far as he could see.

The walls were pockmarked with tiny holes and from one of these Jack saw a thick black leg come out. Then another and another, until the biggest spider he'd ever seen sat on the wall looking at him. The spider was at least six inches across without counting its legs. Out of the other holes came more spiders until the wall was a seething dark mass, like a wave in a storm.

Jack screamed and fled back into the cave. He brushed at his clothes and rubbed his hair, feeling a million legs walk on him though none did. The spiders stayed in the corridor but he felt like they were watching him. He realised what was bugging him about the main cave. There were no cobwebs anywhere in it.

Not one.

5

Jack stood half way between the altar and the entrance to the spider infested passage. He wasn't comfortable with having his back to the engraved slab of stone, but he sure as hell wasn't going to have his back to all those spiders. He could see the black mass of them every time his torch played over the entrance.

He had never heard of so many spiders in one place before. There was that two hundred foot web they'd found in Texas (teaching a bunch of fourteen year olds did have some uses after all) but this was something else. He resisted the urge to scratch, knowing if he did he might never stop. The spiders were not coming into the cave, so he was clear of them, but God…

The silence was oppressive, lying on him like a heavy blanket. He plugged Bruce back in, only to find that the album had finished. As mighty an album as it was he needed something more cheerful and uplifting. He looked through the albums and settled on Led Zeppelin. Crunching guitars and power chords filled the space between his ears. *Perfect!*

He kept glancing up, but could see nothing but the opening up to the sky. Every couple of seconds or so he looked over his shoulder at the altar, but it remained solidly in place. *Of course it would – it's made of stone. Something might have been sacrificed on it, but it was still stone. Stone doesn't move of its own accord.*

And men don't survive a thirty foot fall onto a large bone either.

Jack decided to stop thinking: it was just better that way. He started to sing loudly and badly to the music instead. *Help was on the way*, he told himself. Terry would come through for him: he would soon be home with a cup of tea and be able to laugh at this whole situation.

That bone didn't go through me, it was the angle I was looking at it. It just helped break my fall and saved me.

He was beginning to feel better. He felt strong and could feel his panic about the spiders slipping away to be replaced with boredom. He could smell the flowers from outside, the trees and the pungent aroma of fox droppings. It smelt like a beautiful day out there and it seemed to have stopped raining. *Yep, things were going to be just fine.*

That thought formed whole in his mind as the torch died, plunging him into darkness.

6

His eyes became used to the dark very quickly. The ray of light from above helped, but he could still see the two focal points of the room. He breathed a sigh of relief as he could make out the opening to the passage, which seemed to undulate like the sea at night. Yesterday he would not have believed that he would be pleased to see such a horrible sight, but yesterday was a lifetime ago.

Over the music he heard a soft thump, thump. He grinned: the air ambulance was coming. Underneath the sound of the rotors he could make out sirens getting closer. He pictured them stopping at the gates to the woods, opening them and driving the fire engines through. It would be exciting for people watching, and even though the woods were a mile away from the village, a crowd would have gathered by now. This was a popular walking spot and news of his predicament would have spread.

Switching the music off, he glanced back at the altar. The horned man glared at him as he came to a decision. He ripped his jacket and t-shirt from the hole down and worked a few of the smaller holes bigger. *Nothing went through there, nope, it just ripped as I fell.*

"Mr Stadler?"

A voice from above, loud and authoritative.

"I'm here."

"Hi, I'm John, I'm from the fire service and we're going to get you out. Are you hurt?"

"No. Just a few bruises I think. I can walk."

"Excellent. Give us a few minutes and we'll have a harness rigged up to get you out."

"I'm not going anywhere."

7

Jack wasn't sure how long it took, but it was more than a couple of minutes before a man winched down.

"John?"

"No, I'm Bill. John's up top. Doesn't like to get his hands dirty. Bloody dark down here isn't it?"

Jack looked around the cave, taking in the corridor, mounds of rubble and the creepy altar. "Yeah. My torch died a while back."

"OK, no worries Jack, we'll soon have you out of here. I'm going to tie you onto this harness and then we get lifted out, OK?"

Jack nodded and stood closer to Bill than he had been to his wife in weeks. Bill strapped him onto the harness and then said "Hold on!"

He pressed a button on the radio strapped into his jacket and said "OK, lift away."

The rope tightened and they were in the air. Jack took one last look at the passageway, but couldn't see any spiders there. Before he could really think about that, fresh air blasted through his hair and he had to squint against the bright sunshine.

"It was raining when I left the house," Jack said.

"What?"

"Nothing."

The harness was lowered to the ground and two men ran over to unstrap them both. Another man in a green paramedic's uniform started bombarding Jack with questions and he answered them. No, he wasn't hurt. No, he wasn't taking any medication. Yes, he was in a reasonably healthy state.

The clearing had a fire engine in it, sitting a good thirty yards away from the hole. The air ambulance had landed back on the path.

"You might want to move the fire engine," Jack said.

"Ground's solid," Bill said. "It doesn't even get remotely dodgy until by the hole. You were dead unlucky to fall through that."

Dead unlucky. *That would be about right.* But he felt great. The freshness of the air was almost overpowering: he could smell everything from the wild garlic growing along the path through to the fox and deer scent markings back in the tree lines. A crowd of people were at the top of the hill watching: some waved when they saw him looking. A TV crew filmed the general scene whilst a reporter spoke about the lucky escape. Someone was missing and Jack felt panic rise.

"Where's my wife? Where's Katie?"

Bill looked at Jack in surprise. "Sorry, Mr Stadler, I thought you'd been told."

"Told what?"

"When she heard that you'd had an accident her waters broke. She's gone into labour."

Chapter 2

1

The drive to the hospital was interminable. The paramedic took his blood pressure (normal to a little low) and monitored his heart rate. She kept prodding Jack and saying, "Does this hurt?"

Jack told the truth: nothing hurt, he felt great. She was mystified and kept asking the questions. Had he been unconscious? Any pain in his back or legs? What day was it? After half an hour, they arrived at Barnstaple hospital and Jack leapt out of the ambulance, ignoring any protestations. Two doctors were waiting for him in the bay.

"Mr Stadler? I'm Doctor Baxter. Could you come this way please? We need to examine you," the younger and infinitely better looking one said. The other one took a deep drag on a cigarette.

"I need to see my wife," Jack said. "Then you can examine me all you like."

"But we need to make-"

"I'm fine. Look, I'm not hurt, I've been walking around for hours so I'd know if anything was wrong."

"Adrenaline does funny things to a person."

"I've heard that," Jack said. "But really I just need to see Katie."

Baxter looked at his colleague who nodded, stubbing his cigarette on the grill of the bin next to him. The younger man sighed. "OK, but as soon as the baby is born, I want to examine you fully."

"No problem."

Jack started to run towards the maternity unit. He and Katie had been there for two scans, so he knew where he was going. His feet pounded the floors whilst the ripped t-shirt and jacket made him look like a tramp after an eventful Friday night. He increased his speed, flying past different departments. The maternity unit was in a separate building so he ran into fresh air and across a small car park.

When he stopped at reception, he wasn't out of breath at all. The receptionist eyed him up and down with a sneer on her face.

"I need to see Katie Stadler."

"And you are?"

"Her husband."

"Oh." The receptionists' face changed for the better. "You fell down a hole."

That's not something you expect to hear every day. "Yes. Please, I need to see my wife."

"Follow me, Mr Stadler. She's in room four." The receptionist led the way down a stark white corridor. She stopped outside a plain wooden door but didn't knock. "I'll get you some scrubs. You look a bit of a mess."

Jack could hear panting and groaning from the other side, but couldn't argue with the woman. She opened a cupboard he hadn't noticed and gave him a green tunic. He took his clothes off, momentarily perplexed by the admiring look she gave him, and slipped the tunic on. She knocked on the door.

"Come in!" a woman called, her voice muffled by the thick door.

"You can go in, Mr Stadler."

Jack walked into the room. A curtain hung just inside the door as an extra privacy measure and he pushed past it. The room was dominated by two features: the bed and a water bath. The bath was empty, but the sides were wet and shiny and small pools of water were gathering on the bottom of the bath. A large crane and harness were folded into the wall next to it. *Just how big do these women get?*

On the bed was Katie. She was lying on her back with her legs bent at the knees. She was holding a face mask over her mouth and nose. Clear plastic tubes ran away from the mask into a cylinder standing in a cupboard next to the bed. Two other women, both in green scrubs, stood looking between Katie's legs. All three looked up when Jack walked in.

Katie dropped the facemask to the bed and he rushed over and kissed her.

"You could have shaved."

He laughed. "Gas and air?"

"Yeah, it's shit."

"You've had a bath then." The birth plan, that they'd only completed a week ago, had requested a water birth. They'd seen a film clip where a woman had given birth in one and the baby had just popped out with no fuss. It had seemed easy.

"Yeah, that's shit too."

They both started to laugh but Katie gasped. "Another one."

The older woman spoke then: "Ok Katie, just let this one come. Try to breathe through it and use the gas and air."

Katie screamed then. Jack could feel the blood leaving his face and his earlier elation fading. "What's happening? What's wrong with her?"

"It's just a contraction," the younger midwife said. "She's doing really well."

Just a contraction? Jesus.

"I'm Ronnie," the younger one said. "This is Sue. We'll be looking after you today. Katie is five centimetres dilated, so we've got a way to go yet. I think the baby was waiting for you." Ronnie smiled and Jack felt some of the colour return to his face. Katie's breathing slowed to normal.

"At what point does she get a caesarean?"

Ronnie laughed. "Not for a long time, Jack. She's doing well, let's just let nature take its course and see what happens."

Katie clutched his hand and smiled at him.

"You fell down a hole," she said.

Twice in one day, Jack thought. *What are the odds of that?*

2

Katie's contractions came every four minutes like clockwork. Every time they arrived, Ronnie told her to breathe which didn't seem to help with the pain.

"Get me an epidural," Katie gasped.

"Are you sure?" Sue asked. "It's not on your birth plan."

Katie screamed as another contraction tore into her.

"She's sure," Jack said.

Sue left to call for an anaesthetist, and Ronnie made herself busy, looking at the various monitors that Katie was hooked up to. She left the room to get all the equipment that was needed for the epidural.

An hour later, the anaesthetist arrived. "Sorry it's taken so long, there was a pile up on the A377. I'm Greg, how are we doing in here today?"

On cue, a contraction arrived and Katie wailed. "Please, it hurts."

He spoke to Ronnie for a moment, a brief conversation that left Jack wishing he'd paid more attention to ER. Greg inspected all the equipment that Ronnie had got out and seemed satisfied.

"Ok, Katie – do you mind if I call you Katie – do you know about the dangers with epidurals?"

She groaned, face pale. "Yes, please just make the pain stop."

"Ok, there is a very small chance that –"

"I know. Please just get on with it."

Jack held Katie's hand and nodded at Greg. "Just do it, doc. We know."

Greg didn't bother to correct Jack, but he started preparing for the epidural with impressive speed. He spoke as he worked: "An epidural is an injection into the spine and the drug is like a liquid. It might not go to the right place. There is a very small chance that you will be either temporarily or permanently paralysed as a result. Please turn onto your side."

Jack helped Katie roll over gently. Greg lifted the back of her gown. "You might feel a small scratch and then it will go cold."

Seconds later it was done. "Is that better Katie?"

She nodded. "I can't feel anything."

Greg produced an ice cube and started to run it up her back and legs, reminding Jack of an evening on their honeymoon. This didn't look like half as much fun. Katie didn't react at any point. "I think this will help Katie. It's a good epidural. I'll just wait for the next contraction and see what happens."

He didn't have to wait for long, and this time Katie didn't make a sound. "Excellent. Well good luck folks."

"Thank you." Jack thought he heard a pathetically huge level of gratitude in Katie's voice. As he left, she said "I'd do anything for you!"

Ronnie laughed, and Jack felt himself getting embarrassed. "Ok, now you've got the epidural in, we can add some hormones that will speed all this up. It won't be long now."

3

She was right. Baby Stadler was born two hours later at 5:05 pm. As Ronnie lifted the baby, the room became still. Jack could hear himself breathing. Katie's face drained of all colour and time stretched. Suddenly, the baby made a noise somewhere between a hiccup and a burp and started crying. The tension dissipated instantly and everyone started to smile. Jack cut the cord, taking two goes to cut through the spongy mass. Ronnie put the baby straight on Katie where he latched on and started feeding.

"That's excellent," Ronnie said. "Congratulations!"

Jack stared at the baby feeding from his mother. He was purple and covered in bits of blood and thick mucus. He looked so small and frail. Tiny fingers grasped at the air, opening and closing on nothing. The top of his head pulsed as he breathed in and out and Ronnie covered his head with a small white hat. *Beautiful.* Jack swallowed hard as his eyes welled up. Katie was crying as she looked at him.

"He's perfect."

"Yep, just like his mum." He kissed her head, tasting salty sweat. Ronnie wheeled a see through cot next to the bed.

"We'll come and weigh him later and give him a bit of a cleanup." She left the room quietly.

"What a day," Jack said.

"A perfect day. You're ok and we have a son." She squeezed his hand. "You can tell me about it later." The baby's head lolled to one side, his eyes closed in blissful sleep. Katie suddenly looked exhausted.

"Get some rest, babe." He lifted the baby and put him in the cot. "I'll go phone your mum."

"Great, thanks Jack. I love you."

"I love you too." He kissed her forehead again and walked to the door. She was already asleep. He crept back into the room, found her bag and took her mobile out. He would have to get his fixed, but he'd worry about that later. He crept out of the room and went to phone the world.

4

Jack got home just before nine pm. He had phoned everyone he could think of and had managed not to cry when he told them about his son. Katie had been advised to stay in overnight as her epidural had left her left leg numb. Nothing to worry about, according to Sue. Jack had waited for as long as possible, then left them both sleeping on the maternity ward.

Ginny barked when he opened the door. She was curled up on her bed, big brown eyes looking sad at being left on her own so long. Terry had dropped her off whilst he phoned the emergency services. He also got a little more than he bargained for as Katie's waters broke, but Jack would make it up to him with a pint next time he saw him. Jack bent to stroke Ginny, but she growled a warning at him.

"It's alright girl," he said, reaching to stroke her again. This time she bared her teeth, a gesture that Jack knew meant *back away now*. He stood up and left her alone. *Probably miffed at her crap day.*

He opened a bottle of red wine and poured a large glass for himself. He had contemplated ringing the lads and wetting the baby's head, but the truth was that he was exhausted. The last time a baby had been born, the lads (all six of them) had gone on a massive bender. The night out had involved the top shelf at The Kings Arms. Some of the drinks came out of bottles that probably had last been opened twenty years ago. The night ended with tequila, which was never a good way to *start* a night, let alone end it. John, who was the new dad, had been so ill the next morning that he was sick twice on the drive to the hospital. His wife, Karen, had got out of bed to feed their baby, so John got in. He'd then fallen asleep and Karen had taken the baby for a nappy change, just as the doctors did their morning rounds.

The memory made Jack smile, but also confirmed that he had made the right decision. Now that the adrenaline had left him, tiredness and anxiety had taken over.

"Ah shit!" *I forgot to see that doctor.*

He stripped off in the bathroom, taking a large glug of wine as he turned the shower on. Moonlight streamed through the window – *a great advantage of living in the country, you can see by the light of the moon and stars* – as he inspected his body. There were no marks anywhere on him, not even a scratch where the bone had been.

No bullshit, Jack, that bone went through you.

Jack downed his wine with a shaking hand. He got in the shower and wondered what the hell had happened to him.

5

The shower was almost scalding temperature, but it felt good. He washed then stood under the spray for a very long time. Once dried, he pulled on a thick towelling robe and went back downstairs. He opened the back door to let Ginny out, but she stayed on her bed almost glaring at him.

"Please yourself." He left the door open and poured another large glass of wine. The crystal glass felt heavy in his hands, a far too generous wedding present from a wine loving friend of theirs. He strolled through to the living room and picked up his guitar.

When year nine were pissing him off and his boss was being a pain, his guitar calmed him down. Katie had bought it on a whim last Christmas, but it had been one of the best presents he had ever received. He played every day and had improved hugely since the first hesitant days.

Still, Hendrix is not in danger of losing his greatest guitarist ever status just yet. Jack started strumming, losing himself in the progression of chords. At some point he practised a couple of other songs, but he had drunk most of the bottle of wine so he was kind of hazy on exactly what he had done because somehow it was morning and he was lying naked on the floor of the living room.

Tuesday

Chapter 3

1

He felt terrible. His head hurt and he was trembling. His dressing gown was on the sofa where he had sat last night so he pulled it on. He felt warmer and after a couple of seconds the trembling stopped. His wine glass lay empty on the coffee table, a dark red stain in the bottom the only evidence that it had been used last night.

His guitar lay in two pieces next to him. He swore for a couple of minutes before picking up the neck; the strings were the only thing connecting the two halves of guitar. A large scratch scarred the body through the veneer into the wood underneath. He put it in the wood pile next to his fire: the snap and crackle of burning wood being the only sound that it would make now. How had that happened? *Must have rolled over it in the night, snapping the neck.* Even as he thought it, Jack knew that it sounded impossible, but what else could have happened?

Annoyed with himself for being so stupid, Jack went to the kitchen. The house was cold and he saw why. The back door was wide open. He reached to close it and his hand touched something sticky. Black mud caked the handle and his hand.

Great. Just great.

He collected some kitchen towel and wiped the handle clean, only then realising that the dog's basket was empty. Jack swore again. He went into the garden, calling her name and whistling. Jack climbed the steps that led out of the shade of the house and up to the flat lawn of the garden. The sun was high in the sky and it was warmer outside than in. The garden was bounded by three thick, well established but low hedges and beyond the hedge at the back fields rolled into the distance. Normally there were sheep in the field, but not today.

He found Ginny under a hedge. She was trembling. A large cut meandered across her chest, and she had blood around her mouth. She bared her teeth at him again and started barking.

"Hey Gins." The barking grew more frenzied. "Gins!" She was on her feet now, alternating barks and snarls. Jack backed off and went back the house. *What am I going to do?*

He was saved from answering that question by a knock at the door.

2

He opened the door to see Frank Cooper standing there with his cap in his hands. Frank was the farmer who owned the land behind Jack's house and it had amused both Jack and Katie to see that he always wore a flat cap. Right now, though, Frank wore a very stern expression on his miserable face.

"Hey, Frank, what's up?"

"Morn' Jack. I were wondering if you 'eard or saw anything las' nigh'."

"Last night? Why what's happened?"

"One of me sheep been killed. Found 'er this morn'."

"Jesus, Frank."

"She's been taken apart by a dog, Jack. Ripped 'er throat out."

Jack stared at Frank in horror. Dogs were known to attack sheep but Jack hadn't heard of it actually happening here: people kept their dogs on leads if sheep were around. *Ginny. Oh, God.*

"I'm really sorry Frank."

"Someone say they 'eard a dog barking las' nigh'." He paused, adjusting his cap. "Your dog."

"What, Ginny? She wouldn't hurt a fly!" Jack said. "I've seen her try to catch a few, but never actually succeed." He knew he was babbling now. "Besides she was in all night."

"In all nigh'?"

"Yeah, Katie had the baby." God, Katie – she would be wondering just where the hell he was.

"Good f'you Jack. You must be pleased." There was that famous Devon understatement.

"Yeah, I've got to go actually, I'm late to see her."

"Sure, sure. I'll see you later then." Frank turned to leave but thought better of it. "Jus' so we're clear Jack, I see your dog on my land, I'll shoot 'er."

"What?" Jack's turn to pause. Had he heard that? "Frank? Do you think my dog did this, because I can assure you-"

"Assure me nothing, *boy*, I lost a sheep to a dog. You got a dog, I just sayin'."

"Jesus Christ Frank. Don't you dare come to my house and threaten my dog. You come near her and I will rip *your* head off. Is that clear enough for you?" Jack was now towering over the farmer, voice raised, but not shouting.

Frank did not take a step back, but regarded Jack with clear blue eyes. He nodded once. "It weren't no threat Jack."

He walked to the road and ambled back up the street. He looked like he hadn't a care in the world. Jack slammed the front door and shouted "Arsehole!"

He stormed through into the kitchen to find Ginny lying on her bed. She growled when he came in. He stared at her and growled back. *What are you doing Jack?* Ginny rolled over and exposed her white belly to him. Keeping eye contact, he knelt down and stroked her once. Her tail was flat between her legs and she was trembling again.

"What have you done girl?" he said. As he stroked her, he caught a glimpse of the time from the corner of his eye and panic set in.

3

One o'clock! Katie was going to kill him. He'd said he'd be there by nine. He ran upstairs and started to pull on the first clothes he saw. He spread some hair gel to hide the worst of the bed hair (*bed hair during that exchange with Frank, no wonder he wasn't scared*) and cleaned his teeth.

He sprinted out the door, pausing only to grab his keys and then he was in the car driving as fast as he could. The hospital was thirty five minutes away, but he made it in thirty. The latest Foo Fighters album blared out of the car speakers helping him force the pace. He parked in the first space he saw and sprinted through the car park, down to the maternity unit.

He had to be buzzed in, and ignored the sarcastic "she's been expecting you" from the receptionist. He walked down the corridor until he found the door with Katie's name written on a wipe clean whiteboard. She was sitting up on the bed, feeding the baby and when she saw him her face lit up with the biggest grin in the world.

Not in the doghouse.

"I'm so sorry."

"Nothing would make me upset with you today." She was looking at the baby and stroking his soft hair. "He's absolutely perfect Jack."

He sat in the chair next to the bed and took in the room for the first time. There were four beds in total, but two were empty. The other bed had a small woman who was holding a tiny baby like it was a fine china bowl. Her husband stood up, announced with a boom - and in terms that left nothing to the imagination - that he was going to the toilet. He was easily six foot six. *It takes all sorts.*

Jack lent over and kissed Katie on the mouth. "You look great."

"So do you. How are John and the boys?"

"I didn't go out last night." The words were out before he'd thought through the implications.

"Really? Why are you so late then?"

"I don't know. I drank some wine, played some tunes and then passed out on the living room floor." He decided not to tell her about the guitar. *Something else to add to the list of what could wait.*

"You must have been shattered. Adrenaline and everything."

"Yeah, I guess." *Christ, I'd almost forgotten all about that.* "It was a pretty eventful day."

"You were on the news."

"Spotlight?"

"No the national news. It was quite exciting, according to the nurses." A murmur from her breast made her pause. The baby had come off. "Shh, shh," she said. "Daddy's here."

The baby opened his eyes at her voice and just stared at her. "Do you want to hold him?"

"Of course." Jack took him, trying hard not to look like *he* was holding a fine china bowl.

"Support his neck."

"I know." The baby felt so light in his arms. He rested his head on Jack's shoulder and fell straight back to sleep. Jack couldn't help but smile and felt tears well in his eyes. He perched himself on the edge of Katie's bed.

"Do you want to talk about yesterday?"

"Not really. There's not much to tell." *Getting pretty good at this lying lark, Jack, be careful.* "The ground gave way and I fell in."

"The doctor said there's not a scratch on you."

"Doctor?"

"Yeah, Doctor Baxter. He came round this morning, hoping to examine you properly."

"Well, I'm sure I'll catch up with him at some point."

The older midwife from the day before came in then. "Afternoon, Mr Stadler."

"Jack, please." He remembered her name was Sue.

"Ok, Jack. How are you feeling today? Quite a day you had yesterday."

"I've had less eventful ones," he said with a rueful smile.

"So what about a name then?" Sue asked.

"Still happy?" Jack asked Katie.

"Yeah."

"Good. In that case, he's called Josh."

4

The day passed quickly. Josh slept for most of the afternoon, waking only to feed and for a terrifying nappy change. Katie talked Jack through it like she was some kind of instant expert.

Katie slept herself late afternoon and Jack took the moment to ask if Doctor Baxter was available. Five minutes later, he arrived at the maternity unit. He was even younger than Jack remembered, but that could be down to his clean-shaven fresh face. Jack stood as he walked in. Baxter stretched his hand out in greeting and they shook hands like old friends.

"Congratulations Mr Stadler."

"Please call me Jack. Sorry I didn't get back to you yesterday."

"No problem. We were rammed anyway: bad crash on the 377."

Baxter looked at the sleeping baby and wife and said: "Shall we go somewhere more private?"

He led Jack through the corridors to one of the empty maternity rooms. "Just as well it's quiet here today."

"What do you need from me?"

"Well first of all, I'd like to just do a general exam of you and make sure there's nothing damaged that adrenaline is hiding."

Jack nodded. "Ok, but I think I'm absolutely fine. Not even a bruise."

"That's great Jack, but not many people can walk after falling, what, fifteen feet?"

Jack didn't correct him. This could be awkward enough without explaining that he had fallen nearer thirty feet.

"And there's not a scratch on you. That's a miracle, Jack."

They moved to a bed, and Baxter asked Jack to get undressed whilst he got some things together. Jack stripped to his boxers and lay on the bed. Baxter returned with a stethoscope, blood pressure monitor, small wooden hammer and a range of syringes. He listened to Jack's heart for a minute, before attaching the blood pressure monitor.

"It's all good Jack. Pulse is normal, and so is your blood pressure." He asked Jack to cross his legs and arms and he tapped on various pressure points with the hammer. Satisfied, he picked up the syringe.

"I'd like to take some blood, send it off for some tests."

"Tests for what?"

"Jack, you should be in pieces after that fall but I can't even find a bruise. This might scratch a little."

Jack bit back a shout as the needle slid into his skin. *Scratch a little. Bloody doctors.*

"All done." Baxter said, removing the syringe. Jack started to get dressed, deliberately avoiding looking at the test tube full of blood.

"They won't find anything you know," Baxter said, as Jack pulled on his t-shirt. "They never do in these miracle cases. We've only had to send these results off for the last year: you're my first bona fide case."

"Miracle cases?"

"Yeah, sounds stupid doesn't it?" Baxter smiled. "As I said, there's not a mark on you and you should have at least some broken bones. Therefore, you count as a miracle – medical science can't explain why you're ok. Understand?"

Jack nodded, swallowing hard. *If they knew about the bone, that would make it more than a miracle.* "Who gets the blood?"

"Oh, just some central agency that does the testing. They're based in Kent, I believe. Don't worry, it's all perfectly safe and legal. Your personal records are only accessed if they find something."

"What happens then?"

"I'm not sure: like I say, you're my first miracle. I suppose they put in a request to get more of your blood." He produced a clipboard with a form on it.

"Let me guess, I have to sign?"

"Yeah. It gives consent for the tests to be done, and for you to be contacted if anything is found. You don't have to sign Jack. It's just a legal thing."

"It's not a problem." Jack took the pen from Baxter and signed the form.

5

Katie was advised to stay in another night and had been too tired to argue. Jack strolled back to the car alone, utterly depressed at leaving his is wife and son behind. He held on to the memory of them both asleep: Katie in her too small hospital bed and the baby in his cot. He had been lying on his back, legs and arms drawn into his body and looking a lot like a frog in a white baby grow. The thought made him smile, and he chuckled to himself at how quickly his emotions were changing now: depression to elation in less than a second.

Jack drove home alone for the second night running. The Foo Fighters were a little loud given how tired he felt, so he switched to Lambchop. Kurt Wagner's voice totally fitted Jack's mellow, relaxed mood. He was home by eight, and found two messages on the phone. The first was from John, asking for a night out to celebrate. The second was from Chris, another of the incomers, also asking for a night out.

Jack ate a piece of toast whilst listening to the messages. Ginny lay on her bed looking forlornly at him. She no longer had blood around her mouth, and the cut on her chest was already healing. *What did you do, girl?*

He felt guilty about not walking her that day, and decided to take her to the pub with him. He phoned John first and asked him to ring the others. They agreed on nine o'clock, so Jack went to get changed.

Not for the first time he reflected on the difference between his friends and Katie's. John had not asked anything about the fall or the baby: he knew that there was plenty of time for that conversation in far more convivial surroundings. Katie would have talked for half an hour, then gone out and done it all again.

He tied Ginny's lead to her and left, not even bothering to lock the doors behind him.

6

The Stars was small and far from cosy, but it served beer. The only room was dominated by the fifty-two inch plasma screen that always had sport on it regardless of the time of day. A smattering of tables filled the space between that and the actual bar itself. Two men sat on bar stools alternating looking at their pints and the screen. At the rear of the room was a pool table and John was already there racking up the balls. He waved and shouted that there was a drink already bought for Jack.

Sara, the landlady, gave Jack a kiss and poured him a pint. They chatted for a couple of minutes, then Jack went to the pool table. John clinked glasses with him, before breaking by hitting the balls as hard as he could. Nothing went down.

"Going to be a long game," he said.

Five minutes later, Chris arrived. He bought a drink before coming over.

"What do you get if you cross a baby with soldiers?" Chris said.

Jack shook his head as he bent to take his shot. John groaned and said: "Get it over with."

"Infantry." Chris started laughing but he had one of those infectious laughs that made everyone else smile. "It's the only decent one I could find about babies."

"Decent? Jesus, I'm glad you didn't tell the other ones."

"Did you know there's a whole website devoted to dead baby jokes?" Chris said, shaking his head. "I didn't bring any of those. Didn't seem right."

They all laughed again and raised their glasses. "What do you call a man who fell down a hole?" Chris said.

"Jack." The others all said at the same time.

Jack snorted beer out of his nose. "You heard about that?"

"Heard about it?" said Chris. "It was on the six o'clock news last night. I couldn't believe it."

"Yeah, cameras here and everything, mate. They even interviewed Terry," said John.

Jack potted the black and shook John's hand. "Drink?"

"Very kind of you Jack. I'll have JD and coke." Chris raised his glass in a mock salute.

Jack was relieved at the change of subject that no-one seemed to have noticed.

"Just kidding, man, tonight you don't pay." Chris sauntered over to the bar and started chatting to Sara and the other two locals. He returned with a tray loaded with spirits. He handed each of them a glass and said "Name yet?"

"Josh," Jack said with a shrug. "It seemed right."

"So, to Joshua," Chris said, raising his glass.

"No, just Josh. None of that religious crap for my kid thank you."

"Sorry. Ok, to Josh."

They clinked glasses again and downed the double Jack Daniels in one go. Following the comedy exaggerated gulps after the whisky had ripped the back of their throats out, Jack said, "Where does wetting a baby's head come from anyway?"

"I once worked with a bunch of guys, one of whom wasn't very bright," Chris said. "Anyway, this lad had his first kid and we took him out for beers. This is back in Surrey, years ago. I didn't have my kids then, so I just went along for the piss up."

"You do surprise us," John said.

"Well, while we were out, one of the boys told him that the phrase came from an old tradition where you passed water given to you by your closest friends on to the newborn's head."

There was silence as they took this in.

"So he went home, and his wife caught him standing over the baby's cot with his cock out. She managed to stop him just in time."

"That's not funny," John said.

"True though. The man who told him to do it was his brother in law." Years before, Chris had worked nights in a warehouse, a far cry from the financial manager he was now.

"You must know what it really means." Jack said to Chris.

"Well, some think it originates from baptisms. You know, the pouring of water over a kid's head." Chris, in addition to knowing more jokes than most, also had levels of trivia that bordered on the obscene. "No-one really knows when it started to mean getting lashed. Early 1900s maybe. Of course, to wet has been around as a phrase for drinking since-"

"Enough! I wish I hadn't asked. We going to play or what?"

The rest of the night passed in a blur. Jack explained about falling down the hole, but spent longer talking about the birth of Josh. *Right priority*. He was the last of the group to have children. John had two girls, Chris three boys – all under five.

They played pool several times before getting bored and seeing who could do the most outrageous shots; ordered pizza from the local take away – only condition was that Sara had some; drank more whisky and pints and then stumbled out of the pub at a ridiculous hour. Jack only just remembered to take Ginny with him.

7

They said their goodbyes outside the pub, with Jack promising that they would visit as soon as Katie was home. He walked down a small alley and into the churchyard that represented his route home. As soon as he stepped out of the street, silence and darkness enveloped him like an uncomfortable glove.

"It's dark girl," he said, more to break the silence than anything else. His eyes adjusted quickly and he bent down to let Ginny off her lead. "Just don't poo."

The church sat in the middle of the graveyard, impossibly ancient and imposing. Two paths led around the outside and he chose the bigger, right hand one as that had security lights. He took two steps left for every one forward, stumbling back on track every few paces. He chuckled to himself as he did so. *Too much beer*.

Just then, the clouds broke and the moon and stars came out. He stopped, the clarity of the night sky took his breath away. The moon was bright enough to light the whole churchyard and he could see the Milky Way.

"Wow."

Jack felt a twinge down his left hand side. His hand started trembling. He looked at it, raising his hand in front of his face. His skin was rippling, large waves running across his hand and disappearing into the arm of his coat.

"What the hell?"

It doesn't hurt.

He slowly raised his other hand only to confirm what he suspected: the skin was rippling there too. The ripples reached his face now, arriving with a wave of nausea that threatened to make him collapse. Jack looked wildly up and down the street. No-one in sight, which was not unusual at this time of night in Huntleigh. *Everyone tucked up safe in bed, which is probably a good thing.*

That thought galvanised Jack into action and he started to run. The nausea faded as adrenaline took over. Tarmac blurred beneath his feet as he ran the straightest route, straight down the middle of the road. Within a couple of seconds Jack was sprinting faster than he ever had before, heading for the only safe place he knew.

Home.

Wednesday

Chapter 4

1

Sergeant Peter Knowles opened the door to the medical research wing and was stopped by two soldiers. Their weapons were slung over their shoulders but this didn't worry him; he was expected. Knowles saluted. "Sergeant Knowles for Major Smith."

One of the guards consulted a list and inspected Knowles' ID card. Knowles bit back a tiny bit of frustration: the Major had sent a driver to his home on his day off ordering him to get to base immediately. Knowles lived alone - only his palimony payments for company, he liked to quip - and he had nothing planned for the day, but it still grated to be ordered to work and then made to wait.

Eventually the guard nodded and waved him through. Another armed man led the way. Knowles marched through the stern corridors. It was expected that people would march everywhere in the base, regardless of rank. The Brigadier thought it set the right tone.

The guard stopped outside a non-descript door and knocked twice. *A non-descript door in a non-descript building.* Knowles had not been in this building before, despite being on base for a month since returning from Ghanners.

"Come." The Major's voice was loud even through the door. *What does he want?*

Knowles opened the door and stepped inside. He shut the door then stood to attention in front of the Major's desk. He saluted again and said, "Sergeant Knowles reporting as ordered, sir."

"About time too."

Knowles kept his eyes straight ahead, jaw clenched.

"At ease, Sergeant." Knowles relaxed slightly, but remained standing. The Major didn't offer the only other chair in the room.

"Do you know what we do in here sergeant?"

"No, sir!"

"Good. Best not to ask too many questions young man."

"Yes, sir!" *Don't ask questions? It's cliché day from the pompous twat.*

"I need a team to handle a potentially delicate situation, Knowles, and your name came up."

"Sir?"

"I need you to choose your best men and have them follow orders without question. This is a delicate matter and nothing must go wrong. No media must learn of it, under any circumstances. Is that understood before we go any further?"

"Absolutely sir, you have my-"

"Cut the crap, Knowles. I need a team I can trust, I need it today and I need to know if that's you."

"You can count on me sir."

"Careful Knowles, you don't know what I'm about to ask you."

"No sir."

"Could you choose four men?"

"Yes sir. I would need to know what kind of op it was before I made my final selection." Knowles already knew who he would choose: Meyers; Carruthers; Scarlet; Jones.

"I need you to watch someone for me."

"Bodyguard duty, sir? With respect-"

"No, no. I wouldn't use a field man like yourself for anything like body guard." Smith leaned back in his chair and lifted a folder from the desk. He took a single photograph out of it and threw it to the desk.

"I need this man watched."

"Sir? Again, with respect, that's what the spooks do."

Smith laughed. "No, Knowles, MI5 do not need to know about this man. We need to know if he can help us."

Knowles frowned, looking at the photo of a young white man who clearly hadn't known the photo had been taken. It had the grainy look common to all CCTV images.

"What's he done?"

"It's not what he's done, Knowles, it's what he might do. I need you to watch him discreetly and intervene if necessary."

Intervene? In what?

"This might be the cushiest job you ever get sergeant. You watch this man for a month, maybe six weeks and then come home if nothing happens."

"And what might happen sir?"

"That is why you are watching, Knowles. We want to know everything there is to know about Jack Stadler."

2

An hour later, Knowles had assembled his team in a mission briefing room near their barracks. Carruthers wore his usual scowl, but Knowles knew that underneath the frown lay a man who had an unusually high intelligence for a grav. Scarlet was the polar opposite to Carruthers in intelligence, but was equally large, mean and lacking a sense of humour. Jones was almost the dictionary definition of average, but he knew his way around just about every weapon you could think of. Meyers could drive anything, fast, and through every terrain.

It's like the A-team. Everyone has their uses.

Behind him on the interactive whiteboard was the image of Jack Stadler. "Questions?" he asked.

"What has he done?" Carruthers asked. Knowles had thought that the first question would have come from him. In fact, would have bet next month's palimony on it.

"You don't need to know that," Knowles said, but didn't add *because I don't have a clue.*

"I recognise him." Carruthers had a photographic memory. "Can't place him yet, but I've definitely seen him before."

"Over the next month, we will all get intimately acquainted with Jack Stadler's every move. You place him, you let me know."

"This op is a piece of piss sir. A month in Devon watching a civvy. Sounds like a holiday." Jones grinned at the others as he said it. "I used to go there when I was a kid. Cracking place, Devon."

"Why us?" Scarlet's booming voice asked. "As Jonesey says, this is a piece of piss."

Knowles shrugged. "We don't ask, we do. They say where to go, we say yes."

"Fine," Carruthers said, "but this is wrong. We've got a combined tour of about thirty years, so why this Mickey Mouse op?"

Knowles knew that he could bawl Carruthers out for speaking to a superior officer like that, but he also knew that Carruthers was voicing what they were all thinking.

"The major asked for me specifically. I asked for you specifically." He let that sink in for a moment, *let the guys feel valued.* "It's better than Ghanners isn't it?"

There was no argument in the room against that statement. They had all seen combat in Afghanistan. It was not something any of them were in a rush to get back to.

"There is one final thing though. Nobody knows we are going. Girlfriends and wives out of the loop, no contact until the end of the op."

"No fucking problem," Jones said. *Single again then, now that could be an issue.*

"What's the cover?" Scarlet hated lying to his wife and kids. He did everything he could to protect them from the day-to-day of what he actually did, but that involved just not talking about it. Outright lies were not something he was good at.

"It's our choice. We can be scuba diving in the Seychelles or skiing in Courchevel."

"Yeah, but when we get back in six weeks, my wife will notice the distinct lack of a tan – or panda eyes," Carruthers said.

"Actually, it's a seven week op."

They looked blankly at him. Knowles couldn't suppress a grin: this was the bit that he'd been looking forward to.

"According to Major Smith, this is a seven week op regardless of how long we actually spend in Devon. When we finish, they send us where we want: Seychelles or Courchevel. If we're there for six weeks, then the seventh week is spent there. We finish early, we go for longer."

In the excitement that rose in the room, none of them thought to ask *how* that would happen: what exactly did they have to do to finish early?

3

Knowles packed quickly. Smith had told him the cover story and then outlined the brief for the trip to Devon. They would be five lads on holiday for a month, looking for all the outdoor pursuits that Devon excelled at: climbing, mountain biking, surfing and kayaking.

They were to be soldiers on leave following an extended tour of duty. It was best to keep the story as close to the truth and as simple as possible.

They were renting a holiday cottage two doors away from the Stadler house. The first job was to find a way in to bug the place and they were to keep Stadler under twenty four hour surveillance for at least a month. If they observed anything they felt to be suspicious in any way, they were to bring him back to the base immediately.

The major had been very vague as to what 'suspicious' behaviour they might observe.

Knowles had the usual feeling in his stomach: a queasy sensation like he was going to be sick any moment that he always had just before going on a live op. In Ghanners, he had lived with the feeling twenty-four hours a day. After a week, he had thought he might get used to it. After a month he knew that wasn't going to happen. After a year, he had begun to embrace it, but he never once forgot it was there.

When his patrol had been ambushed, the sick feeling was replaced with out and out terror. Scarlet had saved his life, but they had been too slow to save two of their team. Both had been shot by snipers whilst Scarlet and Knowles had been shielded by a jeep.

Knowles pushed the memory aside.

I am not going back there if I can help it.

Chapter 5

1

Jack awoke in his bed. Bright sunlight streamed through the windows and obscured the time on the alarm clock. He pushed it into the shadows by the wall and saw 07:30 in light blue numbers. Groaning, he went for a shower and was halfway through washing when he remembered what had happened on the way home.

He inspected his arms carefully. No rogue clumps of hair, strange lumps or waves of rippling skin. *No hangover either.* The water was as hot as he could stand it, but it felt as soothing as a massage. Had he imagined it?

No.

What was going on? What had happened? He had no memory beyond the churchyard and seeing the waves coming out of his arm. *Just a trick of the light? The beer messing with my head?*

I need help.

No. I'm fine, just a little sleep deprived and in shock. Get Katie and Josh home and things will return to normal soon enough – or at least, as normal as they can be with a baby.

He turned the shower off then dried and dressed quickly. With a cup of tea he watched the breakfast news. Nothing of note except the usual doom and gloom. The local news didn't mention him at all: he was a good news story which meant a shelf life of one day, max.

He stroked and fed Ginny, then left for his car.

At no point did he wonder why he wasn't hungry.

2

Katie was awake and feeding Josh when he arrived. She had some colour back in her cheeks and she looked more like her old self – or at least her old self with an extra stone. He told her she looked good and kissed them both gently. Josh didn't break stride with his feeding.

"He takes after his old man for feeding," Katie said.

"Don't say that."

"What? He's eating really well, the nurses are dead impressed."

"Old man. I hate that expression – always have." Jack made a face. "It sound like when you're a dad, that's it, life over. Mine feels like it's just starting."

Katie beamed at him. "Mine too."

Josh stopped feeding, looked at Jack for a nano-second then fell asleep. Jack took him gently and Josh nuzzled in to his neck. Years before, he had worked with a man who claimed he'd happily do time if anyone hurt his kids. In that instant, Jack knew exactly what he meant.

"Can you come home today?"

"Yes. Did you bring the car seat?"

Jack nodded. The seat had been fitted the car the day they'd bought it and he had not removed it since. It looked too complicated.

"Could you pack my things for me while I get dressed?"

"No problem. Do you need a shower or anything?"

Katie wrinkled her nose. "Not here. I'll have a bath at home later."

Jack raised his eyebrows with a smirk.

"You can forget that for a start!" Katie said. "I'm going to have to bathe with tea tree oil to help, y'know, the healing." She stressed the word *healing* and Jack felt his insides clench. The vaginal tear had been quite severe but she had been stitched back up before the epidural had worn off.

It's good to be a man.

Once he had packed her bag, they went to the nurses' station and said their goodbyes. Sue, the older midwife, was there and she removed the security tags from around Josh's ankles. He didn't wake, despite all the nurses cooing and fussing over him. Jack felt an insane moment of pride when they said how good looking a boy Josh was, despite knowing that it was probably in their contracts to say that to everyone. Sue said that she would visit them at home on Thursday and then discharged them. It all seemed far too easy to Jack, who had expected much more resistance to the idea of going home.

Too easy. Surely this should be harder? I'm walking out of here with a baby. Shouldn't someone stop me? Point out that I'm nowhere near mature enough for this?

Katie looked at him, beatific smile in place. She held his hand and gave it a squeeze. *I have to be ready, no one else is doing this for me.* Five minutes later they were heading for home via their first car journey as a family.

3

It was lunchtime before they got home. Two days before, the drive had been never-ending. Now it was again, but for very different reasons. Katie made fun of him all the way home, but he knew that she was feeling as anxious as him. She had made him turn the stereo down low, but he had no trouble making out every word – no mean feat as the CD was still Lambchop from the previous evening.

Once in the safety of their home, Katie sank onto the sofa and suddenly looked exhausted. Jack held Josh gently and was surprised to see he was awake. Josh stared at his father, eyes wide with amazement. Then he went bright red and farted loudly.

"You're holding him, you get to deal," Katie said with a smile.

"No problem," Jack answered. He stood in the doorway looking around the room.

"Nappies and wipes upstairs." Jack paused, holding Josh at arm's length. Katie watched him with obvious amusement. "You want a hand?"

"Um. Yeah."

They went up to the nursery room which remained unpainted. They had been planning to paint it that weekend, but things had been brought forward a little. Still, as Josh was going to be in with them for at least a couple of months, they had plenty of time to fix that.

Jack lay him on the change mat whilst Katie got out a nappy and a large packet of wipes. Jack un-popped all the buttons on the sleep suit and pushed it up under his son's back. The slowly rotting stump of the umbilical cord caught slightly and Jack inhaled sharply.

"Sorry little man." Josh didn't appear bothered, just kept staring at his dad. The stump was black from the clip to where it entered Josh's body. It was the most revolting thing Jack had ever seen.

Except for those waves running up your arm last night.

Jack ignored the thought and concentrated on what he was doing. He took the nappy off and was greeted by the second

-third-

most revolting thing he'd seen. The nappy was covered in a thick black substance. It clung to the nappy and Josh's back like tar to a road.

"Holy crap."

"Close. It's meconium."

Jack's memory of those god awful baby books he'd read when Katie had announced she was pregnant. He wiped it and was surprised at how quickly it came off.

Then a large arc of warm liquid squirted across the room, covering Jack's arm and hitting the far wall of the nursery. Katie started laughing so hard she was almost doubled over.

"You already lost your wee cherry!" she said in a bad American accent.

Jack couldn't help but laugh also, even though he was soaked. He reached for another wipe and started to clean his arm. Before too long, Josh was clean and Katie dressed him whilst Jack cleaned up the mess.

4

Later that afternoon, they had their first visitors. John and his wife Karen came round with a present for Josh and bubbly and chocolates for Katie.

"For Katie." John stressed, handing her the box deliberately. Jack started to make some drinks whilst Karen went through to the living room.

"How's your head?" John asked when they were alone.

"Not bad," Jack lied. "Not that great either."

"No, I've been shit all day. Was nearly sick on the way to work."

"Christ, I've not been that bad."

"I'm out of practice see. You'll find out – kids are great for your liver mate."

They made four mugs of tea and went through to join the others. Karen was cuddling Josh, who was predictably enough, asleep with his head resting on her shoulder.

"Oh, Jack, he's gorgeous," she said. Jack felt the lump in his throat come back. "Josh is such a great name too. I like that it's not Joshua."

"I teach several Joshuas," Jack said. "Most are good kids, but we wanted something different."

"Proud-foot Cloud-walker Stadler," John said, to blank looks from the others. "That's different isn't it?"

Karen scowled at him and Jack suppressed a grin. They had toyed with a more outlandish name, but hadn't wanted to make the boy an easy target later in life. Jack had actually taught an Oliver Hardy once. *What were the parents thinking?*

"You've missed all the excitement then," Karen said to Katie.

"Yeah. Husband on the six o'clock news, me in hospital. Bloody typical!"

"You also didn't tell us much about that last night mate," John said.

Jack shrugged. "Not much to tell. I was running with Ginny like I normally do, hole opens up, I fall in like some kind of twat."

It was Katie's turn to scowl. "You've got to be careful with how you speak now." She gestured at Josh who was still fast asleep.

"You're fucking joking!"

"Jack!"

"So, how come you were running across that bit of land then? There's no path there," John said.

"You've had a look?"

"Half the bloody village has, mate. The other half will have by today. You're a bit of a celebrity now."

"Great. I'm famous for falling down a hole." It was one of Jack's bugbears that, as an incomer, lots of people knew everything about him, but he knew very few people in return.

"Hell of a hole though," John said admiringly.

"Tell us more Jack," Karen pleaded.

"Ginny disappeared, and she wouldn't come back, so I ran after her. I don't think that particular bit of land has had anything on it heavier than a rabbit for years. The ground gave way and I fell into the hole."

"You pass out?"

"No, or at least the paramedics didn't think so." Another lie. Jack knew he had passed out, at least for a little while.

Actually, you might have died there for a moment or two.

"I landed on some sort of slab which broke my fall."

"A slab?" Katie looked concerned again. "You didn't tell me that."

"Yeah, a big stone slab, almost like a table."

Covered with weird symbols.

Like the Devil.

"You broke your fall on *stone?*" John's tone of voice said it all. The room had become a little tense in the last few minutes. Jack laughed to try and break it.

"Yeah. How lucky am I?"

That's a very good question Jack. Just how lucky indeed? Lucky enough for your flesh to ripple?

"You ok honey?"

Jack shook himself out of his reverie. "Yeah, sorry, just had a bit of a flashback."

Katie still looked worried. He tried to reassure her with a smile, but it felt false even to him. A change of subject was needed.

"How about we open that bubbly?"

He got up before anyone had a chance to argue and left the room as John and Karen started protesting that the bubbly was for the 'new parents', a phrase that made Katie glow. He quickly got the drink and four glasses then opened it expertly, by twisting the bottle not the cork and was rewarded with a satisfying pop, but no wastage. He filled the glasses and passed them round.

"You ok with him?" Katie asked.

"Oh yeah, I'm an old pro when it comes to drinking and holding kids!" Karen laughed, and much like Chris the night before, it was an infectious laugh. They toasted Josh and drank again.

"I almost forgot." Karen said, after an almighty gulp. "Did you hear about Frank?"

"What?" Katie said.

"He lost another sheep last night. A dog got it. That's two nights running now."

Chapter 6

1

It had been a long drive from Kent to Devon. Five and a half hours sitting in a very nice top of the range Beamer, with Scarlet complaining all the way. Despite the sat-nav, air con, Harman Karden sound system, headrest DVD players and the most comfortable seats Knowles had sat in ever, let alone in a *car*, Scarlet had bitched and moaned about driving a German car.

"You weren't even alive in the war," Knowles had pointed out, but to no avail. If anything, Scarlet upped the level of complaints until he eventually fell asleep near Stonehenge.

Knowles was always slightly unnerved by the ancient stones. What were they for? Why were they there? Who built them? He didn't voice any of those thoughts: the lads would have taken the piss for the rest of the op. A month could be a *very* long time in this company.

Meyers did all the driving – it was his job after all. The other BMW was being driven by Carruthers, who had Jones for company. Knowles suppressed a grin. *Jonesey has probably wound him right up by now.*

He read more of Jack Stadler's file. There wasn't much information in it. He was the same age as Knowles but that was where the similarity ended.

Stadler had been a teacher for three years. Prior to that, he had been in a succession of dead end jobs, including running a bookshop that had failed just before he'd enrolled in teacher training. Knowles had been promoted at about that time, following his third tour of duty. He'd done Ireland for four years, Iraq twice, both times for two years. Afghanistan had been eighteen months, and that had been the hardest.

He remembered the ambushes and the constant daily dread. He remembered children smiling at him whilst their fathers plotted to kill him. He remembered the heat. He remembered not acting fast enough to save lives. He remembered the men under his command who had not made it home.

Too old. He thought glumly. *You're too old for this.* When he signed up, he thought he would be promoted out of the front lines quickly enough, but it hadn't happened. Lots of reasons for this. Someone else picked ahead of him. Another time had coincided with his first divorce. Next time he'd been eligible it had been his second divorce. Neither had left him in a good place. He made Sergeant when someone else had wandered into an IED and had been sent home without his legs. Although he had the respect of his men, he didn't feel he deserved the rank. Now this: a weird assignment to watch a civilian who didn't appear to have done anything wrong.

In fact, just about the only interesting thing about Jack Stadler was that he had fallen into a cave two days ago, the same day his son had been born. Carruthers had remembered this just as they left Kent: he had seen Stadler on the news. *What are the odds?* Knowles had been in service long enough to know that nothing was ever what it seemed, but he had no idea what this was about. Was he a terrorist? Didn't look like your typical sympathiser. Something else? Involved in a plot against the throne? Parliament? No, that would have been one for the spooks and Smith had made it very clear that they weren't to be involved. Maybe he was making bombs? Dealing drugs – *lots* of drugs? Stadler was a maths teacher – perhaps he was a kiddie fiddler? That would be the police. Round and round it went in Knowles' head. They had been given top rated security equipment: listening devices, cameras, seismic sensors and heat sensitive sensors amongst other things. Knowles also had a code word to use that would bring in the helos if something kicked off.

Knowles had never had the power to call in helicopters before and it thrilled him a little. Even on the front line in Afghanistan he had to call FAC in order to get fire support. This was different.

It made him wonder more and more just exactly what they had let themselves in for.

2

They eventually arrived in Huntleigh and the sat-nav took them directly to the holiday home. They drove past the Stadlers' house and all looked at it quickly. It was a normal three bedroom house. The file said it was over two hundred years old, but it just looked like any other house to Knowles. Their rented house looked exactly the same.

Double fronted, with a door in the middle. High windows which let in a lot of light. Upstairs was the same, but with an extra window above the front door indicating the position of the third bedroom. All the houses in the street were painted the same shade of cream; only the front doors showed individuality.

A thick hedge ran down the right hand side of the road, opposite the houses. Knowles knew from the street plan that a field lay on the other side of it. At the back of the houses, at the end of the gardens, more fields rolled away. Woods were at the end of the road, about a mile away from the Stadlers' house, and the main part of the village was in the opposite direction, at the top of a steep hill.

Phone lines crossed above them going to every house and Knowles counted three satellite dishes in the whole street. The road itself was narrow and made more so by the row of parked cars all along it. Two street lights were in view, already on as darkness was approaching. *Lots of dark places in this street. Could be to our advantage that.*

They unloaded all the gear and bags and sorted out rooms. They divided up the three bedrooms, with Knowles pulling rank to get a room to himself. The bedroom he chose had an en-suite, which made the others grumble. Once unpacked they all met in the kitchen. Scarlet and Jones cooked them a meal and Meyers cleaned up whilst Knowles and Carruthers inspected the kit. Once complete, they sat around the table. It was nearly midnight and the darkness outside was complete: even the streetlights had gone out.

Knowles unfolded a floor plan of the Stadler home. Carruthers was examining the bugs and cameras he was going to put in the house. He thoroughly approved.

"Look how small this is," he said holding a dot to the light.

Knowles gestured at the plan. "Now, look at this. There is a back door here, which leads directly to the kitchen. They have a dog, so you'll need this." He threw a can of spray to Carruthers. "Spray onto the dog and it will go to sleep immediately. You'll have to be quick, just in case it's a barker or biter."

Carruthers nodded once and slipped the can into the clip pocket of his black combat trousers. He slid the bugs into another one, and slipped a headset over his ear. A slim microphone swung out when he needed to talk. He pulled a black hat over the top of his head and slipped a set of night vision goggles over the top of the hat, leaving them resting on his forehead. All the while, Knowles continued talking.

"The kitchen leads to a dining room. Then a small hallway which goes upstairs, but across the hallway is the living room. The hallway also has their front door, so you need to get a bug on the door somewhere. Remember, upstairs can wait until they are out and we have more time."

"Why not wait anyway?" Meyers said.

"They have a baby," Jones said. "They might not go anywhere for days."

"Agreed," Knowles nodded. "This way, despite the risk, we get some coverage before morning. The key areas are the doors and the downstairs rooms. Be quick, be quiet and get out if the baby wakes."

Carruthers nodded.

"Good luck. We'll be listening."

Thursday

Chapter 7

1

Carruthers climbed over the fence at the back of their house and found himself in a large field. Thick clouds covered the sky, shrouding all his surroundings in darkness. Night vision goggles gave everything a pale green glow. He moved silently through the field, eyes scanning the ground for any sticks or branches that would break under his feet. At the same time he counted the backs of the houses, stopping at the third one away from theirs. A high hedge surrounded the rear of this garden, but a much lower one bordered the garden on his right. Carruthers vaulted this, landing in a roll. His tightly packed kit didn't rattle, but he still paused to check no-one heard. No lights came on after a few minutes, so he clambered over the fence between this garden and the Stadlers'. He waited, completely covered in shadow for nearly forty minutes. He couldn't hear a sound from the house. Definitely no high pitched crying from a hungry baby.

The back door was half glazed so he could see into the kitchen. The dog was asleep in front of the washing machine. *Cute.* He opened the back door without the need for a key. The whole operation depended on the Stadlers removing their keys once they had locked up. He needn't have worried: they didn't lock the back door at all. *Country folk,* he thought with more than a little contempt.

The dog's head jerked up and its eyes snapped open as soon as he opened the door. It was clearly not used to unannounced visitors coming in through that door and so didn't start barking for a full second. Carruthers used that time to spray the dog in the face with the canister Knowles had given him. The dog emitted one small growl then keeled over. Comedy snoring made Carruthers smile.

Stage one complete. He started to look for a suitable place to hide the first tiny bug.

2

Jack's eyes sprang open and he sat up, instantly alert. Katie stirred next to him.

"What's up?" she mumbled. "Josh?"

"Sshh. Go back to sleep." She grunted and rolled over. At the foot of the bed, Josh lay in his cot, arms in the cross position and mouth open. His white sleepsuit was stretched taut. Pooh bear stared back at Jack, one hand clutching a honey pot. Josh was fast asleep, soft features arranged in an expression somewhere between Einstein and Churchill. Jack smiled at the sleeping boy.

What woke me?

3

Carruthers placed one bug above the door frame in the kitchen and another under the lip of the door that led to the drive. Judging by the dust, it was not a place that got cleaned regularly and the bug had a tiny amount of adhesive in it which meant it wouldn't get dislodged easily. He crept through to the dining room, night vision giving him a clear view of his surroundings.

The Stadlers house was nice. Solid furniture in each room, the type that was neither stupid money nor an Ikea special. A small fireplace was set into the right hand wall. In the bottom of the fireplace, where the grill should have been, sat a wine rack.

Perfect.

4

Jack went to the bathroom and sat on the toilet without turning any lights on. He knew the house well enough to not step on any of the creaky floor boards. He sat there longer than he needed to, enjoying the peace and quiet. He was very tired, but he knew sleep would be a long time coming. There was just too much on his mind. He would have to return to work next week, so he would have to do some planning over the weekend. It was not a thought that filled him with joy. *Imagine if your arm changes in the middle of a lesson: how would that be?*

He stood up and then heard it clearly.

Someone was downstairs.

5

Carruthers eased open the door to the hallway. This was the crucial part. If the door creaked he would leg it. Four bugs were in place, the others would have to wait. It was enough to get them some coverage, give them an idea of what was going on. The door opened smoothly, and he raised an invisible glass to the Stadlers' housekeeping. He placed a bug above the front door and entered the living room.

There was another fireplace in this room, but this was clearly in use. It dominated the room, an open Inglenook fireplace. Carruthers was impressed. A grand-father clock ticked noisily in one corner, next to a 37 inch HD TV which looked very out of place. He went to the corner opposite the TV – no sense risking interference. A lamp stood in the corner, a large one that rose from the floor to the ceiling. He placed the last bug in the lampshade and crossed back to the door.

And then he heard movement upstairs.

6

Jack stood still in the bathroom. He listened as hard as he could. An absurd part of his brain wondered if it was even possible to listen harder than normal. He heard it again. The noise was unmistakeable: someone had just opened the dining room door. Last time he'd checked, Ginny was not able to do that.

We're being burgled. Not with my son in the house. Please god, don't hurt my son.

For the first time in years Jack wished he could sleep in pyjamas. He crept out onto the landing and made his way to the top of the stairs.

He forgot to step over the top of the stairs until it gave a very definite creak.

7

Carruthers didn't panic. Later, he would be proud of that. He stepped calmly into the hallway, hoping the dark would conceal him, knowing his balaclava would protect his identity if it didn't. He glanced up to the top of the stairs and met Jack Stadler's eyes.

What he saw chilled him. He wasn't seeing the face of a family man or teacher.

Stadler was looking at him with absolute fury and hatred in his eyes. He let out a guttural growl and started coming down the stairs fast.

Carruthers knew that contact was not part of the plan. He knew that he could take Stadler, but he also knew that he *shouldn't*. He ran. The dining room wasn't very long and with a couple of strides he made it into the kitchen. He yanked open the back door, hearing Stadler crash his way through the house to try and catch him.

Carruthers stepped into the garden and pulled the back door shut behind him just as something heavy hit it. He fell back in surprise, landing on the floor with a thump and the door was hit again. He looked up at the glass part of the door. An enormous black dog

-wolf-

was growling at him. He backed away carefully, then got to his feet. The dog

-wolf-

had its paws on the door and its teeth were uncomfortably close to the glass.

Carruthers got to his feet slowly. The dog

-wolf-

glared at him, with teeth bared. Carruthers didn't wait to see if it could break down the door. He turned and fled.

Chapter 8

1

Jack stood in the kitchen looking at the back door, the fear slowly subsiding in him. He couldn't remember getting there: from the hall to the kitchen wasn't far, but it was far enough. The burglar was gone, so now what? He looked quickly round downstairs but could see nothing obvious missing. On his return to the kitchen, he bent to stroke Ginny. She was out cold and didn't stir when he touched her.

Strange.

"What's up? Why are you banging about so much?"

"Fuck!"

Katie was standing in the doorway, Josh snuggled into her shoulder. He was looking at Jack with wide eyes, head craned to look at him when he shouted. Lacking any strength in his neck muscles, his head flopped back onto Katie's shoulder.

"Sorry!" Katie moved to him and stroked his bare back. "Sorry. Didn't mean to make you jump. You were making so much noise I thought I'd better come down. You woke Josh."

Jack's heart was hammering inside his chest, but he kept his voice calm. "I thought I heard something, so I came down." *It wasn't me. I was on all fours.*

Katie's face drained of colour instantly. "What did you hear?"

He tried to avoid her gaze, but failed miserably.

"Jack. What did you hear?"

"Someone was in the house. I think I must have scared them away."

Oh yes Jack. Damn near gave him a heart attack when he saw you coming.

Jack ignored the little voice. He had no memory from standing at the top of the stairs looking at the man in black to being in the kitchen with his hands on the door. No memory except for-

What? Chasing him on all fours? Seeing him clearly although it was pitch black?

"Oh my god." Katie held Josh more tightly. "We've been burgled?" Her voice had become higher pitched and she was trembling slightly.

"Nothing's been taken." He held her tightly, her body helping warm him back up. Now that the adrenaline was fading, the cold was seeping in to him. "I think I scared him away."

"We need to phone the police," she said, voice back to normal. She thrust Josh at him and picked up the phone.

"Wait," Jack said. She looked at him, puzzled. "Something's wrong with Ginny. She's not woken up at all since I've been down here."

"WHAT? They poisoned my dog?"

Katie had got Ginny at around the time they had started dating. Whenever she was ill, or did something exceptionally cute, she reverted to being Katie's dog. Of course, Jack did all the walking, feeding and cleaning up after her.

Katie knelt down and stroked Ginny. "She's breathing."

"Maybe they used a sleeping drug on her." Katie gave him a sceptical look so he shrugged. "It happens."

"I'm phoning the police."

2

Carruthers sat in the garden as soft rain, occasionally heavy, fell on him. The garden was a nice size – not too big or small. Steps led down to the house and there was a small patio area at the top before the lawn started. A rusty gas barbecue sat on the patio next to a very old children's slide, which was covered in green slime. It glistened in the rain. The barbecue was attached to a gas canister and a gauge said it was almost full. He couldn't blame anyone for not wanting to cook on the rust bucket. When he was sure no one had followed him, he returned to the house.

Knowles had waited up for him, listening equipment set up in a suitcase in front of him. They had decided to use the suitcase as it could be quickly hidden if any neighbour came knocking. The others were all asleep.

"Well?"

Carruthers didn't say anything. He went to the fridge and took out a beer bottle.

"What are you doing? It's two thirty!"

Carruthers popped the top of the lager and sat down heavily. He took a long swig and finally met his sergeant's eyes.

"I saw Jack Stadler."

"What? You fucking what?"

"I put the bug in the living room. When I came out he was at the top of the stairs."

"Jesus Christ, Sam."

"I swear, Knowles, that I did not make a sound in that house."

Knowles trusted his men: it was, after all, why he had chosen these four. "So what the fuck happened then?"

"I don't know. He was there staring at me, but it was weird, mate."

"Explain weird." Knowles opened a beer of his own. *Fuck it. It's late and I've got a seriously worried man here.*

"It was clockwork. I put the dog out, put the bugs in place, nothing, not a sound. No creaking doors, floorboards, nothing. But there he was. He must have ears like a bat."

Carruthers took a big gulp which emptied his beer. "Then he set his dog on me." *Except that wasn't a dog. And you know it. It was something else. Something just wrong.*

"I thought you said you put the dog to sleep."

"I did. They must have another one, and this was a *big* dog." He sighed. "Don't look at me like that, it was dark and it was a really big dog."

"Did anyone see you come in here?"

Carruthers shook his head. "I went into the fields and along. Nobody came out of the house after me."

"Good. Then we can continue. We're not compromised on our first fucking night."

"Stadler, Knowles, he's-"

"What?"

"He's crazy. The way he looked at me."

Knowles waited. He knew the big man was trying to find the words.

"Do you remember in Afghan? Those children in the mountains after the shooting?"

Knowles remembered all too clearly. He wished he didn't. After the ambush, families had come out and laughed at them. The children were almost feral and they had wild eyes: it was more than being high on the adrenaline rush; the children looked crazy.

"That's exactly what he looked like. It scared me Knowles, really scared me. Made me wonder what exactly the brass are not telling us."

3

"What do you mean there are no available units?" Katie said exasperated. "My husband has just scared a burglar off – what if he is still around?"

"I understand your frustration Mrs Stadler, but all our available units are dealing with other incidents," the dispatcher said, her voice deliberately calm, but nevertheless doing a great job of winding Katie up.

"So what are we supposed to do now?"

"Lock all your doors, check your windows and go to bed. A unit will be with you first thing."

"We have a two day old baby here," she hissed.

"There are no available units right now. I can send one as soon as they become available, but I can't guarantee a time."

"So we wait up and hope that someone turns up?"

"Not hope, Mrs Stadler, someone will be there, I just can't guarantee a time. I'm very sorry, but there is nothing I can do."

"This is ridiculous."

"I will pass your comments to my watch commander, Mrs Stadler. All I can do is apologise."

"Send a squad car in the morning," Katie said and hung up. At that moment she would have given anything to have a handset that you could actually slam down. Pressing a button firmly in anger just doesn't give the same feel.

"Calm down," Jack said. "You'll wake Josh."

True to form, Josh was now asleep on Jack's shoulder. Jack stroked his back and kissed the soft hair on his head. Jack focused on him so he didn't have to think about what exactly had happened earlier.

Katie took one look at Josh and all the anger left her face. "You're right. If I take him up, will you check all the windows and doors?"

"Of course," Jack said handing him over. She went upstairs and Jack locked the back door, engaging the double lock that they had not used since moving to Huntleigh two years ago. A hand on Ginny's side confirmed she was still breathing and then he checked every downstairs window.

He caught a glimpse of his reflection in the glazing of the front door and stared at himself for a moment. *What did happen?* More memories were coming back, but they made no sense.

Running downstairs on all fours? How the hell did I do that?

He climbed the stairs on two shaky legs and got into bed. Sleep was a long time coming.

4

Knowles listened to Katie's phone call to the police. He heard her describe how a tall man in black had come into the house and poisoned the dog. *Interesting that she only mentioned 'the dog', like there was only one.* He smirked as the dispatch officer told her that no units would be available until morning. If Carruthers had left any footprints in the Stadlers' garden, they would be covered by morning. The rain had turned into a downpour.

He was now alone in the kitchen. A lamp lit the room softly and he held a paperback novel in one hand. If anyone looked through a window they would see a man with headphones reading a book. Of course, no one in their right mind would be up at this time, but you never knew who was watching in a small community.

He kept thinking about Carruthers' tale of Jack Stadler looking at him with pure hatred. Carruthers had been right: exactly what did brass know about this? What had they got themselves into?

He'd double checked the file. The Stadlers were listed as having one dog, a Labrador and Spaniel cross. He'd thought that meant it was a small dog and Google confirmed it. At best, it was a medium size dog, something much smaller than an Alsatian. Also, Carruthers had said that he'd sprayed the dog and that this was something else. What did that mean? *Something else: like what exactly?*

The Stadlers' file had been updated on line twelve hours ago to include their baby son, called Josh. How could the brass know that information but not that the Stadlers had bought themselves a huge dog?

They also now had pictures of Katie Stadler and more of Jack. They had information on their friends: a small but tight knit group. It seemed that the Stadlers had taken some time to settle here following their move from London. They were well liked without being popular and none of their friends were 'proper Devon folk'.

Knowles had some recognition of that. Growing up English in a small village in Wales meant he'd never felt part of the community. His parents, when they were alive, saw the same group of friends every week. The routine of it all had numbed him completely.

Whatever you said about the army - once you survived basic - routine, it was not.

Chapter 9

1

Jack woke with the same sick feeling in his stomach that he had gone to sleep with. He got out of bed, disappointed that his legs were still shaking, and went down to the kitchen. Ginny looked up at him, tail wagging furiously, eyes bright. *No lasting ill affects there then.* He ate a bowl of cereal and drank a cup of tea, scalding his mouth as he did so. Next, toast which he demolished in a couple of bites. He was rattling through a cupboard when Katie came into the room.

"You going to say morning?"

"Sorry, felt a bit sick, food has sorted me right out though." He smiled at her. "Josh asleep?"

"Yeah, I just put him down when I heard you get up. He's an angel really. I'm sure the sleepless nights will kick in, but he only woke once last night after-" She didn't need to finish the sentence.

"So, he's asleep, we're alone, you fancy-"

"No chance." Katie said, and winced herself at how harsh it sounded. "Sorry. I'm still a little fragile down there." She unnecessarily pointed as she said that, making Jack smile. He hugged her and made them both fresh coffee.

"We got a plan for today?" he asked when they were sitting in the living room.

"Wait for the police, then see what time it is. I'm going to take Gins to the vets too."

"Ok. Fancy a trip to the pub? Get some food, show him off a bit?"

She looked worried for a second, but then nodded. "It'd be good to take him out for a bit. I'd like some fresh air too."

"Great. We should make the most of this week, I'm back in work on Monday." They had discussed how long his paternity leave should be. He was entitled to two weeks, but the second week was statutory pay and it wasn't worth it. It would be half term in another two weeks, so it didn't really matter anyway.

"You could take a couple of sick days as well you know. You did have a big fall."

"Yeah but I'm fine." *Apart from whatever the hell happened last night.* "That Doctor Baxter said so."

"You don't know what damage you might have done to yourself. Do you have flashbacks?" She paused. "To the cave, I mean."

He shook his head. "No. Weird dreams more than anything." She looked at him quizzically. "I kept dreaming I was running around on all fours."

She laughed. "That's not weird Jack. Turning into a fish and cycling to the moon is weird."

He grinned too. Out loud it seemed absurd that he was worried. *Except you saw the burglar run away scared.*

-and holding a sheep in his powerful jaws, feeling the warm blood squirt into his mouth as he bit its head off-

Jack ran for the stairs and just made it to the toilet as his breakfast splattered into the pan. He heaved until nothing came out and, just for good measure, he heaved again.

2

Meyers felt his stomach churn as he heard Stadler throw up. He lifted the headphones away from his ears and took several quick deep breaths. There were no mics upstairs, so Stadler was clearly being very vocal in his illness. Meyers hated sick more than anything in the world: he hated vomiting himself and he hated clearing it up. His son had been sick for the first two years of his life. An illness that he eventually recovered from, but Meyers' marriage had not.

Right now, he had every sympathy for Katie Stadler.

He'd been listening to their conversation, wondering if he and Sally had been so dull when they'd been together. *Probably.* He wasn't sure what had caused Stadler to be sick, but it could be one of the things that was important, so he kept listening.

Everything could be important.

3

Katie stroked Jack's back and made soothing noises. Even though the retches were almost biblical in their volume, Josh had stayed blissfully asleep. She was relieved to see that most of the sick had landed in the bowl, but on closer inspection she saw that the floor was pebble dashed.

Jack collapsed to the floor, tears in his eyes. "Damn it," was all he managed to say, his voice cracked and weak. There was no colour in his face at all.

"Feel better for that?"

"Better out than in," he mumbled. "Sorry hun."

"Can I get you anything? Water?"

"Water would be great. Thank you." He tried to get up and succeeded on the second attempt. He staggered through to the hallway, paused outside their bedroom door, changed his mind and flopped onto the spare bed instead. Katie brought him water moments later and then he heard her cleaning up the mess. He pulled the duvet over his head and hoped that sleep would give him respite from the thoughts reeling through his mind.

He was wrong.

4

Sheep running terrified as he sprinted towards them.
A man with horns on his head pointing at him.
A bone sticking out of his chest.
A lone sheep falling behind its flock.
Pathetic bleating falling on deaf and unsympathetic ears.
The man with horns raising an enormous sword above his head.
The sheep stumbling as he hit it side on.
A dark shadow cast in the moonlight: a wolf in amongst the sheep.
The sword coming down, hitting his neck and the world going dark.

5

Jack sat up gasping for breath. *What the hell was that all about?* But he knew. Deep inside, he knew. Something had happened in that cave, and it wasn't a good thing. He had changed.

On the verge of hyperventilating, Jack picked a spot on the ceiling and stared at it, concentrating on his breathing only. He felt his heart slow and his breathing came back under control. He felt his neck to reassure himself that his head was still attached and breathed a sigh of relief despite himself.

Jesus, that was one dream. Something in there had felt real and he didn't know what to do about it. The man did not have horns on his head, he had been wearing a headdress. Other people had been in the cave, all kneeling, all wearing skins and furs of various animals. Despite the kneeling, they were all looking at him, terror clear in their eyes. He had laughed as the sword fell.

Jack closed his eyes, trying to get a grip on the images. What had he seen? The execution of the creature he had fallen on? So, what? Now he was possessed by the spirit of the dead animal? He chuckled to himself. *Nonsense, just nonsense.* Except-

Had he eaten one – or two – of Frank's sheep? The very thought almost sent him running to the toilet again, but he forced the bile back down. He almost relished the taste of the bile compared to the imagined taste of the sheep's raw flesh. Almost.

He got out of bed cautiously and went downstairs. He sat on a sofa with a heavy thump. Katie was feeding Josh. She had her top off and held Josh with one hand and a trashy chick-lit book with the other.

"How you feeling?"

"Better," he said, truthfully. He clicked the remote, waking the TV from standby, and clicked a digital radio station.

"No fish biking to the moon this time?" She closed the book and scowled at the TV. "You have to listen to that even when you're sick?" Josh suckled away, oblivious to the world.

"No. It was really bad." He started trembling. "The dream, not the music."

She threw a nursing blanket at him, causing Josh to come away. He looked agitated for a minute until she soothed him. Jack wrapped himself in the blanket.

"Do you want to tell me about it?" she asked. He paused for so long that she thought he didn't.

"I was a wolf. I ate some sheep, but a man dressed as the Devil cut off my head." He hadn't been sure he was going to tell her until the words came out. *Dressed like the figure on the plinth. Not an altar: a sacrificial table. The wolf had been sacrificed to the Devil.*

She looked at him, expecting more, then they both burst out laughing. "You weren't even asleep that long. Maybe your mind is making links to Frank's sheep."

Oh, it's linking alright. That connection has well and truly been made.
"Yeah, maybe."

6

On a pad next to the suitcase of listening equipment, Meyers wrote 'Sheep? WTF?'

This really is a bizarre assignment. He continued to listen.

7

"Did I tell you he came round?"

"Who, Frank?"

"Yeah. After his first sheep had been killed, he came round and accused me of letting Ginny out to do it. Said he'd shoot her if she came on his land."

Katie's mouth dropped open. "He said what?"

Jack nodded grimly. "I told him that if he threatened my dog again I'd rip his head off."

Katie stared at her husband with utter shock on her face. He had never threatened to hurt anyone in the five years they'd been together. "Jack!"

"I know. Crazy huh? He really pissed me off though. As if I'd let Ginny get one of his sheep. What a prick."

"Jack!"

"Well."

They were silent for a moment, then Katie started laughing.

"What's so funny?"

"You. I don't think you've even hit a wall in anger and you go threatening a man who is twice as big as you!"

"He's not twice as big as me," Jack said, smiling despite how he felt. "Maybe one and a half times."

She stopped laughing almost as quickly as she started. "Oh my God, Jack, do you think it was him in here last night? Do you think he poisoned Ginny?"

"I thought that this morning, but I'm not sure." *No last night was something else. Something bad.*

"Yeah, but if he's lost animals-"

"True, but Ginny's ok isn't she? If it had been him, I think," he said, "if it had been him, she'd be dead."

8

Meyers wrote "Frank – farmer? Psycho?" on the pad. At least Carruthers would be relieved that they were already blaming someone for the break-in. They'd all given him some stick for getting caught, and Carruthers had laughed it off. It had all seemed a little false to Meyers though - he could tell that something was really bothering Carruthers.

He'd eventually told them about the big dog, so they were all at least fore-warned. Knowles had made Carruthers go with Jonesey and Scarlet to help him take his mind off things. They were all on Dartmoor, blasting a trail on hired mountain bikes. Knowles had gone to a nearby town to get supplies, leaving Meyers to do the listening. Things had got a lot more interesting since they'd started talking about psycho farmers and threats.

It was his kind of conversation.

9

Katie laid Josh on his bouncy chair and let his head loll gently to one side. His eyes glazed over as she watched and then he was fast asleep.

"I think we should talk to him."

"Why?" Jack said. "What good will that do? You going to ask him if he sent our dog to sleep? It's ridiculous!"

"He threatened her Jack and then the same day she's out cold whilst we have a burglar in the house. That's not right. She barks if someone comes up the drive for god's sake."

He conceded the point.

"I've spoken to the vets. They can see her in an hour or so, she said to just pop up. I'll go and have a shower whilst Josh is asleep. Will you be ok?"

"Yeah," he replied. "I'm feeling much better. Let's all go to the vets, then the pub."

"Is that a good idea?"

Jack forced himself to smile. "Kill or cure, babe, kill or cure!" he said, forcing enthusiasm he didn't feel into his voice.

10

Meyers and Knowles sat watching the Stadlers' house from their front garden. Two mugs of tea sat on the picnic table between them, largely untouched. The garden overlooked the main road, but they could easily see the door in and out of the Stadlers from their spot.

Knowles had returned just as Jack had announced he was going with Katie to the vets and pub and they'd both seen the opportunity that an empty house presented. They sat, watched and waited. A couple of hours passed. The bugs picked up the cries of the baby and the sounds of new parents trying to get organised for a trip out.

Eventually, Jack and Katie appeared at the bottom of the drive.

"Fuck me, I could have done a half marathon in that time," Meyers said.

"In your car maybe."

Katie was pushing an enormous four wheel buggy and Stadler was carrying a shoulder bag branded with Pampers on the side. He also had a dog on a lead. They looked both ways then walked up the road, the proud parents on their first outing with the newborn.

"That dog is tiny," Meyers said. "Well, maybe not tiny, but she's not a big dog is she?"

Knowles grunted and drank some tea. "Carruthers said they had two dogs."

"Best load up with that spray then."

"Yep."

11

Fifteen minutes later they walked calmly to the front door of the Stadler's house. It had been a good idea to wait as the Stadlers had returned once for something.

Meyers picked the lock with a speed and proficiency that would have impressed professional thieves. They had been on the doorstep for maybe ten seconds: an acceptable risk in Knowles' eyes. The hallway was short and had two doors immediately off on either side. The doors were open and they took a room each.

Both held thumbs up. Meyers walked cautiously through to the kitchen whilst Knowles made his way upstairs. He winced and stood stock still when a stair creaked under his foot. Nothing moved. He eased his foot off the step which lessened but did not eradicate the squeak. Still no sounds in the house. At the top of the stairs he looked in one bedroom before Meyers re-joined him. Meyers gave a quick thumbs up as he stepped over the squeaky stair.

They knew from the floor plans that upstairs had three bedrooms and a separate bathroom. All the doors were open except one. They quickly checked the other rooms and then stood outside the closed door. Still no sounds in the house. Meyers held up his spray canister and raised his eyebrows. Knowles shrugged. It was too quiet in the house; it felt empty.

Knowles counted them down with his fingers, trying not to let his nerves show. He wasn't overly keen on dogs: the bigger they were the more nervous he felt. Ridiculous given the training he had and the things he'd done, and he certainly would never tell anyone. After a count of 3, 2, 1 he yanked the final door open and they burst into the bedroom.

It was an untidy room dominated by the king size double bed and the baby's cot. A solitary wardrobe stood against one wall with a large chest of drawers next to it. A huge mirror rested on the chest of drawers, which also had all the makeup, perfume, aftershave and deodorants on it. Clothes lay in semi-neat piles on the bed, and packs of nappies lay on the floor next to a change mat for the baby.

Other than that the room was empty.

12

"Garden?"

Meyers voice made him jump. Knowles nodded and Meyers crossed to the hallway window. It gave him a view of the whole garden. Lawn rolled back to hedgerow and a small herb garden grew beside the kitchen door. A compost heap stood at the very rear of the garden, almost hidden by the lupin tree in front of it. The garden was also empty.

"Big dog my fucking arse," Meyers said.

"He's no bull-shitter," Knowles said. *So where was the other dog?* "Come on. Let's get a move on."

They worked quickly and finished setting bugs around the Stadler house. Cameras were installed in all the rooms, all hidden in smoke detectors or light fittings. Pressure sensitive triggers were put near to each door. They would activate when someone entered a room. It took just under fifteen minutes, but when they were done, they had full audio and visual coverage of the entire Stadler house and garden.

Chapter 10

1

The Kings Arms was the quintessential British pub: a cosy bar sat opposite the main entrance with a log fire that spread warmth throughout; there was always someone at the bar regardless of time of day or night and all conversation died when strangers walked in. Only the landlord broke the stereotypical feel of it all, as he was skinny with pale, almost porcelain skin.

He grinned broadly when he saw Jack and Katie. "First outing with the baba?" He came round from the bar, leaving a miserable looking barmaid Jack had never seen before, and cooed over Josh. "He's got your nose Jack and your face Katie. He's gorgeous!"

"Thanks, Ken. That's nice of you." Jack said, pushing the pram next to a table. He unzipped the cover as the fire was going strong. "What do you want to drink honey?"

"Coffee please." She looked tired. Lots of people had stopped them on the way to the pub: it had taken twenty minutes to do a five minute journey. *Better get used to it.*

"Breast feeding?" Ken asked. Katie nodded. "That's good. My two were breast fed for a year and look at the size of them now!"

Ken's sons were at university now. One in his first year, the other about to graduate. Both were well over six foot, in stark contrast to their father. He sat next to Katie and they started chatting. They paused briefly as two men came in, but Ken continued making small talk. The miserable barmaid brightened at the sight of the two well-built men and went to serve them.

Jack also went to the bar and sat on a stool. He nodded at the two men even though he didn't recognise them. The barmaid, smiling now, came over and Jack caught the faintest of bottom wiggles as she turned away from the two men. He smiled to himself, ordered the drinks and just as he finished another man pulled up a stool next to him.

"Jack," Graham Edwards said.

"Graham." Jack kept his voice level and his smile even. Edwards had once said that John was 'alright for a darkie'. His hand rested on the bar, showing the tattoo APAF on each knuckle: All Pigs Are Fascists.

"Heard you fell into a cave. Saw you on the news."

"Yeah, I also had a baby."

"See, when city boys like you move to the country, you got to watch your step, see? Never know what mischief you could get into." Edwards smirked, winking at the two strangers. "What kind of twat doesn't see a fucking huge hole in front of him?"

I could rip his face off.

Where had *that* come from? Jack swallowed, trying to stay calm. At the same time, it was appealing to just beat the hell out of Edwards. He'd probably be given Freedom Of Huntleigh or something. Jack snorted a laugh.

"Something funny Jackie boy?"

"Graham, my name's Jack, please don't call me that."

"Sorry Jackie boy, didn't mean nothing by it see? Just pulling your leg, like."

Jack stood up quickly and grabbed Edwards's shirt. He lifted the bigger man up and pulled him towards him until they were face to face, inches apart. Jack felt his fingernails grow and saw black hair sprouting on his arm.

"We are not friends. You are a fucking racist twat, now get out of my face and don't come near me or my family again or I will fucking hurt you. Understand?" he hissed quietly. Edwards's mouth dropped open. The barmaid froze, Jack's pint in her hand.

"Jack?" Katie asked. The tension in the bar was palpable.

"Jack," Ken said firmly. Despite his appearance, he was more than capable of keeping peace in his pub: his black belt in aikido ensured that. Jack let Edwards go and the hair receded instantly. He made a fist, feeling the fingernails shrink to normal size. Edwards held his ground for a moment longer, staring at Jack with a sullen grin on his face.

"Anytime Jackie boy," Edwards spat. "Don't you worry, Ken, I was going anyways. Got a job to do, see." Edwards left without another word or glance at anyone in the pub.

"What was that Jack?" Katie asked, trying hard to keep her voice level.

"I've always hated that prick," Jack said.

"Yeah, we all do, Jack, but you can't beat him up in here," Ken said. "It'd take me ages to clean the place up when he was done."

Jack laughed despite himself. In one line, Ken had removed all the tension in the bar.

"Come sit down, Jack. First rounds on me, ok? You eating?"

2

Knowles watched the confrontation with interest. He tried to act like he wasn't watching, but that was hard given how few people were in the pub. The man – Edwards – that Jack grabbed had a good foot height advantage and the build of a labourer. Jack had the build of a teacher, but he had definitely moved first.

Interesting. Not as quiet as he first appears then.

He continued watching as Jack let the bigger man go. Knowles caught a glimpse of something as Jack let his arms drop to his sides. He glanced at Meyers to see if he'd noticed anything, but the other gave no indication.

Am I seeing things?

He watched Jack return to his seat and order food. His left arm was in clear view now and it was a normal pale arm with a thin dusting of hair on it. Knowles shook his head as if to clear it.

"Did you see that?" he asked quietly.

"Yeah, I thought he was going to get a right slapping." Meyers was fond of taking well known phrases and changing them slightly. It made for some bizarre imagery sometimes: usually funny, sometimes annoying.

"No, his arms. Did you see his arms?"

"What about them?"

"Never mind," Knowles said, exasperated. Had Meyers not seen it? Jack's arm looked normal now. Had he imagined it?

No. His arm suddenly sprouted thick black hair. The kind you normally see in the pornos Scarlet liked.

Knowles took out his mobile, but the barmaid shook her head.

"You can do it," she said, "but it's a pound in the fine box." She pointed at a small box on the bar which was covered in a sheet of paper, badly sellotaped to it. The paper had a phone crossed out and 'mobile phine' written above it in WordArt.

He went outside and speed dialled Carruthers' mobile.

"Where are you?"

"About 45 minutes away. We've just finished our ride and-"

"We're in the pub. The Kings Arms. You've got 30 minutes. Get here."

3

As usual, Jack had burger and chips. The burger was smothered in cheese and onions, then he covered it some more in HP sauce. Katie had a bowl of chips with cheese and onion on it. It was all that proper pub food should be: cheap, cheerful, tasty and very satisfying.

They chatted whilst they ate. Katie had been frosty to him at first, but given that she didn't like Edwards either, she let it go. She put Jack's temper swing down to tiredness from the last few days. In all, it had been a pretty eventful week. The accident, the baby, the dog and now this in the pub. She sighed. *Most families don't have that in a year.* She was glad that Ginny had been given the all clear. The dog was lying under the table, asleep.

Ken came and took the plates away when they were done. Ginny woke long enough to steal a chip that fell off the plate and then settled straight back to sleep. Josh had now slept for over an hour.

"We should go," She said, looking at Josh. He sucked his bottom lip in and gave a very heavy sigh, but stayed asleep.

"Good idea," Jack said. He wasn't too comfortable with leaving: Edwards might be waiting for him. Equally if they stayed, Josh might wake and scream the place down. Jack definitely wasn't comfortable with ruining the sanctity of a pub with a screaming baby.

They stood to leave. Ken waved from the bar. Katie went first and held the door open for Jack to wheel the pram through. He was halfway through the door when three men arrived all walking quickly. Jack didn't recognise any of them. They stopped when they saw him coming with the pram and all stood to one side.

"Cheers," Jack said and then stopped, staring at the biggest man. "Do I know you?"

The big man looked surprised. "No, I don't think so."

"Are you sure? You look familiar to me. Did you use to live in London? Sutton maybe?"

"No, sorry." They locked eyes again.

"My mistake," Jack said in a tone that said he hadn't made any mistake at all. He pushed the pram past them and he and Katie started walking home.

"What was that all about?" she asked. "Have you seen him somewhere before in the village?"

"No," Jack said. "I don't think I've seen him around the village."

No, not seen him. Something else. Something as familiar as sight.

Smell.

I've smelt him before.

And with that thought, Jack knew exactly where he'd seen the man.

4

He didn't tell Katie: what would be the point? How would he explain how he knew? *I smelt the man who we just met.* It sounded crazy to him, and he knew it was the truth. No, he needed time to think. Neither he nor Katie had seen the man before which meant he had to be someone who had just moved here or was on holiday.

He has been in my house. He drugged my dog. Jack gripped the pram handle tighter and took a deep breath. *I need to stay calm for Katie's sake. And Josh. Otherwise I'll go back and rip him apart with my bare hands.*

He shuddered at the thought, at the same time that it gave him a thrill. When he'd held Edwards in the pub, he'd felt the power surging down his arms. He knew he would have won the fight against the bigger man: he didn't know if he'd be able to restrain himself. All his life he'd objected to bullies and others who liked to throw their weight around. It seemed that whatever had happened to him would now make it possible for him to stand up to these cowards. It thrilled and horrified him in equal measure.

I have to be careful. Whatever this is, it could scare a lot of people.

Plus, I don't really know what this actually is. Am I turning into an animal like some kind of old story? What happens if I just embrace this?

Chapter 11

1

Jack regretted his pint when a mid-afternoon slump kicked in just as Josh was letting rip with a huge wail. He would stop momentarily if he was fed or held, but then the screaming would start again. They both rushed around trying to get things to console him but to no avail. He eventually fell asleep just before six in the evening.

They both flopped onto the sofa with the news in the background. Katie looked exhausted.

"Jesus," she managed to say.

Jack chuckled. "Yeah. Just think, he's not even teething yet."

"That's not even approaching funny. Not even on the same planet."

"I know. But that's the first time he's been tough: maybe we've been lucky so far."

"Yeah."

She looked like she was going to say more, but the phone interrupted her. She answered it.

"Hi, John. Yeah, he's here. Pub at eight?" she looked at Jack who nodded with a grin. "He'd love to. Bye!"

She flopped back onto the sofa. "Another boys night. Lucky you!"

"I won't go if you don't want me to."

"Don't be daft. Go, enjoy. We won't get too many nights out for about the next year, so make the most of it."

"Oh, I'll just have a couple."

"You're a terrible liar Jack."

2

Scarlet wrote 'pub 8 o'clock' on the pad, and threw it at Knowles who was playing dice with the others.

"Ok, who wants to go to the pub tonight?" he asked.

"Not me," Carruthers said. "I'm sure he recognised me."

"We've been through this," Knowles said. "There's no way he could have recognised you."

In response Carruthers shrugged. He'd known he'd been made the moment he saw Stadler coming out of the pub. He had no idea how, but Stadler had known who he was. *It was the look in his eyes, pure hatred, just for a second.*

"I'll go," Scarlet said. "I fancy a night out in the sticks."

"Me too," Jones said.

"Ok. You two are up. Take radio earpieces and stay in contact. Go early."

"Early?" Jones smiled. "Well, ok, but only if you twist my arm."

"Go to the Kings Arms. If they are not there by 8:30, go to the other one."

3

Jack was exhausted before he even reached the pub. Josh had woken in a better mood, but after bathing and dressing him then clearing everything away, a wave of tiredness had almost drowned Jack. The last thing he wanted to do was go to the pub. He resolved to have one drink, then go home.

John was waiting for him, two pints in front of him in the Seven Stars. He pointed at his watch.

"Don't mate, I'm knackered."

"You look terrible."

"Yeah. Josh has learnt how to cry."

"Oh. Yeah that's tough isn't it? They're drugged up to their eyeballs for the first couple of days."

"You could have warned me."

"And spoil your fun?"

Jack laughed and instantly felt better.

"You know," John said between sips of his beer, "this is a strange time."

"How so?"

"Well, anyone who has been a parent starts doling out advice and anyone who hasn't gives you that look of pity."

Jack smiled. "I'm not getting much pity yet."

"You will," John replied. "Trust me. People can't help giving you advice or telling you 'My Shell's cousin's sister had a baby just like yours'." He said this last in a high shrill voice, making Jack laugh out loud. John smiled. "You know, it's all bollocks – he's your kid, whatever you do must be right." John drained half the glass in one mouthful and shrugged. "Unless you're putting out cigarettes on him or making him support Chelsea. There are some sick people in the world: your job is to protect Josh from them."

Jack felt uneasy at this, his stomach churning with anxiety. *What if I'm one of the 'sick' people now?* He tried a smile, but he knew it was far from convincing.

"Grandparents been yet?"

"No. We asked them to give us space for the first week. We needed to get our heads round the fact that he's actually here. I go back to work on Monday, so Katie's mum is coming down then. Mine will be down at the end of the week."

They fell into a comfortable silence then. The sort of silence that takes years to feel natural, but one of the reasons Jack liked John so much was he didn't feel the need to talk just for the sake of making noise. He could relate to that. "Something has happened to me."

"What?"

"When I fell down that hole. Something happened."

"Yeah, you didn't get hurt and it was a miracle. You're a bloody lucky bloke, now get your round in."

Jack did as he was asked and sat back down with a heavy sigh.

"You got something you need to share Jack?"

"I'm changing John. Today I held Graham Edwards up by his shirt."

"That cunt? No doubt he had it coming."

John rarely swore, so to hear *that* word was a shock to Jack.

"Jesus, John."

"Well he is isn't he? I could have used a nicer word but what would have been the point? Call a spade a spade I say."

Jack looked at him, mouth open until John laughed. "He is a racist twat isn't he?"

They drank some more, then Jack started to speak.

"It's more than just having a bit of impatience with Edwards though, John. I've been having these really violent fantasies, thoughts really. I wanted to tear his face off."

"Tear his *face* off?" John spat his beer out. "Wow, that is very John Woo."

"Like I said. I think I'm changing." He decided not to say anything about his fingernails growing and arms suddenly sprouting fur. As much as he liked and trusted John, it felt like too much. He drained the last of his drink. "Sorry, man, I'm knackered. I'm going to have to go home."

"Sure," John said emptying his glass too. "Try not to kill anyone on the way home now."

"You staying?"

"I'll have another, see who shows up."

"Alright. Cheers mate." Jack paused as he stood up. "I'd appreciate this being just between us. Ok?"

John nodded as if to say he'd already assumed that. "See you."

"See you."

Jack left the pub. Five minutes later, two men who had been sitting on the next table stood and followed him out.

4

Jack took the shortcut home. He walked down the alleyway that led to the churchyard. A security light should have come on to light his way, but it didn't. Jack swore softly, but his eyes adjusted rapidly to the gloom and he kept walking. Even with his night vision, he still didn't see the dark shape until it was too late.

A bar swung at his leg and he heard a crack as it connected above his knee. He howled in pain and fell to the floor, clutching his knee. He rolled onto his back and raised his arm as the bar came again. The bar connected with his arm and he heard the bone snap.

"Not so fucking tough now are you?" A deep voice came from the shadows. Jack heard the clatter of the bar hit the ground. "Come on Jackie boy, try pushing me around now." His face took the full force of the hit and his nose broke. Blood spurted out of his nose, covering his mouth and chin. Tears welled in his eyes.

Pain is just in your head Jack. Let it go.
-embrace it-

The shadow straightened and looked around. He aimed a kick at Jack's side, but was surprised when Jack caught it. Jack pushed with all his strength, and the shadow crashed to the floor. Jack tried to stand, but his leg gave way.

"You should leave."

The big shadow got back to his feet surprisingly quickly "Leave, Jackie boy? Not until you've got no shit left in you to kick."

"No."

The man stopped moving. Despite the darkness engulfing him, Jack could see the arm drawn back, fist ready to fly.

"You need to leave. I will not be responsible if you do not."

A laugh rang out. "I'm going to enjoy this."

He strode to Jack and bent to pick him up. Jack waited until their faces were level, then he let *it* embrace him.

5

Scarlet heard the noise and it shocked him: not a noise you expect to hear in a sleepy Devon village. At first he thought it was some old biddy's TV turned up way too loud. A scream followed by a howl that echoed around the buildings and carried far into the night. It certainly wasn't a human cry and he would give good money that it wasn't a common animal sound. A quick glance at Jones confirmed that he felt the same.

"Shit," Jones muttered quietly, "I wish I'd brought a gun."

"I did." He pulled out his standard issue Browning pistol. He made ready now – largely to make himself feel better.

"You got a spare?" Jones hissed.

Scarlet shook his head, then pointed at the dark alley that was the quickest way back to the Stadler house. Given the road was well lit, it seemed an obvious route. Scarlet went first walking slowly into the dark with his gun outstretched before him. No movie style heroics, he had both hands on the grip and looked down the sights all the way.

Jones followed closely behind him and kept his mic in the open transmission position. He gave a running commentary as they walked into the dark.

"Not exactly sure what we just heard, Knowles, but it sounded like there's an animal in the churchyard-"

"Of course that was a fucking animal, city boy," Scarlet said.

"You keep aiming that gun, let me do the talking. Scarlet is right, guys. That was one hell of a howl, whatever it was. I don't mind admitting being a teensy-weensy bit scared right now."

"For fuck's sake, Jonesey," Knowles said.

"Ok, it's really dark here. It's so quiet too. It's like that animal has sent everything away. We are walking towards the churchyard like a right couple of lemons who have never seen a horror film."

"What are you worried about? It's just an animal. There's hundreds of the buggers round these parts. You're worried because it's dark." Knowles' voice sounded calm and reassuring in his ear. "Either of you armed?"

"Scarlet has his Browning. It didn't sound much like a cat or dog to be honest."

"So what did it sound like?"

Good question. "Like nails on a board sir."

"Worse than that," Scarlet muttered.

The dark now enveloped them totally. Behind them, a lone streetlight glowed, a beacon of safety against the encroaching dark. Jones felt the urge to sprint towards the light, but fought against it. *Pull yourself together man. You've been to Ghanners – this is a quiet village in Devon.*

They could make out a security light above the gate, but it didn't come on. Scarlet knelt and felt small shards of glass on the ground underneath the light.

"Broken deliberately," he said, "and covered up badly." He reached into his pocket and pulled out his mobile phone. He switched on the flashlight function and weak light shone onto the path.

"Well, *that* makes me feel better," Jones said, and then to Knowles: "This is looking like a pretty good ambush spot."

"Someone after Stadler? Or the other way round?"

"Good question."

"Well, find out Jonesey. Now."

Jones let go of the mic and made a wanking gesture with his free hand. Then he switched the mic back on and said: "We're on it."

Scarlet pushed the gate with his left hand and it creaked open. Inside the churchyard, the path split to go two ways round the church. He was about to order Jones to go one way when he saw the body on the floor.

6

The body was lying in a pool of blood that was still spreading like an oil patch on water. As he got closer, Scarlet could tell it was a man by the build. It would be a frightening woman to be that tall and heavy. The meagre light played over the remains.

Half of his face was missing – a huge chunk had been removed that ran from just under his eye socket to his jaw line. His cheek had been torn clean off, leaving teeth, bone and muscle exposed to the air. His eye was open and staring, barely held in place by the remaining skin. The other side of his mouth was open in a scream. His ribcage had been pulled apart and even in the dim light Scarlet could see that things were missing.

"Holy fuck." He fought down bile. Even with everything he had seen in war zones, this was something else. *You don't expect to see someone ripped open in Devon.*

Jones looked at the body and threw up, wet bile splashing noisily onto the floor.

"Thanks for that Jonesey," Knowles said.

"Sorry," Jones gasped. "Forgot to switch the mic off."

"What's going on? Where's Stadler?"

"No idea. We've found a body. It's not good, Knowles."

"Body? Where the fuck is Stadler?"

"Fucked if I know. He left before us and we followed him to the churchyard. That's where we are now, with a dead man."

"Fuck the dead man, where's the target?"

"Knowles, if you could see this you wouldn't say that." The words were out before Jones had a chance to process them. *Fuck it, I'll take the bollocking later – this is serious.*

"Tell me."

"There's a dead man lying in the middle of the path in the churchyard. He's got half his face and most of his insides are missing."

"Shot?"

Jones and Scarlet locked eyes at that. Scarlet shook his head, not that Jones needed confirmation.

"No. It's like he's-" *Do I really want to finish that sentence?*

"He's what, Jonesey?"

"He's been eaten, Knowles. It looks like something has had a right good chew on his bits."

They both heard the hiss of static on the earpieces. Jones imagined Knowles staring into space, trying to figure out what to do next.

"Has anyone seen you two?"

"Don't think so, but you can never be sure in a village like this."

"Ok, get out of there. Make sure you aren't seen. You need to find Stadler."

Jones and Scarlet moved quickly. They skirted the dark edge of the pool of blood and then ran to the other side of the churchyard. Sticking to shadows, they exited the churchyard by the gate on the other side of the graves. Once back in streetlight they walked normally down the street, heading for their house. There was no sign of Stadler, or anyone else.

Or anything, Jones thought. He checked his mic wasn't transmitting before he spoke again. He didn't want to sound crazy to everyone.

"Do you think Stadler did that?"

"I don't know. That looked like an animal attack didn't it?" Scarlet said, but by his tone Jones knew that he was trying to convince himself.

"Yeah, it did. But why are we watching this guy? What's he done?" Jones looked over his shoulder as he talked. Was something moving back there? "Maybe he's a right crazy fucker who likes to eat people?"

"No way Stadler could have beaten that guy. He was a monster! Stadler couldn't have beaten him with Carruthers helping and Knowles as back up."

Jones laughed at that, but it didn't make him feel any better. "Listen, what if he's, you know, like the Hulk or something?"

"The Hulk? What are you, twelve?"

Jones looked over his shoulder. The street behind him was almost perfectly black apart from the dotted pools of light from streetlights. Cars were parked sporadically along the street. *Plenty of hiding places.*

"So where's Stadler gone?"

"Maybe he went to the other pub? Maybe he went the other way home? Just cos he went that way when we were watching earlier doesn't mean he always goes that way."

"We should have left sooner." Jones looked behind him again. He thought he heard a noise, like a can being kicked down the street.

"Then he would have made us. Maybe he's expecting us or someone to be following him. Look, it's not a problem, we know where he lives."

Jones had to agree with that and they came to the end of the street. They crossed the main road and walked a short way to their house. In doing so, they walked past the Stadler house. A single light burned from behind curtains on the second floor.

Somewhere, a dog barked, making Jones jump out of his skin.

"What the fuck is wrong with you?"

"Nothing. This just doesn't feel right. I think there's a lot we don't know about Stadler. That body just gives me the creeps, man."

"Well, let's see what Knowles has got to say."

8

Meyers was on listening duty when they got in. He waved at them and carried on listening. Knowles gave them a beer each and told them to sit down.

"Stadler's not home. His wife is in the bedroom with the baby. He keeps crying." Knowles sat down in an armchair facing them. "Talk to me guys."

Scarlet ran through what had happened, with occasional help from Jones. Knowles listened, nodded at appropriate parts but didn't interrupt.

"So, was he killed by Stadler?"

"I don't think Stadler could have killed the man. He was at least twice as big as him," Scarlet said. Jones nodded agreement. Sitting in bright light, four walls surrounding them and in the company of his friends, he felt the tension ease out of him. *No way could Stadler have done that, no way.*

"We saw Stadler argue with a big guy in the pub earlier. Well, kind of argue. More a disagreement. Ok, maybe handbags were used," Meyers said.

"Same guy?" Knowles asked. Scarlet and Jones both shrugged: no idea. "So, we got an animal attack?"

"Animal attack?" Meyers said. "They were talking about that earlier. Some sheep have been killed."

"So, there's definitely a wild animal in the area?" Jones asked.

"Wild animal? It's Devon for fuck's sake, not the Masai Mara!" Scarlet said.

Knowles threw a satellite phone to Scarlet. "It's encrypted, they won't be able to trace the number. Call the police, just tell them where the body is."

"Yes sir." Scarlet went out to the garden to make the call.

"You ok?" Knowles asked Jones.

"Yeah. You know, where we've been –" he paused and drank long from his bottle. "I never thought I'd see something as bad here."

Friday

Chapter 12

1

Katie sat in the living room, phone in one hand, Josh in the other. He was feeding with loud sucking noises and she was trying to fight back panic. Jack had not come home and he had not done that before. In their entire relationship, once they had started living together but before Josh had been born, Jack had only spent two nights apart from her. One of those had been his own stag do.

Where are you Jack?

Josh had woken for a feed twice in the night, but she had assumed that Jack was sleeping in the spare room and had been so tired herself that she'd gone straight back to sleep both times. The panic had started when she saw the neatly made spare bed. Josh's insistent crying prevented her from ringing the police immediately. She thought about ringing John. She didn't want him to think that she was a nagging, insecure wife. Eventually, she gave in to her worries and phoned him. Karen answered.

"Hey, how's the little man doing?"

"He's great Karen, finding his lungs, y'know."

There was a pregnant pause that Karen broke. "What's wrong Katie?"

"Is Jack there?"

"No. Why? Did you have a fight?"

"No, but he's not here."

"Don't worry honey, he's probably nipped out for a run or to get the paper."

"Ginny is here so he hasn't gone for a run." She didn't add that Jack rarely read a newspaper so that was unlikely too. "What time did John get back last night?"

"I don't know, I went to bed. Hang on a second."

She muffled the mouthpiece and Katie could hear her talking to John. "Hello? He got back at about 11, which probably means half past. He said Jack left about an hour before him."

"Oh God."

"I'm sure he's fine. He'll come back in a minute and ask what's wrong with you."

"Maybe," Katie said, but she wasn't convinced. She hung up and sat staring into space. Josh continued his noisy feed without breaking stride.

A police car roared past outside with its siren blaring making her jump. Sirens were heard so rarely in Huntleigh and usually meant someone had had a heart attack or stroke. A police siren was a once a year event at most. Her heart rate quickened further.

Where the hell are you Jack?

2

Jack woke slowly, sounds and sights taking their time to reach through his senses. He was lying in a field: grass tickled his nose and mouth. He sat up quickly.

Too quickly.

His stomach churned and blood rushed to his head. The nausea passed after a moment, but the disorientation remained. *Where am I?* The multi-coloured houses and unfamiliar view threw him for a moment, until he realised he was looking at the back of his street. His house, with the white cob walls and grey tiles stood in stark contrast to the greenery around him. He was in Frank's field, the one that ran behind his house. On his right, proud on top of the hill, he could see the tall spire of the church.

The church.

Edwards.

Oh shit.

There was a faintly metallic taste in his mouth – a taste that was horribly familiar to Jack. He'd last tasted it when building a fence in his garden. He had slipped with the saw and cut across the back of his hand. For a moment he'd thought he'd got away with it, then blood welled out of the wound and he'd licked it like you do when you're a kid.

Same taste.

Jack turned to be sick, but nothing came up. He had expected his stomach to do a somersault, but it didn't. Instead, he felt instantly energised, like he had run three miles and eaten a good breakfast.

That's probably not a million miles from the truth.

He stood up, this time with no head rush or nausea. He felt his arms and could feel muscle rippling there. *Bare arms.* He reached down to his legs and felt hair and muscle. His breath frosted the air, but he wasn't cold.

He looked around the field. He couldn't see his clothes anywhere. The field was empty: no sheep, no dogs and no clothes. *Best get indoors as quickly as possible – how the hell am I going to explain this?*

He ran across the field and vaulted the fence into the neighbours' garden. From there he jumped over the hedge into his own garden, cursing the conifers they'd planted at the rear of their garden. He moved quickly to the back door, hoping that no-one had seen him. That would take far too much explaining. He pulled the handle of the back door.

It was locked.

3

Katie turned the television on. The silence was killing her slowly – even Ginny wasn't making a sound. Josh had gone to sleep so she'd put him in his cot. The TV seemed unnaturally loud even when she turned it down. She had tried to sit still, but lasted less than a minute before she was up and pacing again.

On the TV, she flicked to the local news channel. A female presenter with an obviously fake tan and too many teeth grinned out at her whilst wearing something that wouldn't have looked out of place in an old people's home. Katie almost turned it off but then she saw the ticker tape scrolling across the bottom of the screen.

..body found in Huntleigh, Devon…. Suspected animal attack…. Police-

She let out a cry and another police car roared past. Sirens and lights shattering the peace. *Oh God!* She forced herself to calm down. Jack wouldn't – *couldn't* – be dead. No way, not after everything that had happened this week.

How do you know for sure?

She ran upstairs and pulled on yesterday's clothes. Josh was still asleep so she scooped him up and almost sprinted back downstairs. She laid him on the sofa, silently thanking God that he stayed asleep. Back in the kitchen she set up his buggy and turned back to the living room.

A man was standing at the back door staring at her intently.

4

Jack looked at Katie through the glass. She had never looked so beautiful to him. Her dark hair sat tussled around her face and her eyes almost glowed. Clothes hung loosely, but clung in the right places to emphasise her newly curvaceous figure. For a moment, he thought of her on their wedding day, but then she screamed.

"It's me." It came out so low it was almost a growl. She unlocked the back door and started to hit him, tears rolling down her face.

"You fucking bastard! Where the fuck have you been? I've been worried fucking sick!" Each word was punctuated with either a punch or a slap.

He pulled her to him and held her tight until the struggles stopped. She rested her head on his shoulder, tears of relief running down her face. Her body was warming him and-

"You've got to be fucking kidding me," Katie said pulling away from him. "Where have you been?"

"I woke up in Frank's field," he mumbled in the low voice again.

"Frank's field? Where are your clothes Jack? What happened?" She started to cry again. "They found a body. I thought it was you."

A body?

Edwards.

Jack held her tighter. "I don't know what happened, Katie. I was walking home and someone hit me. I think it was Graham."

"Shit, Jack." Her vocabulary had always been second only to sailors.

"I know. I ran and woke up in Frank's field."

You almost believe that don't you?

"I was so worried." All the anger seemed to have left her now.

"I'm sorry honey."

"What happened to your clothes?"

"I don't know." That, at least, was the truth.

81

She pulled away from the embrace and looked at him carefully. It was her bullshit detector and it was in full flow.

"Jack?"

"I'm cold. I need a shower." Her face fell. "Please Katie. We'll talk later."

5

They sat on opposite ends of the sofa, a distinct chill covering the distance between them. Jack was now in jogging bottoms and a t-shirt. His hair was still damp, but he managed to scrub away the dirt and smell of the field. Katie was clearly still fuming.

"I had a few beers with John and left early, like I said I would." The words came out slowly, like he was thinking carefully about each one. In truth, he had no idea what he was about to tell her.

"I cut through the church yard, but Edwards was there. At least, I'm pretty sure it was him. He hit me round the back of the head with a bar or a bit of wood or something and then started to kick me on the ground-"

"You haven't got any bruises."

"I know. I can't explain it. Anyway, I got up and hit him a few times then I ran. Next thing I know, I woke up in the field."

"Maybe you're concussed."

"Maybe. I was thinking of ringing that Dr Baxter who saw me after the fall. He said it was a miracle I wasn't more hurt. Maybe this is the same thing."

Even as he said it, he didn't believe it. *No, this is all to do with that bone.*

Then there was a very loud, very firm, knock on the door.

6

"You better come quick, Major Smith is on the blower." Carruthers burst into his bedroom. Knowles sat up quickly, took off his headphones and pulled on some shorts. He had slept with headphones for years. *Choose an album, put it on repeat and go to sleep.* It had drowned some of the noise in Ghanners. For a second, the only noise in the room was a tinny version of 'Sweet Child O'Mine', then he switched the music off. He was out the door and downstairs only thirty seconds later.

"Stadler's been out all night. His missus is having a fit. It's like listening to the end of a squaddie's marriage too."

"Hang on a second," Knowles said, taking the satellite phone from Meyers. "Morning, Sir."

"Sit rep, sergeant."

"Stadler seems normal sir." He paused, unsure what to say next. *Oh, Carruthers saw a big dog that none of us have seen since, I saw his arm sprout hair and Jones and Scarlet heard an animal and found a mutilated body. Yep, he's normal alright.* "Happy new dad, wife looks good. They seem happy. I've just been informed they're having an argument, but it's only just started." He winced as he said it: *This isn't going to look good.*

"Someone has been killed."

"Yes sir."

"What is Stadler's involvement in this?"

"Unknown sir. We lost eyeball on him last night."

"Why are you there, Knowles?"

He didn't answer; he knew a rhetorical question when he heard one.

"Sort yourself out Sergeant. I want a full report within the hour."

The line went dead.

Carruthers gave him a stern look. "Why did you lie?"

"What am I supposed to say? It's all a bit fucked here isn't it? And we don't know for sure that Stadler is involved."

"If it looks like a duck, quacks like a duck and tastes good with hoi sin sauce, it probably is a duck," Meyers said.

"Turn the box on."

Four of them watched TV in silence for a couple of minutes, whilst Meyers continued to listen to the Stadlers' argue. The twenty-four hour news channel was leading with the latest crisis in Afghanistan, but the ticker tape at the bottom said that a mutilated body had been found in a village in Devon. Knowles swore quietly.

"What are you going to do?" Scarlet asked.

"Tell Smith the truth."

Five minutes later, he used the radio to call Smith back. Carruthers took over from Meyers, whilst Knowles told Smith everything that they'd seen so far. *Well, not the part about hair growing on his arm – that's just too weird.*

Smith seized on one part of his story, excitement obvious in his voice. "A big dog?"

"Yes sir. None of the rest of us had seen it but-"

"There is a dead body and you've seen a big dog. You don't think the two are related Sergeant?"

"We don't know what to think, sir. The dog has only been seen once. We looked all over the Stadlers' house, but could find no trace of it."

Carruthers started waving his arms frantically, trying to get Knowles' attention.

"Just follow your orders, Knowles. You are to keep Stadler under close observation. I want eyes on that man at all times – am I clear?"

"Yes sir."

"No more mistakes, Knowles."

Carruthers waved even more frantically. Scarlet wandered over and listened in on the spare set of headphones. His mouth dropped open. Knowles finally saw Carruthers.

"Sir, I think we have a situation developing."

"Go, Sergeant. Remember – eyes on, no matter where."

7

It was John. He came in as soon as Katie opened the door without waiting for an invite. He made a beeline for Jack, sweat rolling down his face. He tried to get his breath back, but failed miserably.

"Do you want water John?" Katie asked, a concerned hand on his back. John shook his head.

"Jack," he gasped, "what have you done?"

"What have I done?"

"They've found Edwards in the churchyard."

Katie let out a gasp.

"He's been ripped apart apparently. Father Keeling found him when he went to open the church this morning."

Katie sat down, her face pale.

"What's that got to do with me?" Jack said.

"How do you know this?" Katie asked simultaneously.

John turned to Katie first. "I went to get the paper, like I always do." John liked fresh air in the morning. "I saw a couple of police cars turn up and went to have a look. I heard them talking about it – I'm glad I didn't see the body. Father Keeling is a bit shaken up apparently."

"I still don't see what this has to do with me," Jack said, but there was something in his voice: a lack of conviction that the other two heard clearly.

"They found your clothes around the body. They were also ripped to pieces. I recognised them as they were carrying them away in evidence bags."

"What?" Katie asked. "You said you ran away from him."

"I did," Jack said. He was close to tears.

"I thought you were dead, that's why I ran all the way here." John had finally got his breathing under control. "But when I saw you…"

"You what? When you saw me, what?"

"Edwards is dead, Jack. Your clothes are all over the scene."

"Do you think I killed him?" Jack tried to put indignation into his voice, but failed. John looked at his friend with a pained expression on his face.

"Last night, you said you'd happily kill him."

"That was just talk, wasn't it Jack? Tell him."

Jack put his head in his hands. *What the hell do I do now?*

"I did not kill Edwards. I don't mean to speak ill of the dead but he was a complete wanker and you know it. I'd loved to have punched his lights out, but not this. I didn't kill him."

John and Katie exchanged uneasy glances. Katie was grateful that Josh was staying asleep.

"I know he hit me, I remember that much. I don't know what happened next, then I woke in the field."

"You woke in a field?" John asked.

Jack nodded. "Yeah. I was naked. At least I know where my clothes are." He attempted a smile but it fell on stony gazes.

"What are you not telling me, Jack?" Katie asked, a single tear rolling down her cheek.

"Nothing Katie. I swear I didn't kill him."

No, something inside me did. Something I can't explain – something I don't understand.

"So who – or what - did? And who ripped all your clothes off you without leaving a scratch on you?"

8

The soldiers listened intently. They had all heard similar tones in their partners' voices over the years: I don't believe you. *Be careful what you say next Jack, Knowles thought, this might be the point of no return for your marriage.* For him it had been a point blank refusal to talk about Afghanistan that had done for his marriage. From his wife's point of view, she hadn't seen him for six months and then he wouldn't talk to her. From his perspective, there was nothing he could possibly say: he wanted to believe he was protecting her, but in reality he was protecting himself. No point in dragging those memories up. His wife had used the exact same tone of voice when berating him for excluding her from his life.

She had no idea.

Was Jack linked to the animal attack? Knowles wasn't sure, but it was a hell of a coincidence that Edwards was killed just seconds after Jack had left the pub. Then there was the bit that had got the others excited: what exactly had happened to his clothes?

He watched the grainy images on the monitor and listened more.

This op was getting weirder by the second.

9

Jack took a deep breath and considered his options. *You don't really have any choice here, Jack. Tell the truth.*

"I did hurt myself when I fell," he began and then stopped. *They are not going to believe me.*

"What?" Katie gasped.

"I fell onto a table made of stone, like a slab. It had carvings on it and there were bones on top. One of them went right through me."

"I should go," John said standing up.

"Sit down," Katie shouted. "I want you to hear this too."

John sat down without another word but with an expression on his face like someone had asked him to chew on a wasp.

"I pulled it out without thinking really, but there was no cut once I'd pulled it out."

"What do you mean? How can it go right through you without leaving a mark?" Katie's voice was breaking. The single tear had been joined by a few more.

"I didn't say that. I said that there wasn't a cut afterwards. It definitely went through me."

"Do you have any idea how that sounds?" Katie said, voice rising now. Jack nodded. He felt exhausted.

"Yeah. But I swear it's true. The bone went through me without leaving a mark."

"How do you know it went through you mate? You were concussed maybe, seeing things-"

"No," Jack said more sharply than he'd intended. "I know exactly what happened."

"Did you tell the doctors this?"

"No."

"Why not?"

"Because then they'd be looking at me like you are."

10

Knowles looked at Scarlet. "Get your climbing gear together. You're going into that cave tonight."

"Why?" Scarlet looked puzzled.

"Let's have a look at what he fell onto."

"Come on Knowles, he's lost the plot."

Knowles shook his head. "The Major said that we were to watch him. We can do that, but I want to know more. If he's telling the truth, then that cave is important. If he's crazy, then we lose a few hours and you get to go caving at night. Could be fun."

Carruthers sniggered. "If he's telling the truth. Priceless."

"Square that away Carruthers," Knowles barked.

"Ok, who comes with me?" Scarlet said.

"Carruthers and Meyers," Knowles said without a moment's hesitation.

11

Katie started to cry, quietly and without histrionics. It was worse that way. Tears rolled down her cheeks, more of a flood than the earlier trickle. Jack felt his stomach knot and his heart rate go up. His legs started trembling.

"Jack, I think we need to take you back to the hospital," John said, his voice barely above a whisper.

"I'm not crazy," he said, tears of his own welling. "I'm not. I don't know what's happening to me, but it all started there, in that cave."

"The fall must have done more damage than you first thought," John said, a little louder now, as if for Katie's benefit.

Jack just shook his head. "No. I'm fine. That doctor said I was his first miracle."

"Tell me about the cave," Katie said, wiping tears away. Anger was back in her eyes now.

"Like I said, I landed on a big stone slab. It had carvings on it."

"What kind of carvings?"

Jack shrugged. "Not sure really. One kind of looked like the Devil, but with really big horns."

Both John and Katie's mouths dropped open. In different circumstances it would be comical.

"Jack, seriously mate, you do know this is out loud and everything?"

Nobody laughed.

"What has this got to do with your clothes being ripped?"

"I don't know," Jack said. "I'm just saying that weird things have been happening since I fell down that hole. Bad dreams for a start."

"BAD DREAMS ARE FUCKING NORMAL JACK!"

John held up his hands in the universal 'calm down' gesture. "I think I should leave you to it." This time he got up and almost bolted for the door. Neither Jack nor Katie made any attempt to stop him.

"You had a traumatic day," Katie hissed. "Bad dreams are normal. Your clothes falling off you and ending up in shreds next to a dead man is not."

"I don't know what happened!" It was Jack's turn to shout.

But you do know Jack. Oh yes, you remember it all.

"I want you to go back to the hospital. Right now Jack."

"What?"

"You heard. Go back and see that Doctor Maxler-"

"Baxter."

She glowered at him and he realised a little too late that this wasn't the time to be pedantic.

"Josh will be awake soon. We will go to see the doctor, make sure you're ok."

"There's nothing wrong with me."

"Jack, please."

He realised then that she wasn't angry at him, well not *that* much anyway. Angry Katie wouldn't have stayed in the room with him. The post-birth hormones wouldn't be helping her emotions either, but he was wise enough to keep that thought to himself.

"I can't just turn up and get an MRI scan."

"No, but you can go see that doctor and get yourself more thoroughly checked out."

He conceded defeat by raising his hands in a close mimic of John's actions earlier.

"I'll go and get Josh, you ring the hospital. I'll drive."

Chapter 13

1

They barely spoke on the long drive to the hospital. Josh slept all the way, head slumped to one side at that horrible angle only newborns seem to manage. The head support in the seat seemed to be in danger of contravening the trade descriptions act. It took them just under an hour but seemed a lot longer. Jack remembered the journey taking him just over thirty minutes several days and a whole lifetime ago.

He spent most of the journey trying to think of ways to break the ice. He didn't even dare turn on the CD. He knew that Katie was worried about him and that currently, concern was manifesting as anger.

He couldn't blame her.

He ran through the events of the last few days over and over again. He couldn't deny the facts: something had happened to him; something horrible and strange. He couldn't grasp the reality of it. Was he turning into an animal? Was he losing his mind? Something else?

This is just absurd Jack. Turning into an animal? You really have lost it.

More facts: running on all fours; the strange dreams; the taste of blood in his mouth; waking up in a field with no clothes and ripped clothing being found next to a dead man.

As they neared the hospital, Jack became more and more certain that no doctor would be able to help him.

2

Katie tried to keep her anger in check. He was lying to her, she knew that much: what she couldn't figure out was why. What was he trying to hide? From her, the mother of his child. She knew she was being more than a little emotive with that thought, but she couldn't help it.

She had been terrified to see him on the doorstep with no clothes on. Looking almost feral with dirt caked over him. Now she thought about it, was it just dirt? Could some of the dark streaks have been blood? That had been before John had turned up with his bombshell. But that really was what this boiled down to.

What exactly did she think Jack had done?

Attacked and killed a man? *Not Jack, no way.*

The man who had taken her to a bookshop for their first date could not kill a man. He had taken her to Waterstones in Piccadilly Circus. It was huge, covering six floors, but that hadn't been the reason for going. Jack had just smiled when she'd looked confused. A date in a bookshop? Hardly gets the pulse racing.

Turned out there was a cocktail bar on the sixth floor. They'd sat and drunk absinthe all afternoon. They'd done it the European way too: melting sugar cubes covered in absinthe into the shot glass through a slotted spoon. It had felt a little like cooking up drugs - not that she'd ever done that.

There was no way *that* Jack would have killed a man.

3

Knowles and Jones tailed from a very long way back. The entire family had got into the car so they had decided that both of them should follow. They also had inside information on where the Stadlers were heading. No alarms and no surprises. Knowles sang it to himself. *Who had sung that?*

"So what do you think is going on here?" Jones asked.

"I don't know," Knowles said honestly.

"Come on, after all we've been through – you must have more info than us."

"I really don't. Stadler came to our attention when he fell into that cave. I think it was because he was unhurt. Our op is purely surveillance."

"Yeah, but surveying what?"

"I don't know."

"Do you think he killed that man?"

"Jonesey, we've both killed people, but it was in the line of duty," Knowles said after some deliberation. "Kill or be killed. But it doesn't matter-"

"That shit stays with you."

Knowles nodded. "Yeah. It does. If he did it, then God help him."

4

The hospital was as busy as usual and they had to wait nearly five hours to see Doctor Baxter. He seemed much younger to Jack than he had the first time they'd met. He had a day's worth of stubble and big bags under his eyes. He fought back a yawn, but – much to Jack's annoyance – brightened considerably when he saw Katie.

"It's Mrs Stadler isn't it?"

"Yes," she said, smiling at him. The man was handsome, in a public school boy kind of way. Jack could feel his pulse quickening and a cold sweat ran down his back.

Stay calm Jack. You know who she's going home with.

"So, Jack, how are you feeling today?"

"I'm fine, Doc." Jack tried to keep his voice neutral, but judging by Katie's stern look he had failed miserably.

"Well, what can I do for you?" Baxter looked between the two of them, his face almost comical in its puzzlement. "Is there something wrong with the baby?"

"His name is Josh," Jack snarled. He felt his pulse increase a little again. Josh was asleep in a sling tied to Katie. They looked beautiful together, the new mum and the content baby. *All babies are beautiful when asleep.*

Katie put her hand on Jack's leg. He felt his muscles tense at her touch, but in a good way. He felt the heat of her hand and it seared up his leg into his groin. His pulse shot through the roof and the sweat was now pouring down his back.

"No, there's nothing wrong with Josh," Katie said, smiling at the doctor again. She looked stunning and Jack knew that Baxter could see it too. "We're here about Jack."

She shifted her gaze to Jack and inclined her head towards Baxter. Jack sighed and tried to get his pulse to slow down by deep breathing. It didn't work. Baxter leant forward, hands on his knees.

His gaze was firmly on Jack, but his hands were millimetres away from Katie's bare legs.

"Something happened last night," he started slowly. "I-"

"Go on."

Jack tried not to let the interruption annoy him. "I was attacked by a man. I was hit on the head then ran away and woke up in a field. I can't remember how I got there."

"Where on your head?"

"Back, and my left leg too."

"Well let's have a look at you. Is it ok to roll your trousers up or do you need to take them off?" Baxter was looking at Katie as he spoke. He was smiling at her, eyes lingering on her legs. *Stop fucking my wife with your eyes.* Jack tried to bury the thought, but too late. *Always too late, Jackie boy.*

"I think you should leave. I want another doctor," Jack gasped. He could feel his insides moving, his bones beginning to stretch.

"Jack-"

"Mr Stadler, Jack, are you ok?"

"You need to leave-"

Jack started to change.

5

It was approaching dark. Jonesey put out his cigarette and went back in to the waiting area. Knowles sat reading a gardening magazine. It was a very incongruous sight. Jones suppressed a grin and sat next to him.

"Where are they?" he asked.

"They've just been taken by a doctor," Knowles said as if it were obvious. "Third curtain down the hall on the right. The doctor came out and got his kit, then went back in."

"Why do they do that?"

"What?"

"Get their kit after you're in the curtain. You'd think they'd have it all to hand."

Knowles shook his head. "For fuck's sake, it's been a long shitty day, you watch the curtain." He threw the magazine onto the coffee table and stood up.

"Where you going?"

"For a slash. Just watch the curtain, Stadler doesn't leave without us, ok?"

Jones nodded.

"And get us more coffee."

Knowles was halfway to the toilet when the screaming started.

6

Katie watched hair sprout along her husband's arms and his nails grow, curving into claws. Her mind couldn't cope with what she was seeing. The hair was now thickening, matting together until it resembled fur. She looked at his face, her heart hammering so hard against her chest she thought it might escape.

His eyes were a bright yellow, almost golden colour. The pupils were an enormous black circle in the centre of a sun. The remaining white bits were red-rimmed and laced with blood-vessels. His teeth were far too large for his mouth and as she watched they too grew and sharpened. The strange thick black fur was sprouting along his chin and now his mouth – *no, face* – was stretching to accommodate those terrible teeth. His skin was rippling, like waves off shore.

She couldn't help it. She felt her bladder go, warm liquid splashing over her legs and feet. She opened her mouth and screamed.

7

Baxter started moaning as soon as he saw fur sprouting on his patient's arms. In five years of medical school and three years of practical experience he had never seen anything like it. Jack Stadler was changing in front of his eyes, his entire body going through some kind of metamorphosis.

This is going to make me rich.

The first step would be to get this written up and then published in one of the journals, but which one? The mental health ones would be a waste of time as this was clearly happening- it certainly wasn't all in Jack's head. Infectious diseases? Hereditary genetic disorders?

He was still thinking when *something* seemed to explode out of Jack. A thick, hairy arm topped with razor sharp claws swung at him and took a large chunk out of his face.

8

Katie screamed louder as Jack swung his arm at Baxter. The younger man fell backwards, blood pouring out of the large cuts in his face. He had three lines running from his jaw line, across his nose and other cheek. Skin flapped loosely around the cuts and Katie knew that Baxter would no longer be good looking.

He fell to the floor, pulling the curtain off its rails and rolled around there holding his face as if trying to stop the skin falling off. He pushed hard on the cuts, but blood poured out through the gaps in his fingers, pooling around his head like an obscene halo.

She turned Josh away from the thing that was standing where her husband had once been. Tears rolled down her cheeks and she couldn't stop screaming. She stepped through the curtain into the corridor and started sobbing in between the screams.

Doctors and nurse were sprinting towards her. Somewhere a fire alarm was urging people to clear the building. Its klaxon sounded as if it were under water because all her senses were being dominated by the thing. She felt the huge presence behind her, felt hot air being blown onto her neck and turned slowly.

Two well-built men not in hospital clothes were running towards her, but it seemed as though everyone was running to her so that hadn't been what had got her attention about these two. She recognised them. They had been in the pub yesterday, watching Jack. She couldn't focus on that now. Couldn't focus on anything other than what was happening behind her.

She continued to turn, forcing herself to look at the thing that had exploded out of her husband. *Jack.* Her eyes skated over what he was doing, refusing to take it in. Something warm splashed onto her face.

Oh God, Jack, what have they done to you?

He opened his mouth and roared when he saw her looking.

"Get away from my son!" she screamed as loudly as she could. "Get away, get away, get away!"

Then the world was sliding, getting dark and she fell to the floor.

9

Knowles turned at the scream, hand straight to his weapon. He had a brief moment of panic and felt the surge of adrenaline that had been a near constant companion in Afghanistan. He forced his hand away from the weapon – analyse first. Doctors were running down the corridor, towards the screams. The public were on their feet, or those who could stand anyway, and were edging towards the door. Jones was looking at him and pointed down the corridor. *Watch me, follow me.* He wanted to run, but a group of people blocked the way. He reached over and smashed the cover to the fire alarm with his elbow. The people looked up at the sound of the siren and then, muttering all the way, they started to head for the exit.

God help them if it had been a real fire.

He saw the doctor who had greeted the Stadlers fall back into the corridor, ripping the privacy curtain as he fell. Blood was pouring from multiple wounds on the doctor's face and the man was trying to stem the flow with his fingers. Knowles could tell he was wasting his time.

He saw Katie Stadler stagger backwards, screaming and shielding the baby as best she could. *Something* fell on the doctor's prone body and buried its head in his neck in an obscene parody of a lovers' kiss. Blood geysered out of the wound, showering Katie - not that she seemed to notice – and he knew that the doctor was gone.

"Get away from my son!" he heard her scream. "Get away, get away, get away!"

The thing had reared on its hind legs, clearing her head by at least a foot. Thick black fur covered its body and sharp teeth filled the mouth. Blood dripped out of the open orifice creating an image that Knowles would find hard to shift every time he closed his eyes.

Katie collapsed, somehow shielding the baby as she fell. The thing fell to all fours and sniffed at her, like a dog at a bin. Knowles could hear the baby – *him* – crying over the fire alarm. The thing turned to look at him as he sprinted closer, and too late, he wondered if rushing towards it was a wise move. Too late, he reached for his weapon.

It pounced and hit him full force in the chest. He fell backwards smacking his head on the tiled floor. His gun clattered away from his hand. Stars exploded into view and he grunted, expelling the last air from his lungs. He was pinned by its paws and his entire view was filled with two rows of razor sharp, blood stained teeth.

"Fuck!" he screamed as the creature roared, lowering its head.

Bullets tore into its flank. He heard the distinct *pop! pop! pop!* of a Browning firing. The animal – *wolf* – roared in pain and then leapt off him. He rolled quickly and swept up his gun. He fired three shots in quick succession, aiming at the thing's back. It howled again and ran past Jones, heading for the doors.

The hordes of people heading for the doors all paused as one. The thing ran past them all, accelerating as it ran into the night. It let off a final roar before it disappeared – a high pitched, guttural and completely animal sound that chilled the blood.

"What the fuck?" Jones gasped.

"Thanks man." Knowles stood slowly, checking himself for cuts as he stood.

"You hurt?"

"No."

They both turned to where Katie and Baxter were lying on the floor. Baxter's eyes were wide and unstaring. His blood was still expanding, running into Katie's hair and face. A nurse in a blue uniform had lifted the baby and was trying to soothe it. Another nurse was checking Katie's pulse. Around them were signs of panic and bedlam. Doctors and nurses tore up and down the corridors, shouting instructions at each other. A crash cart was thundering down the corridor, the doctor pushing it white faced. Some patients were crying and the ones the wolf had run past were extremely pale.

"Where's Stadler?" Jones asked, surveying the pandemonium.

Knowles paused for several seconds before answering. "I think he just left."

They looked at the door and the shocked faces surrounding it.

"Jesus."

"Yep."

10

The wolf ran and ran. The ground passed quickly under its feet. As soon as it left the hospital, it crossed a road, ignoring the screech of brakes as it went. It was soon in a field, then woods. Birds took to the air noisily ahead of it. Deer and other nocturnal creatures scuttled away through the undergrowth. The scent of salt filled the air as it breathed and it followed the smell.

Blood stopped leaking out of its side as it ran. If it had been running on a road, it would have heard the clatter of the bullets landing after they had been pushed back out of its body. It felt stronger and stronger as it put more miles the hospital further behind.

Eventually it broke through the tree line and saw large mounds rising ahead of it. The ground became softer and the salt scent became almost overpowering. It slowed to a fast walk, sticking to the natural shadows. It climbed the sand dunes and avoided a small fire and tent in a hollow. The smell there. Something familiar.

It soon found an empty hollow away from the camp. It sat on its haunches and looked at the sea. The sound of the waves was calming. It lay down, head on its paws, gaze fixed on the horizon. Soon its heartbeat slowed down, breathing became more regular. It watched with no emotion as the fur began to seep back into its limbs.

Jack sat up and began to cry.

Chapter 14

1

Knowles was bored of talking to the police. His statement had been taken twice, and now this third guy looked like he was about to start from scratch all over again. He could feel bruises on his chest from when the wolf had floored him and he needed to get back to the house before the others left for the woods.

"So Mr Knowles, how are you doing?"

"Fine," he snarled. "As I said to your colleagues."

"I'm Detective James Wilson. I just have some questions for you."

"I've said everything to the other officers, I just need to get home."

"I appreciate that, sir, but we have a dead man and a vicious animal on the loose. There is also another missing man, who is presumably dead given that all we have are his ripped clothes. We need to make sure we have every avenue covered before we let you go. The fact that the evidence here matches a scene from Huntleigh, where you are staying, is quite interesting, don't you think?"

Knowles sighed heavily. Leaving now would bring far too much unwanted attention to him and their operation. "Make it quick, please."

"The animal jumped on you?"

"Yes."

"Your friend scared it off."

"Yes."

"He shot it twice."

"Three times."

"Then you shot it."

"Twice."

"A witness said you fired at least three times."

"Yes, but I only hit twice."

"Are you a good shot?"

"What?" Knowles raised his eyebrows at the question: that was a new one.

"You seem a little bitter at only hitting it twice."

"I'm a soldier, I'm supposed to be a good shot. By missing I might have hit a civvy."

Wilson looked down at his notebook and nodded slowly. He flicked a page and scanned his notes. "You used a Browning, is that correct?"

When the other man nodded he continued: "I thought soldiers only had guns assigned to them when they were on an operation."

"Yes." Knowles stared at the policeman.

"So how come you've still got your gun, Sergeant?"

"I've just come back from Ghanners – um, Afghanistan. I didn't turn it in."

"And neither did your colleague?"

Knowles sighed again. "Look, we fancied doing some shooting when we were down here. Maybe some pheasants."

"Deer?"

"No, no, no. Just some birds," Knowles said. "Look, it was a good thing we had the weapons isn't it? God knows what it would have done if we hadn't shot it."

Wilson smiled for a second. "Oh yes, most fortuitous. Still, we have a problem."

"We do?"

"Well, you claim to have hit the wolf twice, your friend thinks he hit it three times in the side."

"And?"

"A trail of blood goes across the car park and into the woods. We've had a team trailing it, but they got back just before we started speaking."

Knowles knew that they would have been using UV torches to make the blood show up. Judging by the expressions on Wilson's face, they hadn't found the wolf.

"The blood stops, but there's no body. No dead wolf."

"Shit."

"Quite. So, where did it go?" Wilson tapped his pen on his notebook. "See, that's what we call a mystery."

Throughout his career, Knowles had met people like Wilson. People who talked very slowly and explained every little thing as they talked. People who assume that, because you are in the military, you are stupid.

"Us policemen, we don't like mysteries." Wilson tapped his pen again. "And the worst thing is, when I told you there was no body, you didn't look at all surprised."

2

Wilson eventually, bored of Knowles, interviewed Jones, who stuck to the script like an actor on first night. Frustrated, he let both soldiers go after taking contact numbers for them both.

He reviewed his notes. One dead, one missing and all the witnesses claim to have seen a huge wolf running through the corridors. This was his first corpse since moving to Devon a year ago, and already he didn't like it. Murder, or death by an escaped animal, either way it was a mess.

When he'd been in the Met, he'd seen a murder a day – often more, and that had been why he'd put in for a transfer to Devon. There were only so many dead junkies and prossies you could see. His last case had been a man who had been set on fire because he'd owed money to drug dealers. No witnesses. The burning man had run into the street where he'd been run over by some poor sod on his way home. Wilson had put in for a transfer the next day. *Too much, too much.*

The doctor – Baxter – had been partially eaten. That was a first for Wilson. The missing man was Jack Stadler, but his clothes were in tatters next to the dead doctor. His wife was now in a bed in the maternity ward with his baby being cared for by the nurses. The baby was not yet a week old.

What a mess.

He asked for directions to the maternity ward and made his way through the packed car park. A news van sat in the ambulance bay, but it didn't matter – the hospital was closed to emergency cases now. The whole of A&E was a crime scene and would be closed until the SOCOs were done.

It wouldn't be long before more media vans arrived – this would be a great story, like the Beast of Bodmin but with actual bodies. He had maybe an hour before this turned into a media circus and then dealing with the press and crackpots would take up all his time.

What a mess.

3

Katie sat up in bed, disorientated by her surroundings. A blue curtain surrounded her bed, giving everything a pale hue. The bed was narrow and uncomfortable, like lying on a concrete slab. To her left sat a clear plastic cot and Josh lay fast asleep in it, his head facing her and low soft snores coming from him. Relief washed over for a second before-

-Jack-

She started crying, huge sobs that racked her body. A nurse ran in and hugged her. Katie was in no position to resist and she allowed the nurse to rock her like a newborn.

"There, there."

"Jack!"

The nurse continued to make comforting noises until the sobs subsided. "Can I get you anything?"

Katie shook her head. "I want to see my husband."

The nurse looked distinctly uncomfortable. "How much do you remember, Mrs Stadler?"

Before she could answer, the curtain was pulled back by another nurse who was accompanied by a tired looking man in a suit.

"She's just woken up," said the first nurse, lips thin.

The man flashed his badge. "I just need to ask some questions."

"Now?"

"Yeah. We have a dead man – I need to know what she knows so we can find the killer."

"Go easy on her."

"She's not a suspect," Wilson said, as if this would make everything alright.

"Katie, this is Detective Sergeant Wilson."

Both nurses left. Wilson pulled over a chair and sat down. He took out his notebook and a pen.

"Hi, Mrs Stadler. I appreciate that this isn't a great time for you, so I'll be as quick as I can."

Katie nodded, fresh tears rolling down her cheeks. She went cold inside: she had not been interviewed by the police before.

"What do you remember?"

She shook her head and started sobbing again. Wilson looked at Josh as if aware of him for the first time.

"He's – he? – very cute." Wilson smiled at Katie. "I have two of my own. I suppose you've already been told this, but make the most of them at this age, they grow up so fast."

Katie tried to smile at him, but more tears rolled instead.

"Mrs Stadler, uh, Katie, I don't have much time. I need to know what you can remember."

Katie nodded. "We came to see the doctor. He was so nice." Her bottom lip quivered and she paused. "Then the animal came and–"

This time she didn't succeed in getting herself under control. Wilson scribbled in his notebook.

She took a deep breath. "I didn't know there were wolves that big in Devon."

"There are no wolves in the UK, apart from in zoos. We've got people ringing round to find out if any have escaped."

"Have they?"

"None yet," he admitted, "but the night is young." He looked at his watch. Only seven o'clock. Just over an hour past the attack. "Wolves are not known to attack humans – anywhere in the world." *Thank God for Google.*

"But–"

"I know. Every witness said it was either a wolf or a really big dog. Katie, I'm really sorry about your husband but–"

"Jack? Where is he?" *You know, Katie.*

"Nobody told you?"

"What happened to my husband?" Panic was very clear in her voice.

"I'm sorry, Katie, I thought you knew. You were there –"

"Tell me."

"He's missing, presumed dead. His clothes were found next to Doctor Baxter. They were shredded and covered in blood. Our SOCOs are on the way to examine it all, but it doesn't look good."

Katie went white. "He's not dead, he can't be," she said firmly.

"I'm sorry Katie."

"Jack is not dead, Mr Wilson, you need to find him before he gets hurt."

4

Wilson closed his notebook and put his pen away. He'd covered a page in doodles. It was important that Katie thought he was writing pertinent notes, but he's realised quickly that she had nothing to tell him. Crying relatives were the worst part of the job. He stood and put the chair back against the wall. On his way out, he paused by the cot and looked at the sleeping baby.

"What's his name?"

"Josh."

"Good name. Sleep well young Joshua."

"No, it's just Josh."

"Sorry." He paused again. "We will find your husband, Katie." Even as he said it, he knew he shouldn't have. "With your permission, I'd like to go to your house."

"Why?"

"It's where he'll head if he's still alive."

"Then I'm coming with you."

"I don't think that's a good idea, Katie."

"You got a warrant?"

"No," he admitted. "But I can get one."

"How long will that take?"

Wilson said nothing, but his face gave it away.

"So let me come and I'll give you permission."

Wilson shrugged, but knew she was right. Time was crucial here. The media would be here any second and with them any chance of a quick, easy end to this would disappear. He hoped there was nothing seriously wrong with Katie. It would be a nightmare if she died whilst with him: the paper work would be a bitch.

"Come on then."

5

Knowles sat in the car with Jones. They were watching from a street opposite the hospital car park. They had a good view of the only entrance to the car park. Neither Stadler would be able to leave without being seen.

"This is fubar."

Knowles had to agree with him. He knew what he'd seen with his own eyes, but he had a hard time believing it. *If it looks like a duck, quacks like a duck, then it probably tastes good with hoi-sin sauce.* That was what Meyers had said. It didn't make anything easier to believe though.

"Hello, what's this?"

Jones' voice shook him from his reverie. Katie Stadler was getting into her car. Near her, a man was talking to the uniformed police manning the cordon. He flashed his badge twice before they started to move. Katie had already bundled baby Josh into the back and was soon setting off past the cordon of police cars. Moments later another car pulled out, clearly following her.

"Let's go." Jones had already started the engine.

"Keep back, we know where they're probably going."

"Who's in the other car?"

Knowles shrugged. "Some useless copper, probably."

They were barely five hundred yards away from the hospital when the radio buzzed. They could hear a voice shouting in the background, but it was too muffled to make out. Knowles clicked receive.

"Sit rep," he said, far more calmly than he felt.

Scarlet started talking fast – and it was not good news.

Chapter 15

1

Jack stopped crying when the cold made him start to shiver. His clothes were long gone, lying in tatters back at the hospital. Every time he closed his eyes, he saw Katie shrieking and shielding Josh from him (*no, not him, the other thing*).

What am I going to do now?

His options appeared to be very limited. Firstly, he had killed a man (*two men, Jackie boy, two men*) and terrified his wife. He had attacked yet another man, been shot and run away from the scene – all in the view of about forty people.

Katie. God, please forgive me, Katie.

No-one had actually seen him kill Baxter, of that he was sure. Except Katie of course, but surely she wouldn't tell people that she'd seen her husband turn into a wolf? Who would believe her?

No-one. So she goes into a mental home and Josh goes into care, never knowing who his real parents are. Not bad for a night's work, Jack, not bad at all.

Baxter. Did he have a family? A wife? Children? *Think, think. What can I do?* He could turn himself in but who would believe him? What if he changed into that thing in one of the cells? Would he eat all the prisoners? The police? He felt calm around Katie, the creature wouldn't come then – he was certain of that. He screamed as loud as he could for a few minutes until his throat started to burn and tears filled his eyes again. Katie was not going to a mental home, Josh not going into care, not while there was breath in his lungs. He would sort this out somehow, but he would not let his wife suffer.

How Jack? How do you solve this problem?

Easy: one step at a time.

First problem: clothes.

2

Steven Wexley looked at the sausage and took a tentative bite. He nearly scalded the inside of his mouth and chewed noisily, mouth open. He tried to blow on the sausage piece as he chewed and ended up looking like a horse.

The fire was going strong, although it had been a slow starter. The wood around here wasn't as dry as he'd first thought. Gathering it had taken an hour as the sun had gone down. He'd waited for the minimal tourists to bugger off before pitching his tent. Rain had helped with that. He was far enough down the beach that he didn't think anyone would find him, despite the light from the fire. He sat in the opening to his tent, sheltered from the wind, but exposed enough to feel the heat from the fire. A noise came to him on the wind, somewhere between a roar and a scream. No one in sight.

The smell of the sausages was overwhelming his senses. He tried the sausage again and this time it was at an edible temperature. His stomach had just started grumbling at the lack of food today, so the sausage tasted fantastic.

There were two more sausages left in the packet. He had planned to keep them till morning, but that first one had tasted so good he couldn't resist. Not being able to say no had got him into this state in the first place.

He had put the next sausage on his stick and in the fire when he realised that a naked man was staring at him.

3

They regarded each other for a few seconds. The only sound was the popping of the fire and the crash of the surf behind them. Jack sized up the man in front of him and decided that a fight was probably not the best option.

"I need some clothes."

"No shit," the other man said. "It's cold out here. You on a stag?"

"Something like that."

"Get closer to the fire, son, it'll help."

Jack did as he was asked. The heat from the fire helped take the immediate chill off his bones, but the wind still felt cold. A seagull called out in the distance and was answered by several others. *Nice to be wanted.*

"I need some clothes," he repeated.

"So you said, son, so you said." The man nodded, his grey beard bobbing up and down in the firelight.

"Can you help?"

"Maybe, son, maybe."

Silence fell between them again. Jack took deep breaths and tried to keep calm. It was not easy. The wind blew again, and he shivered.

"You want a sausage?"

"No thanks." Jack nearly added *I've just eaten*, but managed to stop himself. He didn't want to throw up.

"Your loss. There's nothing quite like a sausage cooked on an open fire." The man bit into a sausage and fat dripped down his chin, settling in his beard. "I'm Steve, by the way."

"Jack."

"So, your mates stripped you and left you. Not good mates I'd say."

Jack shrugged.

"So what's this going to be worth to me?"

"What?"

"Well, I ain't got much, son; I give you some clothes, I got even less." More fat dripped onto his beard.

"You want money?"

"Yep."

"How much?"

"How much you got?"

"Not a penny on me."

That awkward silence fell between them again. Then Steve threw back his head and laughed. "Hey I like you Jack, you got a sense of humour." He continued to laugh even as he bit into the sausage again.

"I can get you enough money to buy you food for a week," Jack said.

"And whiskey."

"And whiskey."

"Don't look like that Jack. I ain't no drinker and that's not how I ended up like this – but a little whiskey keeps the cold off at night, know what I'm saying?"

Jack nodded. He already had an idea how much whiskey would have helped keep him warm tonight. *Last time you had a drink you killed a man.* Jack closed his eyes, but could see Baxter as clear as day on his closed eyelids. *And don't forget him either, Jack: you weren't drinking then.*

"Want some now?"

"No thanks," Jack said. "I'm not a good drunk at the moment."

Steve laughed again. "Well, son, I don't come across too many people who *are* good drunks. Have a whiskey." He fished around in his tent and came out with a bottle of cheap whiskey. He uncapped it and took a long swig then offered it to Jack.

Jack hesitated, then took the bottle. *Anything to get rid of the taste.* The whiskey burned his throat going down, but he welcomed the feeling. He could feel the hot liquid cleaning is throat and stomach: no trace of Baxter would now remain.

"When you getting married?"

"I am."

It was out before Jack had a chance to think.

"So, your mates strip you when it's not your stag? You got mates like what I had son."

"Please don't call me son."

"Why not? You young enough to be my son."

"I don't like it."

"Well whoopee fucking do, Jack. I don't like living in a tent, but there's fuck all I can do about it."

"Please don't upset me – you wouldn't like me upset."

"What are you? The Hulk?" Steve started laughing again. "Relax, son – Jack – I'm only joshing you."

Jack breathed deeply again, and felt his heart rate slow down. "Sorry. I've had a shit day."

"I've had a shit life," Steve laughed. "So what happened? Your woman kick you out?"

"Not yet," Jack said.

"She will, son, fucking bitches never stand by their men when the going gets tough."

Jack waited, knowing there was going to be more. With men like Steve, there was always more.

"Take me, right, I put a little too much on a horse and she goes nuts, kicks me out. Work sacked me 'cos I was on a website what I shouldn't have been on and that was that. Me in a tent on a beach in fucking Devon. Ain't fair. The bitch could've helped me, got me into one of them programmes, but no, off you go Stevie, twenty years down the pan cos the wrong horse won the 2:30 at Epsom."

For God's sake. "I'm sorry to hear that."

"Yeah, she never complained when I won did she? Maybe you should leave your bitch before she chucks you out."

"Maybe."

Jack was a little surprised to see tears in Steve's eyes and his cynicism disappeared. He swigged more whiskey and passed the bottle back.

"So what is your story Jack?"

"You don't want to know."

"Well now I wouldn't have asked, would I?"

"My wife and I were on holiday. She found out I'd been having an affair and she's kicked me out. I didn't have time to grab clothes – she had a knife." *Getting pretty good at this lying thing Jack.*

"Was this other piece of tail worth it?"

"No."

"So what's your plan?"

Jack paused for only a second. "I'm going to go and beg."

Steve laughed again. "I do like you Jack, you're my kind of man. I got some clothes you can have. They might smell a bit, but you can have them."

4

Steve had not lied about the smell. Jack trudged through the woods, feeling his skin itch. He was heading for the road, and he knew the way but he didn't really want to know how he knew. *Following the scent of cars.*

He had promised Steve money, but they both knew that they would probably never see each other again. Jack kept walking, thinking about the kindness of strangers and those who have nothing left to give. *Is that how people get redemption? Generosity to strangers?*

In which case, he had a lot of giving to do.

He stepped out of the woods and onto the coastal road. He had driven this road many times with Katie and knew it well. Last time they had travelled it, it had been a blisteringly hot day. Katie had worn very little and it had possibly been the day Josh had been conceived. *Happier times – much happier.* He had to see her. It probably wasn't a smart idea, but he had to know his wife and child were safe.

He turned right and started heading towards Barnstaple, ready to stick his thumb out if a car passed.

5

Steve ate his last sausage and waited for his phone to ring. He lay back in his tent, shuffling around so his head was at the opening. He stared at the stars – so clear here. He picked out Orion's belt easily and then used the Plough to find the North Star. He was just closing his eyes when the phone rang.

"Yep."

He listened for a while.

"Yeah, I made contact. I don't think he knew I'd led him here."

He inspected his fingers whilst the other person spoke.

"I think he's still in denial. He's going to try and meet up with his wife. He's heading for Barnstaple now."

Licked the last of the sausage grease off them.

"Yes we could meet him there, and yes I think he'll make a great addition to the Pack." He smiled in the dark. "I could smell the blood on him – he's already killed."

He hung up shortly after that. Following Jack would be easy – he had made no attempt to hide his trail and the smelly clothes showed the way better than a flashlight. He collapsed the tent and gathered everything into a kitbag. A wry chuckle escaped his mouth. What a tale he had told Jack! All the little details that had made it. The 2:30 at Epsom! How he would laugh when he told Jack the truth. How they hadn't found enough of the silly bitch to identify, let alone bury.

He whistled throughout. He always was at his happiest when recruiting.

Chapter 16

1

Meyers parked the Beamer outside the gate into the woods. He killed the lights and they were plunged into darkness. Stars were bright in the sky and the moon was brighter. It was just after eight in the evening.

"Fuck, it's dark," Meyers complained.

"No street lights," Carruthers said.

"No shit," Scarlet said.

They got out and he opened the boot. They took out a rope and a flashlight each, then Carruthers lifted a portable winch. Meyers took an empty kit bag and they set off into the woods.

As soon as they were through the gate, the path split – one route went off to their left and the other went straight on. Without pause they went straight, torchlight bobbing ahead of them. Eventually they came to a small clearing.

"It's this way," Meyers said, gesturing over the clearing towards the tree line.

"What are you whispering for?" Carruthers said loudly. "There's no-one for miles."

Birds erupted from the trees above them. Carruthers chuckled as Scarlet jumped. Meyers shrugged and they trudged across the clearing. He stumbled once on some overgrown gorse and the others laughed at him. Eventually, they found the hole that Jack had fallen down several days before. A rough circle of police tape surrounded it. They climbed over and then Meyers played his flashlight into it.

"Fuck, its dark."

Carruthers gave him a pained expression as Scarlet said, "No street lights."

"Let's get it done," Meyers said.

Scarlet put the winch down and tied a brace around a nearby tree. Meyers and Carruthers attached their ropes to it and attached the ropes to the abseiling belts they were wearing.

"I'm set," Scarlet said. Without another word, Meyers jumped backwards into the hole. He fell for a few feet and then the clips on the belt prevented him falling any further. He fed the rope through and abseiled to the floor. At the bottom he shone his light around the cave and shouted, "Clear!"

Carruthers landed softly next to him a few seconds later.

"What are we looking for?" Meyers whispered.

"The bones and anything else we find." Meyers noticed that Carruthers was also whispering down here. The cave felt that way. His torch picked out the stone slab that Jack had landed on and they went over for a closer look. Meyers got down on his haunches and inspected the slab carefully. He gasped when he saw the carvings on the side.

"Fuck me, it's the devil."

2

Carruthers knelt next to him, shining his torch even closer.

"No, it's not."

"Look at it, man, it's the devil. What the fuck is this place?"

"It's not the devil. It's more likely to be Cernunnos."

"Who?"

"The Green Man. He's the Celtic god of nature and living things."

"How the fuck do you know these things?"

"It's called an education. You should try it."

"Whatever."

"Cernunnos was perceived as a threat by the Christian church. He stood for all things like fornication-" he saw the look on Meyers' face. "-shagging – and so they demonised him."

"We should call you fucking Google."

"He's not a sign of evil, Harry, it's the opposite. The fact that this carving is here means this place is really old."

Meyers stood up and swept the room with is flashlight again. "It's cold."

"Yeah." Carruthers stood up. "What's that?"

Meyers moved his light back. "A tunnel."

They looked at each other. "Shall we?" Carruthers said.

"S'pose." They edged towards the opening, torches focussed on the opening.

"You okay down there?"

They both jumped. Scarlet's voice had come from the walkie-talkie hanging on Meyers' belt. Meyers looked up at him and keyed the radio. "Shut the fuck up man, you scared the shit out of me."

"Just hurry up, it's cold up here."

Carruthers was now at the opening, but something made him pause. Later he would not be able to say what, but he was glad. In light of what happened to Meyers, he was very glad.

Meyers stood next to him and looked into the tunnel. It was as if the light went no further, swallowed in a pit of darkness. He felt a shiver down his back and suddenly wanted to be *anywhere* rather than in that cave. Even Afghanistan. One look at Carruthers confirmed that he was thinking the exact same thing.

"Well?"

"Shh." Carruthers held his arm out, preventing Meyers from going any further. He angled his torchlight down one wall and that seemed to allow the beam to penetrate the gloom.

As they watched, a thick black strand as long as Meyers' arm came out of the wall followed closely by another. Leg by leg the biggest spider they had ever seen squeezed itself out of a cavity in the wall. It sat in the light, as if it were watching them.

"Fuck," Meyers said.

Behind the spider, another set of legs appeared, then another and another until the wall was covered with spiders. None of the spiders moved after coming out of the wall. They all appeared to be watching the soldiers with mild curiosity.

"Have you ever-"

"No," Carruthers said. "Never."

"Come on Google, you must know of spiders that big."

"There's a tarantula that grows up to a foot across, but these must be twice that."

"Look at them sitting there. What are they doing?"

"Sizing us up."

Meyers looked at his colleague. "Tell me that was a joke."

"They're not coming in the cave. Why not?"

"I don't give a fuck. I'm glad they're not. I might have to use this bad boy otherwise." He took his Browning out of his coat pocket and mock aimed it into the tunnel.

"What did you bring that for?"

"Well, after last night, I thought better safe than dead."

"What are you planning on doing? There's hundreds of spiders in there, maybe thousands."

"Yeah, but I'll take a few with me." Meyers lowered his torch. "This is giving me the shits, man, let's get the stuff and get out."

He had no argument from Carruthers on that.

3

"That's strange," Carruthers said.

"What?"

"There's no skull."

They were standing back at the slab, which Carruthers was beginning to think was an altar. He was looking at the bones on the slab.

"Look, this is a rib cage and these could be tibias and fibulas."

"What?"

"Legs."

"Arms?"

Carruthers shrugged. No point in telling Meyers he had reached the end of his anatomical knowledge. He moved his flashlight up and down the remains several times and then examined the floor around the altar. He couldn't see a skull anywhere.

"Maybe it's rotted away."

"Quicker than the rest of the body?"

Meyers conceded the point. He threw the bag at Carruthers. "Come on, man, let's hurry it up before those spiders get a little braver."

Carruthers had to agree. This cave wasn't the most pleasant he had ever been in. He lifted the bones carefully into the bag, slipping each one into a clear plastic bag as he did so. He saved the largest one for last. It had blood crusted across the tip of it.

"This must be the one Stadler landed on. Maybe he was telling the truth."

"Hurry up!"

Soon he was done and he zipped the bag closed. He slung it over his shoulder and nodded. The bones were heavy, not as heavy as Meyers but they agreed not to overload the winch.

Meyers lifted the walkie-talkie. "Bring him up."

The motor kicked into life and Carruthers started to rise into the air.

4

They both heard the noise, even above the sound of the motor. It was like rustling leaves in an autumnal field or like paper being crunched up but much, much louder. Meyers turned quickly, flashlight aimed at the tunnel opening. The spiders were pouring out of the opening. They spread out in all directions, running across the cave floor, ceiling and walls.

"Fuck!" Meyers screamed. "Hurry up!"

He looked up and saw Carruthers clear the top of the hole. He imagined them rushing to get him unclipped, but he knew that it was too slow. The spiders were beginning to converge on him from all directions. They seemed even bigger in the open than they had in the tunnel.

"Fuck! Fuck! Fuck!"

He aimed his gun, but it was pointless. There were just too many. He shot one anyway and laughed as it exploded, showering its companions with blood and ichor. The rest of the spiders paused at the sound of the gun, then continued their inexorable progress towards him.

"Harry! Quick, tie it on!" Scarlet could see the spiders and panic was clear in his voice. He dropped the end of the rope. Meyers clipped in and yelled, "Go, go, go!"

He felt his feet leave the ground and he broke into a huge grin. "Ha! Fuck you!" He fired again, the report echoing around the cave.

The spiders jumped on him.

5

"Pull him up! Pull him up now!" Scarlet cried. They both started to pull on the rope, helping the small winch. They could feel the weight on the end of the rope increase as more spiders jumped on Meyers and pulled harder. Meyers' screams echoed round the cave below.

"Keep pulling!" Scarlet said and let go. He stood to one side and pulled out his Browning. "Come on you fuckers!" he roared.

Carruthers hauled the rope hard and Meyers's body came into view. At first Carruthers couldn't process what he was seeing. Meyers was covered in spiders. There wasn't a spot on him where clothes or skin could be seen. The spiders moved like waves on the ocean: a black tide that swept over Meyers' body. Outside the confines of the cave, the spiders didn't seem quite so big: most were maybe half a foot across, but one was at least twice that.

Mother and young.

Carruthers and Scarlet watched in horror as Meyers spun on the rope. Then he reached out with his hand and screamed. The sudden movement made some of the spiders fall, and they could see part of his face. He had a large bite mark on one cheek, it was large and swollen already. It had puffed up close to his eye, making him squint out.

"Help me," he croaked as a spider crawled onto the empty space. For one horrible moment, Carruthers thought that one of the spiders was going to crawl into his mouth.

Scarlet reached out and grabbed hold of Meyers's outstretched hand. A spider immediately ran onto his arm, but he didn't flinch. He raised his free hand and fired once. The spider exploded as the sound of the shot echoed around them. Birds flew out of the trees and something large ran through the undergrowth away from them.

Most of the spiders scattered at the sudden loud noise. Scarlet stamped on two that came near him. Carruthers let go of the rope and started stamping at the ground around him. Meyers fell to the ground with a thump and would have slipped back into the cave had Scarlet not remembered to grab hold of him again. The spiders fled back into the cave, but some still had hold of Meyers.

Carruthers went to his fallen colleague and kicked at the remaining spiders. He caught hold of one just right and it flew through the air, falling into the cave again.

Scarlet joined in kicking at the spiders on Meyers's body. Several times his foot connected with something more solid than a spider, but he didn't care. He didn't think Meyers would either.

"We need one of them!" Carruthers yelled.

"What?"

"We need an intact body, for the venom." He slapped a spider away from Meyers and it lay still on the ground next to the soldier. "This one will do." Carruthers retrieved a plastic bag from the kit bag and fighting revulsion he lifted the spider into it.

"Knowles, we have an emergency situation here. Meyers is down, repeat Meyers is down," Scarlet shouted into the walkie-talkie.

"Sit rep," Knowles calm voice came back.

"It's crazy, really fubar."

"Talk to me Scarlet."

"He's been attacked by spiders. We need casevac."

"Spiders?"

"We need casevac now Knowles. NOW!"

Scarlet clicked the walkie-talkie off without waiting for a response. Carruthers was kneeling next to Meyers, checking for a pulse. Meyers was unconscious now, which Carruthers felt had to be a blessing.

"He's alive, but the pulse is faint."

Meyers was drooling, thick strands of spittle coming out of both sides of his mouth. Thick red welts covered every bare piece of skin they could see. They all had holes in the top where spider fangs had punctured the skin.

"Have you ever seen anything like this?" Scarlet asked quietly.

Carruthers shook his head. "We need to get him out of here. This little fella will help." He waved the plastic bag containing the dead spider. Scarlet picked up the kit bag containing the bones and winch whilst Carruthers gave Meyers a fireman's lift.

They ran back to the car as quickly as they could under the weight they were both carrying. When they reached the car, Scarlet was a little surprised to realise he was more out of breath than Carruthers. *Damn, he's good.* He turned the radio back on at the car.

"How's the air vac sergeant?"

"Three minutes. Where are you?"

"At the gates to the woods. There's a field next to us they can land in."

"Roger that. I'll pass it on. What happened to you lot?"

"Knowles, this is really fucked up. You won't believe us."

"Try me."

Carruthers touched his arm. "Look."

Scarlet turned back to face the woods and felt his legs turn to jelly. He lifted the radio to his mouth. "Uh, we have a new situation. Get that casevac to hurry."

In the starlight, they could see a black tide coming towards them, following the path they had just run down. They heard the rustling of bodies pushing for position and the click of many legs on stone.

The spiders were coming.

6

Scarlet dropped the radio and raised his gun. It was the ultimate in futile gestures. The black mass continued towards them, that horrible click-click getting louder and louder. Scarlet fired a single shot at the head of the wave. A spider erupted and there was a momentary gap in the wave. It was soon filled as the spiders surged to fill the hole.

"What are we going to do?" he gasped.

"Listen," Carruthers said with a calm he clearly didn't feel. In the distance they could hear the steady *thump-thump* of an approaching helicopter. They didn't bother to look for lights as the helicopter was probably running tactical. In any case, it was difficult to drag eyes away from the approaching spiders.

"Get in the car," Scarlet said. He rummaged in Meyers' pockets until he found the keys. Up close, he could see how pale Meyers was, and he seemed to be trembling under his clothes. "What's happening to him?" he asked.

Carruthers barely glanced at him. "It's the venom. He's been poisoned."

"There aren't any poisonous spiders in Britain. Don't be a twat."

"There aren't any that are a foot across either, but that doesn't seem to be bothering that lot."

Scarlet clicked the car open and started to lift Meyers, but then Carruthers said, "Wait." The helicopter sounded nearer now. *Not long. Not long. Hurry, please hurry.*

Scarlet stopped mid lift and looked to where Carruthers was pointing. The spiders had stopped advancing. They stood about twenty feet away from the soldiers, not moving. Then the back of the mass peeled away and spiders scuttled in all directions.

Scarlet dropped Meyers heavily and drew his Browning again. He aimed in all directions, twitching every way like a teenager without Ritalin. "Shit, shit, shit," he yelled.

Carruthers was silent. He stood unmoving, watching the spiders wheel around them. Eventually they stood at the centre of a circle of spiders. That horrible scratching sound stopped as they became motionless. The edge of the spiders looked to be a perfect circle, although the illusion was broken upon closer inspection. Odd spider limbs stuck out giving it a rougher appearance. Carruthers shuddered.

"I fucking hate spiders," Scarlet said. "Why aren't they moving?"

"It's the bone," Carruthers voice was still calm. "They didn't attack until we took them, now they're waiting again."

"What the fuck is with this place, man?"

A spotlight suddenly illuminated the gloom, as bright as the sun in the dark woods. They shielded their eyes and braced themselves against the sudden down force of the rotors. The spiders suddenly scattered and they were alone on the road within seconds.

"That's just fucking wrong," Scarlet said. "Where did they go?"

Carruthers picked up the radio by Scarlet's feet. The helicopter came in to land in the field next to the woods. Thirty seconds later a man wearing medic stripes ran over to them.

"Did you see that?" Scarlet asked.

"See what? I'm Pete. What you got for me boys?"

"We have a man down, spider poison."

"Spider bite? Jesus, you got me out of bed and halfway across the country for a spider bite?"

"You didn't see the spiders?" Scarlet was incredulous.

"What spiders?" Pete looked around the ground and shone his torch all round him.

"These ones." Carruthers held up the clear plastic bag containing the spider corpse.

"Fuck me, that's a big one," Pete said and smiled. "Said the nun to the bishop."

Scarlet grabbed Pete by the throat and pressed his Browning to the other man's cheek. "I'm not in the mood for shit jokes, sunshine. My man is hurt. Sort him out."

Pete stepped back as Scarlet released him. They glared at each other for a second. "Where is he?"

Carruthers gestured at the ground behind him. Meyers lay still, not even twitching any more. Pete knelt next to him and felt for a pulse. He swore silently and immediately opened his bag. He took out a drip and a needle. He ripped the top of a bag of medicine, then injected Meyers straight in the middle of the chest.

"He's gone into a coma. We need to get him to hospital, now."

"Go," Carruthers said, still using the unnaturally calm voice.

Pete took a folding stretcher out of the bag and they rolled Meyers onto it. Then he and Carruthers lifted it and ran over to the helicopter. Carruthers threw the spider corpse bag into the cabin after Meyers was secured.

"That's what bit him."

"We'll be in touch," Pete said. The helicopter rose into the air and was gone.

Carruthers ran back over to Scarlet, who was looking on the verge of panic. He kept scanning the tree line.

"They're out there man, I can feel them watching me."

"They won't come any nearer now."

"How the fuck do you know that?"

"I don't. I'm guessing they were following the bones."

"Following the bones? For fuck's sake, do you know how that sounds?"

"Yep." He lifted the bag of bones into the car and got in the driver's side. Scarlet sprinted around the car and leapt in the other side. It was almost comical the speed with which he had moved. Almost. "As long as we have the bones, we'll be alright."

"How can you stay so calm, man?"

"Calm?" Carruthers said. "This has been one of the worst nights of my life. I fucking hate spiders."

Chapter 17

1

A lorry driver took pity on Jack and picked him up. A wrinkled nose as Jack climbed into the cab showed a moment's regret, but Jack buckled his seat belt before the driver could change his mind.

"Where to, mate?"

"Barnstaple. Are you going anywhere near the hospital?"

"Right by it."

Jack jumped out by a set of traffic lights near the hospital. The hospital car park was absolute bedlam. Ambulances sat in bays with lights flashing. Police cars had cordoned off the main road into the hospital and a TV crew filmed from beyond the line of police cars. He arrived just in time to see Katie leave. He also saw another car follow her out. Two police cars had been moved out of the cordon to let them through.

They are heading for home. What are they looking for?

Was Katie in trouble? That had been an unmarked police car following her - he was sure of it. Was she an accessory to murder? Were they looking to blame her for what he'd done?

No. They were looking for things that might help them find him.

Jack was still standing in shadows, looking at the chaotic car park. Nobody had seen him, but crowds were starting to form around the police barriers. He had to keep moving before anyone noticed him.

He headed down a side street, just as a car rushed past him. Shadows engulfed him and he hoped he hadn't been seen. The car sped on.

Jack continued walking to the town centre. He scanned the pavement, picking up any change that he saw on the floor. The town centre was bright and loud. Bars, pumping out noise and light pollution, were filled with people drinking, laughing and dancing –

but mostly just drinking. He passed a drunk man being sick and a couple pressed up against a wall doing things that really should be done in private. Jack walked on, ignoring everything around him. He was in no mood for a Friday night in town.

A group of young men, the eldest no more than twenty, poured out of a pub and started arguing on the street ahead of him. He skirted the edge of them, head down scanning the pavement for more change.

How much for a bus these days? He was nearly up to a pound. *That was enough, surely?*

If he'd been paying more attention, nothing would have happened: many people would still be alive and he might have made it home.

2

Paul pushed Roger the way that drunken men do: far too hard to be taken as a joke, even though that was what was intended. Roger pushed him back and soon they were play fighting in the street. The rest of the group shouted at them, cheering and pushing them back together if they got too far apart.

A man with shoulders hunched walked around the edge just as Paul fell into his path. They bumped into each other and the man kept his head down.

"Sorry mate," Paul shouted, laughing. The man kept walking, not acknowledging the younger man at all. Paul glanced at his friends who were now looking at the man. "Oi! I said sorry."

He kept walking. Paul looked first at Roger then at the rest of his friends, with a mock wounded expression on his face. He started to follow the man and his friends fell into step behind him. Paul walked swinging his arms and his shoulders, swaying slightly from side to side.

"Oi! Mate. I was fucking talking to you."

"You tell 'im Paul."

"Go on mate!"

Paul reached out and grabbed the man's shoulder.

3

Jack turned when he felt his shoulder being pulled. He turned slowly, surprise on his face. Five young men stood watching him, each dressed in the Friday night uniform: shirts and jeans. Three were smoking, the stench of tobacco almost overwhelming him. All were drunk, fumes of lager and tequila seeping out of them.

I don't have time for this. I need to get to Huntleigh. I just need a few more pence.

"I said I was fucking talking to you."

"Smack 'im in the mouth, Paul, teach 'im some fucking manners."

Paul grinned at his friends.

"Sorry. I didn't realise you were talking to me. I apologise." Jack pushed Paul's hand off his shoulder and turned to leave. Paul grabbed him again, harder this time.

"Bit fucking late for apologies init?" He made an exaggerated sniffing sound. "You a right smelly cunt, ain't you?"

"Please. I don't want trouble."

"Well you found it, you-" Paul paused, searching his not very extensive vocabulary for an alternative adjective, "smelly twat."

Jack breathed in deeply several times. It made no difference to his heart rate.

"You need to leave," he groaned. "NOW!"

Silence greeted his shout, before the gang all started laughing.

"Well, what the fuck are you going to do then?" Paul snarled and pulled back his fist. He punched Jack as hard as he could in the face.

4

Knowles had the radio scanning the police frequencies, trying to get any information at all about the Stadlers when he heard the call.

"He's tearing him apart! Help us, please, God help us!"

A woman's voice came next, calm and authoritative. "Try to stay calm sir, we have units en route." There was a pause, then: "All units, all units, proceed to junction of Bear Street and Boutport Street in Barnstaple. Caution advised, I think we've found our animal."

Knowles looked at Jones. "How far away are we?"

"Less than five."

"Fancy another crack at the wolf?"

"What about Carruthers and that lot?"

"Medic on route, e-vac if they need it. They'll be ok."

"I hit that wolf you know."

"Yeah, me too. This time, we do the job properly."

Jones grinned and spun the car round.

5

Steve met up with the other two members of the Pack on the bridge into Barnstaple. All three had been sent to find out who had been scented in the area. Steven had been the lucky one who had made contact. Now Lucy and Anton were itching to meet the new recruit.

Lucy was petite, polar opposite to Anton. As they walked into the centre of Barnstaple, they reminded Steve of the old "lower, middle, upper class" sketch from the years back. Lucy and Anton were lovers – Anton had turned her once he had been turned himself. He couldn't bear to be without her for long. She had embraced the lifestyle with a passion that was enviable, but all the same, the lovers made Steven feel sick at times.

"What's that?"

Lucy pointed up the street. There appeared to be a brawl ahead. Two men were running towards them, one of them yelling into his mobile phone. Behind them, two men lay on the floor whilst another had curled up into a ball.

"It's him," Anton said in his monotone deep voice.

"No shit," Steve answered.

"What do you want to do?" Steve liked the way Lucy always deferred to him.

"Let's just see what he's capable of."

6

Jack reeled from the punch and stumbled backwards. Paul was on him in a flash, raining blows on his head and body. His lips were curled in a snarl and he was shouting as he punched. The rest of the gang were also shouting, their voices mingling into a cacophonous roar.

"Do 'im! Fuck 'im up!"

"Look at 'is nose, man, that's fucking funny!"

"Jesus, Paul, mate that's enough."

"Don't be gay! Smack him again Paul!"

Jack could barely hear the shouting over the thunder of blood in his ears. *Not again.* He reached up with a powerful hand and caught

Paul's hand as it flew towards his face. He twisted the hand around, feeling the power in his arm. Something snapped. Paul screamed.

"My turn," Jack growled in a voice that wasn't quite his. Fur burst along his arms and he punched Paul with his free hand. Paul fell back, slipping to the ground, his left arm limp by his side and left hand at an angle that was just wrong.

The mob fell silent instantly.

"Holy shit," Roger said, he held his hands up. "Hey, we're going mate, no bother, eh?"

"Too late," Jack said in that same low growl. Claws grew out of his fingers. He grinned at the group. "You could try running."

He swept his arm out and caught Roger on the side of his face. Claws dug deep into the man's cheek, tearing the flesh and leaving it hanging off his face. Blood spurted out, splashing Jack's face and arms. He licked at the blood and grinned revealing long teeth.

Roger screamed, long and loud, then collapsed clutching his ruined cheek. Two of the other gang members turned and fled. One of them was fumbling with a phone as he ran. The third stood still, face white. Jack sniffed him, drinking in the smell of his fear. Paul groaned on the floor and Jack pounced. He bit into his neck and more blood splashed onto the street.

The street was dark here and Jack fed almost in private. Roger was unconscious on the floor, next to a small pile of bin bags. Blood was still pouring through his fingers and later he would need over sixty stitches and a skin graft to repair the damage. Every time he looked in the mirror, he would remember the night and thank god he hadn't been bitten. He didn't ever tell anyone what had happened to him.

The unmoving man had curled up into a ball and was rocking, muttering to himself. Jack paid him no heed. He ripped more of Paul's throat out and spat it across the street.

"Now who's a cunt?" he roared in that strange other voice of his. The clothes ripped off his back and he fell to all fours. He threw back his head and howled: a high pitched noise that echoed around the buildings. Jack had gone and in his place stood an enormous black haired wolf.

7

"He's fucking huge," Steve said, almost in a whisper.

"He's bigger than-" Lucy started.

"Yes."

They watched as the wolf finished eating the man. It ignored the other two but instead howled again, a sound that they were all familiar with. Steve started walking towards him, eyes wide and a large grin on his face. This wolf was bigger than Alex, hell, probably bigger than Callum, something that Steve planned to use to his advantage. *Alex has been in charge for far too long.*

"What are you doing?" Lucy hissed.

"He's magnificent!" Steve cried.

"Yeah, and dangerous."

"Not to us."

The wolf looked up as Steve approached. It bared its teeth and emitted a low growl. Lucy and Anton jogged up behind Steve.

"Be careful," Lucy said, putting her arm on Steve. "This is not what we were expecting."

Suddenly, the air was full of the sound of sirens and three police cars sped around the corner. Blue lights flashed and lit up the street, bathing the wolf in an eerie glow. Its fur seemed to absorb the light, giving the impression of a shadow surrounded by blue light. It lowered its front to the ground, tail between its legs. Underneath it was the corpse of its unfortunate attacker.

Two policemen jumped out of each car and used doors for shields. Behind the wolf, more sirens were approaching.

"Armed police!" they all shouted, slightly out of time with each other resulting in a cacophony of noise. One of them decided to take charge: "Please don't go any further. Move slowly back towards us."

When none of Steve, Lucy or Anton moved, he spoke again: "That animal is dangerous. Please step back slowly. No sudden movements."

"No shit," Steve said for the second time in as many minutes. Lucy and Anton looked at him, waiting for his order. He grinned at them both. "We're not losing this one."

He shrugged his shirt off.

"What are you doing?"

Lucy returned the grin and unbuttoned her dress, turning deliberately towards the police.

"Miss, please come away from the animal!"

Anton rolled his head, clicking his neck. Then he removed his shirt and started to unbutton his trousers.

"For fuck's sake, get out of the way!"

Steve threw his head back and howled. The other two joined in. The sound drowned out the noise of the approaching sirens.

"I have a shot. Sir, I have a clear shot!"

One of the police officers stepped out from the cover of the car door. He held his hand out towards the three strangers. "Come with me, quickly!" Desperation was clear in his voice.

"Jesus!"

"What the-?"

"Miller, get your arse back here!"

Three wolves stood where there had once been people.

8

Jones spun the car into the top of Boutport street, pulled the handbrake hard and the car slid to a halt facing back the way they had come. Knowles was out of the car the second it stopped. His 9mm was in his hand, aimed down the street.

At the other end of the road, three police cars blocked it off. About fifty yards from where he stood, a huge wolf was howling as it straddled a man. Another man was curled into a ball near it and a third man lay unconscious in the foetal position. Knowles tried to focus – it was difficult due to the police lights and street lights – and saw that the man under the wolf was dead. He actually doubted if it had once been a man at all.

"Jesus."

Knowles could only nod in response to Jones. Years ago, Knowles' wife had dragged him to an art exhibition and he had been fascinated by the carnage present in some of the pictures. The street looked a little like that: a painting by Bosch. *Wrong, just way wrong.*

Beyond the enormous wolf, three more were standing staring at the police. The police were huddling behind car doors, guns aimed into the street. They all had identical expressions. They were out of their depths, several times over. Knowles had seen similar expressions on the faces of the so-called Afghan police force. One of the officers was standing in front of his car, his face clearly white even at this distance.

"Get back," Knowles muttered, more to himself than as a shout. So far, it didn't look like anyone knew they were there and Knowles didn't plan on changing that until he had to.

The first wolf, sleek and lean with white fur, leapt at the policeman. He fell to the floor, screaming. The other two wolves leapt at the police cars. One landed on the bonnet and immediately leapt off again, knocking another policeman to the floor. It then reared up and bit the other officer in the neck. The final wolf landed on the roof of a car and howled. It then jumped on the nearest officer.

The two policemen left dropped their guns and fled down the street. Knowles couldn't blame them.

Throughout it all, the police didn't fire a shot.

"Sarge?" Jones' voice had a tremor in it. Knowles had not heard that before. "Knowles? What do we do?"

"Shoot. If it moves, shoot it."

They stepped forward as one, guns trained on the largest wolf. It still wasn't doing anything, just straddling its kill. It was watching the other three wolves intently. Knowles moved to the left, Jones to the right. Neither said a word.

The three wolves came back to the centre of the street, blood smeared around their mouths. The sleek white one was in the front, and it lowered its head and upper body. The other two followed suit. All three had their tails between their legs. The white one turned its head and gestured at the brown one on its left flank.

It was an oddly human gesture.

The brown one padded closer, keeping its ears flat and tail between its legs.

Neither soldier said a word. There were four people – including themselves - near the wolves. The other two could be alive – they had to be careful.

The brown one nibbled the enormous wolf's neck and licked at its face, then rolled onto its back, exposing its belly. The white one stood up on its hind legs. *Can wolves even do that?* Knowles thought. Its fore legs seemed to be lengthening, fur disappearing. In a matter of seconds, a man stood naked in the street.

"We're like you."

The brown wolf was also losing its fur. When it stood up, a naked woman was inches away from the wolf's mouth. Despite everything,

Knowles clocked she was stunning. Brown shoulder length hair and a lean, firm body.

"Shit," Knowles said.

It broke the spell. The big wolf roared and swiped at the woman. A large red gash appeared across her stomach, and for a moment nothing else happened. Then the gash opened and blood poured out, followed by what looked horribly like her intestines. The woman had time to scream a name.

"ANTON!"

She fell to the floor and the wolf pounced. A ripping sound cut through the night as the wolf closed its jaws. When it lifted its head, Knowles could see the woman's head, briefly, before it closed its jaws. A loud crack made him gag.

"NO!"

The other wolf had turned into a large well-built man. He started forward, but he was restrained by his friend.

"We have to go!" The friend shouted. "We leave. NOW." Anton gave one final glare at the large wolf, tears in his eyes. Then, both men turned and ran, stooping to collect clothes that Knowles hadn't seen before.

The wolf turned its head to Knowles.

"Shit." This time he was prepared and this time he would not miss. He started shooting. Bullet after bullet tore into the wolf's hide. It screeched in pain. He heard Jones start shooting, both weapons roaring in unison as bullets shredded the wolf's body. It howled and howled, then whimpered and crashed to the floor. Its legs twitched several times. Knowles weapon clicked empty, and Jones kept firing until his was empty too.

They walked to the body of the wolf.

"I have never seen-"

"Not now," Knowles said. "We have to get out of here."

"What about-" Jones gestured at the two men. He checked their pulses. They were both alive – one unconscious (who had clearly lost a lot of blood), the other catatonic.

"Not our problem," Knowles said, kicking the wolf carcass with his boot. "This is, though. This is what they wanted us to get."

"They knew?" Jones was incredulous.

"Possibly. Possibly not." Knowles looked up and down the street. Blue lights still flashed at the end of the street, but he couldn't see any sign of the police bar the dead ones. He reckoned they had another couple of minutes at most before the rapid response vehicles arrived. The media might even beat them to it. *What a mess.* "We'll take the body and get it back to base."

"How the fuck are we going to lift that thing?" Jones had his back to the wolf and Knowles, trying to put the unconscious man into the recovery position.

"Not going to be a problem."

Something about the Knowles' voice made Jones turn round. He immediately wished he hadn't. Lying on the floor, caked in blood, with bullet wounds covering his torso lay Jack Stadler.

9

Steve and Anton ran hard, feet pounding the pavement. Steve kept looking back over his shoulder and could see Anton crying as hard as he was running. The big wolf wasn't following. He heard the gunshots and increased his pace. Anton kept pace easily, hovering just behind his left shoulder.

Some drunks outside a pub cheered at them as they passed, but they continued, ignoring the shouts. It reminded Steve of the need to stop and put clothes on. He veered into a side street and they stopped, gasping for breath. A fine misty rain began to fall. They started to pull on the clothes that they'd managed to salvage.

"Lucy," Anton said. "I will kill him."

Steve sighed. The big man spoke few words normally and he had half hoped that this would have made him mute.

"He's actually bigger than you," Steve said. "Besides, I think the police have beaten you to it."

Anton shook his head, "No. I can still smell him."

It was true. The air was still full of the scent of the big wolf. "Doesn't mean anything."

"I can still smell Lucy." Anton started to cry again. Steve pulled him close and hugged him. The big man was shaking – a combination of grief and anger.

"Hey! We got a couple of faggots here!"

The shout came from the top of the side street. Steve looked up and saw a gang of four men walking into the street, grins on their faces.

Looked like Anton was going to get a chance to vent after all.

10

Knowles lifted under Jack's shoulders and Jones picked his feet. They staggered over to the car and threw him into the boot. Jack lay in the dark of the boot, looking like a giant pale worm. Bullet holes covered his body, chunks of flesh missing in parts.

"No blood," Jones said.

"What?"

"I haven't got any blood on me."

"It's all on the floor."

Jones wasn't convinced.

They went back, picked up the woman and put her into the boot next to Jack. Knowles slammed the boot shut and stepped back, wiping his hands on his trousers. The lack of a head made him want to gag. He pushed the remains of her intestines back into the gaping wound of her stomach. *Plenty of blood from her.*

Jones gunned the engine and they drove away, sticking to side streets until they re-joined the main road half a mile away from where the bodies were. They didn't encounter any police.

"Probably realised they were out of their depth," Knowles mused. "Let's get back to Huntleigh, call back to base. I'd say our mission is over."

Jones nodded agreement. They were halfway back when the banging started.

11

"What's that?"

The road was pitch black, no street lights or any light for miles in either direction. It had started raining as they'd left Barnstaple and a fine mist had reduced visibility to less than fifty yards. Jones couldn't even see a house in the distance. *Bloody country.* A lay-by came into view and Jones swerved into it, brakes squealing as he stopped the car.

Thud! Thud!

Both men looked into the back of the car. The sound was definitely coming from the boot.

"Now what?"

Knowles shrugged. "Fuck knows." He reached into the glove box and pulled out his Browning. It was empty, but still felt reassuring in his hand. You could, after all, give someone a hefty smack with the butt.

"I hate this op," Jones said as they opened their doors and got out. "I used to love Devon, now it just seems fucked up. Is this what inbreeding does to you?"

"What?"

"I mean, how many of them have been fucking animals?"

Against his better judgment, Knowles had to ask: "What are you talking about?"

"Those wolf-people. How many people fucked a wolf before that happened?"

"They turned into wolves, Jonesey. They weren't 'wolf people'," Knowles gritted his teeth. They were both standing by the boot now. He was thinking of Carruthers and his big dog story. Carruthers hadn't wanted to admit the truth either. He couldn't blame him.

"I know," Jones said, his voice quiet. "I just didn't want to sound-"

"Crazy."

The two men stared at each other for a couple of minutes. The knocking sound brought them back to the roadside.

"Open it," Knowles hissed. He drew his hand back, ready to swing down if anything jumped out of the boot. His hand was curled over the top of the barrel, middle finger through the trigger guard. He had one leg slightly in front of the other. Jones clicked the boot button and the Beamer's boot swung open.

Jack Stadler sat up, screaming. Knowles brought the gun down, swinging his arm in a downward arc. The blow connected with Stadler's temple and he crumpled, lying still in the boot. The woman lay under him, and Knowles was relieved to see she was still headless. Her blood had caked Stadler.

"HOLY FUCK!" Jones shouted. "I can't take this. Jesus, I just can't take any more of this!" He put his hands on his head and stepped into the road.

Knowles peered at Jack until he was sure he wasn't going to move again. "Calm down, Jonesey."

"Calm down? Calm down? Are you fucking nuts?" Jones said, his voice breaking. "He was dead. He was fucking dead. We put about thirty bullets into him."

"He was also a wolf."

"Is that meant to make me feel better? Now we've got a zombie wolf guy in the boot of our car?"

They were silent for a second and then Jones started laughing. "I think I've gone crazy."

"You haven't," Knowles said, suppressing a grin. "You do need to get me a flashlight though."

Jones retrieved a flashlight from the glove box and handed it to his sergeant. Knowles shone the light into the boot. He ran the torch up and down the man's body and swore again.

There were no marks on his body. Where there had been holes was now smooth skin. Stadler did not have a scratch on him. *Now who's crazy? This is impossible.* The light made something glint in the boot. Knowles peered closer, reaching into the boot.

"Careful!" Jones hissed.

Knowles straightened, holding something small in his hand. "Jesus."

It was a bullet.

Chapter 18

1

"Jack?" Katie shouted as soon as the door was open. She thrust Josh into Wilson's hands, ignoring his brief cry of protestation and ran into the house. Ginny looked up from her bed, wagged her tail a couple of times and then rested her head back on her paws.

The house had that horrible stillness that places get when they are empty of life. Each room felt more oppressive than the last. She turned on all the lights as she went. For some absurd reason she was relieved to see everything in its right place: *no burglary to add to the day's woes.*

The light made her feel better and it seemed to alleviate the stillness. The tight knot of fear in her stomach was still there; it would take more than a few lights to loosen it. *Will it ever go?* She looked in all the bedrooms, even behind curtains and then went back to the kitchen. Wilson was still on the doorstep holding Josh, looking more than a little out of his depth. Josh was staring at him with wide eyes.

"He's not here," Katie said, taking Josh from the relieved policeman. She shushed the baby and he snuggled into her neck. She felt tears well and a primal urge to protect her child. She hugged him tightly to her.

"Are you ok?"

She thought about lying, but her face would give her away anyway: "No."

"Do you mind if I have a look around?"

She shook her head again. "I have to feed Josh anyway."

She led him into the house. Ginny growled when he stepped in, but Wilson made a fuss of her and she went quiet. *Some guard dog.* She sat on the sofa, switched the TV on and started to feed Josh. She could hear Wilson upstairs. A weatherman told them nothing surprising for March and then the local news started.

2

Wilson searched every room. He looked at old bills left lying on the bed in what was clearly the spare room. Jack Stadler had no debt according to the statements. *There goes reason number one to disappear.* He found some pictures of groups of people, all smiling or pulling faces. Either Jack or Katie were in every one. They looked happily, sickeningly in love. *What are you looking for, James?*

He stopped by a bookcase and scanned the books. Binchy and Tartt jostled for shelf space with thrillers by Connolly, Lansdale and McDermid. A whole shelf had hardcore science fiction by the likes of Alastair Reynolds and classics by Asimov and Clarke. He also spied a first edition Watchmen and the Sandman graphic novels. *So, Stadler is a geek like me.*

He gave up and went back downstairs. Katie was watching TV, Josh latched on to her breast. He looked away, embarrassed for some absurd reason. He caught the TV out of the corner of his eye and focussed on it.

The story was on the news – and it had got worse.

3

"This has been a trying day for the residents of North Devon. The day started with the shocking news of a death in the sleepy village of Huntleigh. It was not the death that was shocking, more the manner of it: the deceased, whom the police have named as Graham Edwards, a local builder, was apparently attacked by a wild animal.

Then this evening, over forty witnesses saw a wolf run through the corridors of Barnstaple A&E. A doctor was killed before the wolf was scared off by some of the witnesses.

Things then proceeded to get worse as the wolf made its way into the centre of Barnstaple and there it injured another passer-by then killed a further eight people, including three policemen. A ninth person is in such a severe state of shock that one doctor I spoke to likened it to a coma or catatonic state. There are rumours, currently unfounded, that there is more than one wolf involved and that we might, in fact, have a pack of wild wolves roaming this once peaceful countryside."

The picture switched to the anchorman. "We now have a live link to our correspondent, James." In the background a young man clutching a mic hard enough to make his knuckles white, appeared. "Good evening James. This is pretty shocking stuff."

"Yes, indeed it is Huw. The town is in a state of shock and several people I spoke to are locking themselves away until this is resolved."

"Any ideas on where this pack of wolves has come from?"

"It has not yet been confirmed that there is more than one animal involved – that is a rumour going round at the moment, although it is one that is being whispered louder and louder."

"Ok," Huw tried not to look annoyed, "where did the wolf come from? Indeed, can we confirm that it is a wolf?"

"Yes, more than forty witnesses all said it was a wolf. There are very few theories as to where it came from, but I think the most likely one is that an irresponsible person bought the wolf as a pup and has released it into the wild."

"I thought that wolves were scared of humans?"

"Yes, in places like America and Canada, wolves have learnt to be scared of humans – they tend to shoot them – but if, indeed this wolf was brought up in a human household it would not have that fear."

"But wolf attacks on humans are very rare?"

"Yes, indeed they are, Huw. That is the reason some think it was a pack, rather than a lone wolf."

"What have the police said?"

"Nothing official yet, Huw. Several officers are believed to have been witnesses to their colleagues' deaths and are being interviewed as we speak. We expect an official announcement soon, but it might not happen until morning."

"Thank you very much, James, we will hear more from this story I'm sure."

"Yes, indeed we will. Thank you Huw. Thank you."

4

"He had the same name as you."

"Huh?"

"The reporter. Same name as you."

Wilson looked at Katie, bewildered. *Of all the things in that report, why fix on that?*

"He said 'indeed' a lot. Do you do that?"

He didn't reply, just watched as tears rolled down her cheeks. She wasn't sobbing, just crying. Silent tears, his mother had always called it, when you're just too tired to cry properly.

"Jack's dead isn't he?"

"You don't know that Katie."

"Yes he is and yes I do. He's dead."

"A body hasn't been found yet." He hated the words as soon as they came out, it just sounded so cold. *A body*. That was her husband.

"No."

"Until they find a body there is hope."

"You don't really believe that do you?"

Back at training, all those years ago, they had always advised stretching the truth if it kept witnesses or victims on side. Not lying, stretching the truth.

"No. I'm sorry, Mrs Stadler."

She nodded once, the motion splashing tears onto her sleeping son. "I think you should go now."

Wilson also nodded once and without another word he left. He stepped into the street, relishing the fresh air. The house had felt like a morgue. Fine misty rain fell, changing the street, making it look like it was in soft focus in a bad film. A car drove slowly past, two pale men looking at him as they passed. There was something familiar about both men, but he couldn't place them for a second. The car stopped a few doors down.

"Back to Barnstaple," he muttered and started to trudge back to his car. He had the keys in the ignition when he realised where he'd seen the men before. *Coincidence?* Not many police believed in coincidences. He got out of his car and walked back down the street.

Chapter 19

1

"He's not dead," Alex said. The Pack fell silent so they could hear him speak. Steve regarded him with cool eyes.

"I saw it with my own eyes Alex."

Anton stayed quiet: grief had rendered the big man almost incapable of rational thought. Almost.

"Then you are mistaken."

Steve gritted his teeth. "He was hit by over thirty bullets. Nothing-"

"He's not dead."

Steve sighed. This was going to be difficult. Alex, as befitted his alpha status, was the largest of the men in the pack. He had dark shoulder length hair and Mediterranean olive skin. Steve thought he looked like the hero on the cover of an awful romantic novel, a look Alex had cultivated without irony.

Alex stood now and surveyed the clearing. Steve and Anton stood to one side, with the others sat on either the ground or a fallen tree trunk. Three women: Sophie, Alex's mate, glowered at the other two as if they were responsible for Lucy's death. Her long dark hair matched Alex's and her blue eyes shone with intelligence. She was the oldest of the female wolves and the most beautiful. Steve had to admit they looked good together. He had tried with her a long time ago, and he sometimes still heard her shrill laughter. *Such hatred with such beauty. Not uncommon.*

The other two were twin sisters, both turned at the same time. Amy was the slightly shorter and prettier, Louise the more fun. Steve had tried with both of them too and failed. Amy now had her arm around Anton. *She didn't waste any time.* The remaining two were recent additions but Steve hadn't made his mind up about them yet. He hadn't bothered to learn their names either.

"Our latest member, Jack, is still alive." Alex grinned at them all, perfect teeth glinting in the moonlight. The soft rain had settled on his hair like dew. *All he needs is a billowing white shirt open to his waist.*

"Not possible," Steve said.

"He is special, Steve. He is like the old ones."

Silence greeted the remark. Steve sighed and Alex glared at him. They'd been here before and it had ended in tears then.

"Why do you always think that?"

"I don't, but this time I am right."

"Like Berlin?"

Alex scowled. Sophie hissed at Steve. He smiled at them both.

"Berlin was-" Alex paused, searching for the right word. "-disappointing."

"We agree on something then."

Alex punched him, and Steve fell to the floor. Louise gasped and Amy hugged Anton harder. Alex jumped on him and put an arm across his neck.

"Remember your place old man, or we'll see how you do on your own," he whispered in Steve's ear. He stood and let the older man get to his feet. Steve kept his head down as he stood. *Give respect now, but your time is coming. Oh yes.*

"We will find Jack Stadler now," Alex said. "He has been taken to Huntleigh. We can be there within an hour if we go now."

"And we will kill him!" Anton roared.

"No," Alex said, and gave Anton one of his special smiles. "We will worship him."

2

Wilson stepped into the shadows as a short man came out of the house and went to the smart looking BMW. He caught a glimpse of something pale as the man shut the boot. His breath caught in his mouth. The man looked up at the sound and stopped for a moment, looking up and down the street. The car beeped twice and amber light filled the street for a moment. Wilson pressed himself further into the shadows. The man went back into the house.

Wilson let out a long breath. He hadn't seen that man before, but he was with the two soldiers from the hospital. *What are you looking for James?* He asked himself for the second time that night.

He crept closer to the BMW. *Nice. Roughly two years' salary.* If he owned one, he wouldn't be driving it round country lanes in Devon. He also wouldn't have a dead body in the boot. And he definitely wouldn't have a headless woman there.

He took his phone out of his pocket and hit speed dial 1. He had reflected many times on the fact that his work was the first number in his phone. *Must get out more.*

"It's James Wilson here. I need back up urgently to Park Place, Huntleigh."

"That's not great timing James. Have you seen the news?" The dispatch officer sounded harassed.

"Yeah, that's my case. I think I have a related thing here."

"Explain."

"Two suspects interviewed in the hospital have just left their car in Huntleigh with a body in the boot."

"Jesus."

"Yep. How soon for back up?"

"Half hour. Hopefully sooner. Don't do anything stupid."

Wilson hung up and then inspected the house: from the outside it looked like the Stadlers', two downstairs windows facing the street and a front door. He hunched over and walked to the windows. A TV sat against one wall, with a large fireplace next to it. The room was almost identical to the one he had just sat in. He crept along to the other window and peered around the edge of the wall.

He was just in time to see a man get shot twice in the chest.

3

Knowles opened the boot with a sick feeling in his stomach. Stadler was still unconscious and the woman was still dead. And headless. Knowles felt much calmer on seeing that, even though he knew it was absurd.

Jones appeared next to him. "Can we just get this done?"

They lifted Stadler out of the boot and carried him into the house. They put him on a kitchen chair and Carruthers started to tie him up. Scarlet went outside, locked the car with a nervous look up and down the street. Satisfied no one had seen anything he went back inside.

"Any news on Meyers?" Knowles asked Carruthers.

The big man shook his head. "It didn't look good."

"Giant spiders, huh?"

Carruthers nodded this time. "I wouldn't have believed it if I hadn't seen it with my own eyes."

"It was fucked up," Scarlet said.

"Trust us, you ain't seen shit," Jones muttered. "Is he tied up?"

Carruthers gave Jones a look. *Don't question me.*

"Check him carefully," Knowles said.

"He's tied up," Carruthers said, with more than a little impatience.

"I gave you an order."

Carruthers muttered something that neither Knowles nor Jones caught, but he checked the binding all the same. It was tight enough to be digging into Stadler's wrists.

"How much of that sleep drug have you got left?"

"Enough to stop a herd of stampeding elephants."

"Go get it."

"How much?"

Knowles looked at him like it was obvious: "All of it."

Carruthers left to get it. Scarlet clapped his hands together, the sudden noise making everyone jump.

"I need a beer after all that." He took three bottles out of the fridge and opened them all. He handed them out and then took a long sip from his. He opened a fourth when he heard Carruthers footsteps on the stairs.

"Sit down, lads." Knowles pointed at the sofas. He waited until they were all seated. He stood next to Stadler, the spray sleeping drug in his hand.

"Ok, gentlemen, we've all been through a lot together, so you need to trust me here. Jonesey can back me up too." It was his turn to take a long drag on the beer. "We saw Stadler turn into a wolf tonight."

"Fuck off!" Scarlet exclaimed. Jones and Knowles just stared at him. "Ah, shit."

"We knew something was off about this op from the start, lads, and we've just discovered it. We don't know if brass knew this, but no matter, we now have to get him back to base. Suggestions?"

"Sarge, seriously, come on," Scarlet said.

"It's true, mate," Jones whispered. "I saw it too."

"So the other body in the boot?"

"He ate her head."

Scarlet went very pale. "You are fucking kidding? Oh, you're not. Oh shit."

"She was one of them too."

"One of what?" Carruthers demanded. "What are you talking about? You taken crack?"

Knowles laughed, but it lacked mirth. "I wish. Seriously."

Silence settled on them until it was broken by Scarlet. "This is too much, I'm off to bed. For fuck's sake you two, this is a really bad joke. There's a woman in the boot of that car without a fucking head and all you can do is wind us up."

"We're not joking."

"I saw him didn't I?" Carruthers said, his calm voice filling the room. "When I planted the bugs, the dog that chased me. It wasn't a dog, it was him."

"Yeah," Knowles answered.

"I knew I recognised the smell."

They all jumped and turned. Jones had his gun out before he even realised what he was doing. Stadler was looking at them with cold eyes. Given the circumstances, he looked very calm. Jones took a fresh ammo clip from the table and slid it into place, then took aim at Stadler.

"In the pub. I said I recognised you." He looked straight at Carruthers. "It was because I knew how you smelled." He started crying. "What is happening to me? How can I recognise you by smell?"

"You don't know?" Knowles asked, surprise creasing his forehead.

"Put the gun down, Jonesey," Carruthers said.

"I'm a wolf aren't I?"

Knowles and Jones exchanged nervous looks.

"Please. I just want to see my wife and son."

"You've killed many people, Stadler." *The pleading in his voice is possibly the most pathetic thing I've ever heard.* "We can't let you see them."

"Who are you people?" This voice was deeper, no hint of a plea. The tears had stopped, like someone had turned off the tap.

"We're the army. We were sent to watch you."

"Did you do this to me?" Again, very deep.

"Jonesey, your gun. Put it away."

Knowles shook his head once. "We didn't know anything about you a week ago."

"How do you do that with your voice?" Scarlet asked.

"This started a couple of days ago." Stadler started crying again. "Jesus, only a couple of days ago. I have a son." His voice was high pitched now, broken by sobs.

"You've killed people you sick fuck," Jones snarled.

"What? I-"

"You bit a fucking woman's head off," Jones shouted. "And she wasn't a fucking woman, she was like you, all fucking wrong".

Before he really knew what he was doing, he fired his gun twice. Two bullets hit Jack square in the chest.

4

"What did you do that for?" Carruthers roared.

Jones stayed quiet for a moment. "Just watch." All trace of anger had dissipated now.

"We don't shoot our prisoners," Carruthers said. "Put your gun away."

"No," Jones said and stared at the bigger man. His lips were a thin line of defiance. "I'm never putting a gun down again."

A huge crash rang through the house before anything else could happen.

"Armed police! Drop your weapons!" a man shouted. He ran into the room, holding a dark shape before him. Knowles caught his arm as he came through the door and spun him quickly. The man cried out and fell to his knees. Knowles kept hold of his arm as he fell and used it to lever the man fully to the floor. He let go of the dark shape and it rolled to a stop by Scarlet's feet.

"Torch," he said, picking it up.

"Who are you?" Knowles growled, and then got a good look at the man's face. "Oh, shit." He let him go and stepped back. The other man jumped to his feet and drew his fist back.

"Don't," Knowles said. "Lads, this is Detective Wilson."

Wilson turned to Jones. His eyes flicked to the gun. "You are under arrest for the murder of this man. You have-"

"He's not dead."

Wilson, Carruthers and Scarlet all looked at Jones with disbelief on their faces.

"Detective, this is Jack Stadler. I believe you are looking for him," Knowles said, gesturing at the man in the chair. Blood had dripped and splattered onto the lino underneath the chair.

"And you shot him." Wilson said, still alternating between the gun and Jones but his voice was stronger this time. "I have backup on the way. You won't get away with this – I saw you shoot him."

He heard a sound a little like the dull thud when coins drop onto lino. He turned to the noise – it had come from near Jack. He saw something glinting under the chair and it hadn't been there a moment before. A movement drew his eyes to Jack. As he watched, the holes in his stomach seemed to shrink until they weren't there anymore. No scars, no marks at all.

Jack opened his eyes. He threw back his head and screamed. Sweat poured out of every pore and his muscles strained against the bindings. He started rocking the chair back and forth, screaming all the while.

Knowles reacted first. He grabbed Wilson and pushed him back to the front door. Scarlet stood immobile, open mouthed, just staring blankly at the revived man. Jones raised his gun, but seemed to take forever to do it. Carruthers raised his fist, but that too seemed to be in slow motion.

"What-" Wilson shouted, only just audible above the screaming.

Carruthers' fist connected with Jones' jaw. Jones spun from the impact, loosing off a shot that blew a hole in the plaster of the kitchen wall. Carruthers followed up with another punch to Jones' cheek and the smaller man hit the floor, eyes closed.

"We don't shoot prisoners."

"Shit!" Scarlet yelled.

"Oh my God," Wilson said. It was almost whispered, but Knowles got the gist even if he didn't hear every word. He spun to face Stadler.

Stadler's muscles were rippling and black fur was sprouting along his arms and legs. His teeth appeared to be growing, and his eyes were turning yellow. He looked at Knowles, recognition clear in the horrifying glare.

"Help me."

Knowles jumped forward as Stadler turned into a huge black wolf. The ropes broke at the same time that the chair gave way under the sudden increase in weight. The wolf opened its mouth wide, large white teeth just millimetres away from Knowles head. He had time to think about Grandma from Little Red Riding Hood and then he sprayed the wolf's head with the sleeping drug. He emptied the entire supply in one go.

The wolf howled, even managing to top Stadler's scream for volume and turned and ran for the back door. It ploughed head first into it, breaking its hinges and causing the door to buckle, but not break. It convulsed once, then collapsed.

Silence.

Carruthers helped Knowles to his feet. "Thank you."

"You didn't have to knock him out."

"I didn't need to take a dump this morning neither."

Knowles shook his head and went to Scarlet. "You ok?"

Scarlet didn't seem to recognise him. "You ok?" he repeated.

Scarlet nodded once. "He turned into a wolf. Like a real, fucking huge wolf. He turned into a wolf."

"Yep," Knowles said with a calmness he didn't feel. "We all saw it, so we're not going to talk about it being impossible, ok?"

Carruthers and Scarlet exchanged glances then nodded.

"We are going to deal with this until we get him back to base."

"What do we do then?" Scarlet asked.

"We're going to get royally pissed and forget this shit happened."

"What do you mean back to base?" Wilson demanded. "This man – uh, thing – is responsible for the murder I'm investigating."

"You want to put him in a cell like that?" Knowles sneered. "Good luck, Detective. At least he'll half your crime rate."

"You can't take him away," Wilson said. "What is this? Some army experiment that got messed up?"

"No," Knowles said.

"Why should I believe that?" Wilson demanded. "You'll not get away with this. You can't cover this up, it's too-"

From outside, they heard a long, high pitched howl. It was joined by other howls almost instantly. The noise was coming from all around the house.

Wilson went white again.

"There are more of them," Knowles said.

5

"Do we have more drugs?" Knowles asked.

Carruthers shook his head. "No, you told me to put it in there."

"What does that mean?" Wilson asked, his face still pale.

"We're screwed," Knowles muttered, staring at the back door. "Get the toys," he ordered Scarlet.

Scarlet sprinted for the stairs, then stopped. He threw something at Carruthers. "Car keys," he said and continued upstairs.

Carruthers moved quickly. He picked up Jones in a fireman's lift and ran to the front door. He beeped the car open and dumped Jones on the back seat. He looked up the street but saw nothing. He opened the car boot then ran back into the house.

"Grab Stadler," Knowles ordered.

Carruthers grabbed Stadler's feet and didn't pause to consider that they were feet, not paws. "A little help," he snarled at Wilson. The detective didn't move.

"My back up will be here in about ten minutes," he said.

"We don't have ten minutes," Carruthers pointed out.

"He's right," Knowles was still looking at the back door. It was buckled, and the hinges were loose, screws clear of the plaster. *One well-placed blow and that whole door is coming off.* "They are coming."

Nobody had to ask who. The statement galvanised Wilson. He lifted Stadler under the arms, straining with effort. With Carruthers, he carried the body to the car and threw him into the boot, next to the decapitated corpse.

"Good," Carruthers said. "We're going to be ok."

The wolf hit Wilson in the back, sending him crashing into the big man. Both of them fell into the BMW and slid to the floor. The wolf roared once then bit down onto Wilson's leg. He kicked at it, but its jaws were locked. He started to scream.

Another wolf jumped out of shadows and landed next to Wilson. Carruthers rolled clear and stood just in time to see the second wolf rip Wilson's throat out, silencing the screams. He ran back to the house while the wolves fed. He reached the front door and turned to shut it, just as the wolves jumped. He pushed the front door, hitting the first wolf with it. The wolf yelped, rolling away in case it got hit again. Carruthers slammed the door again.

It clicked shut just as the second wolf hit it.

6

Knowles edged closer to the back door. From outside came the blood curdling roar of a wolf. Scarlet arrived at the bottom of the stairs.

"Knowles!"

Scarlet threw a pistol at Knowles who caught it in one hand. Knowles kept his eyes on the glass of the back door. All he could see was his reflection staring back at him. He pressed his face up to the glass to try and see more in the back garden.

A wolf jumped at the glass, hitting it hard enough to send the door flying into Knowles. He grunted as it hit him and fell backwards, with the door and wolf on top of him. He started to scream as the wolf bent its head to the glass. Large teeth snapped closed inches away from his face, a trail of saliva falling onto the glass. *This is it. After all that shit in Ghanners, I'm going to get done by a fucking wolf in fucking Devon.*

Shots rang out in the kitchen and the wolf whimpered and fell to the side of the door. Knowles kicked the door off him, aiming the shattered frame at the wolf. It was lying on its side next to him, thick blood pooling around its neck. He fired three times, the last shot taking the back of the wolf's head off.

"You ok?" Scarlet came and stood next to him.

Knowles was breathing heavily. "Yeah," he said, "Jesus I thought that was it." He took a deep breath. "Watch it. If it moves, shoot it again." Knowles turned back to the front door just as Carruthers leapt through it. He saw Carruthers use the door to smack a wolf back into the street, before slamming the door shut. Knowles heard a thump as a wolf hit the front door. Carruthers looked at him, face white.

"Wilson?" Knowles said.

Carruthers shook his head. He held up two fingers. "We need to shoot our way out that way."

"Knowles," Scarlet said. "I think this one is dead."

Knowles looked down at the wolf. Its brown fur was now matted with blood and it wasn't moving, not even twitching. He bent down and tried to find a pulse.

"Where do you check for a pulse on a wolf anyway?" He muttered, standing back up. "I think you're right."

"Stadler didn't die," Carruthers said.

Another wolf leapt through the door and hit Scarlet side on. His weapon was knocked out of his hand and the wolf bit down hard on his arm. Blood sprayed out of his wrist as an artery was severed. Its claws raked across Scarlet's neck, thick red lines appearing in their wake. Knowles shot the wolf twice in the side of the head, both at point blank range. The wolf's head exploded, showering both Knowles and Scarlet with blood.

Scarlet stood up but his legs buckled. He put a hand on the kitchen table to steady himself, blood pouring out of his arm and neck. "I don't feel too good," he said and his legs gave way. Knowles caught him under the arms, and fell back under the weight of the bigger man. They stumbled to the floor.

Carruthers opened a bag and pulled out a medical kit. He unwrapped a bandage and gave a thick pad to Knowles.

"It's too late," Knowles said. Scarlet's eyes were open and staring at the ceiling.

Carruthers threw the pack down and swore. He sank to his knees and held his head in his hands. A wolf howled from outside, and a timely bang indicated the ones by the front door were still there.

A wolf padded up to the back door. It sniffed the air, then lowered its head and growled at them. Knowles aimed at its head and squeezed the trigger once. It jumped back and the bullet thudded into the wall behind it. It bared its teeth.

"Run," Knowles said.

Carruthers turned to run to the stairs just as the front door caved in and a wolf growled at him. He squeezed off three shots and two hit the target. The wolf buckled and fell blocking the door momentarily. Another wolf snapped its jaws in the street. Carruthers aimed at it, but the weapon clicked. He didn't have time to wonder which idiot hadn't reloaded it, he fled for the stairs.

Knowles was only a second behind him. He fired into the doorway, but the wolf leapt out of the way easily. He got to the top of the stairs just as Carruthers shouted, "Move!"

Knowles flattened himself against a wall as Carruthers threw a mattress down the stairs. It hit the wolf square in the head and both tumbled to the bottom of the stairs. It spun from underneath the mattress and growled up the stairs. Carruthers threw the bed frame down next. It smashed against the wall and split in half, blocking the stairwell.

They ran into Knowles' bedroom and slammed the door shut. Carruthers flipped that bed up against the door and started pushing the wardrobe to block it. Knowles looked out of the back window.

Two wolves were dragging Scarlet's body to the garden. They stopped at the top of the steps to the patio. One of them looked up at the window, then dipped its head and started to eat.

"Shit."

Carruthers stood next to him. He pointed at something in the corner of the patio. "Shoot the gas."

Knowles opened the window and aimed at the barbecue. The gas canister was a reasonable size and so it was an easy target, even in the dark. He fired once. The round smashed into the canister and it exploded. Fire engulfed one of the wolves and Scarlet. The wolf screamed and whined. It ran around in erratic circles as its fur and then flesh burned.

The other wolf was hit in the side by shrapnel. White hot metal shredded its side, cutting through flesh like a knife through butter. It too screamed and leapt away. Fire caught the ends of its fur and it yelped in fear.

Knowles aimed again and took its head off. The other he left to burn.

"Two down."

"How many are left?"

"No idea."

They both heard a growl behind them. The wolf was at the door. They heard it sniffing around the bottom of the blockage.

"Now what?" Carruthers said, alternating looks out of the window and back to the door.

"Wilson said his back up was on the way."

"Yeah, I don't fancy being here when the plods turn up though. They'll get massacred or the wolves run away and leave us to explain this mess."

"Out the window we go then."

"Yep."

The fire was dying down now. Smoke and the stench of burning flesh filled the air. Two charred wolf carcasses lay next to the ruined barbecue. The child's slide had been blown across the garden and was lying next to the rear hedge. They used the light of the fire to check the coast was clear, then jumped.

Knowles went first, landing awkwardly on his ankle. His gun flew out of his hands and landed in a bush. Knowles fell to one knee and stifled a yell. He tried to stand, but white hot pain shot up his leg. Carruthers landed next to him with a thud.

"That's fucking great," he said. "My gun."

Carruthers was already searching the bush. He shook his head after a couple of seconds searching. "We gotta go."

"I know," Knowles nodded. "My ankle's fucked."

They looked each other square in the eye for a moment. *This is it. Self preservation. I don't blame him.* But then Carruthers broke the stare by putting his arm around Knowles shoulders. *He's a better man than me.* They walked down towards the ruined back door. Carruthers peered into the kitchen and it was deserted. He helped Knowles over the threshold and they nearly slipped in a trail of blood.

They were halfway across the kitchen when they heard the first growl.

Blocking the way to the front door were two wolves: one grey and the other large and brown. Behind them, another wolf padded into the kitchen. This was the largest of all, with thick black fur covering its body.

Knowles sagged against Carruthers. "I'm sorry."

"Nothing to be sorry about."

The black wolf stopped several feet away from them. Its fur started to slide off its body and it stood up. Its head started to shrink in on itself until it was human again. The man standing before them was very handsome, with the requisite square jaw and piercing blue eyes. Knowles would have hated him anyway.

"Not such big men without your guns," the man said.

"Let's kill them."

Knowles turned his head and wasn't surprised to see the grey wolf had turned into an older man. The brown wolf stayed, hackles up, tail between its legs. He had seen dogs look like that, usually before they attacked other dogs.

"Yes Steve, we will kill them, but they will suffer."

"Do them now, Alex."

Alex glared at Steve and Knowles recognised the expression: he had looked at Carruthers the same way many times.

"Do us now!" Carruthers snarled. "Come on, I can take the pair of you!"

"You have no idea what power we have," Alex laughed.

"The power to bore me stupid. Come on," Carruthers shouted. He puffed out his chest and roared.

"Carruthers-" Knowles began.

Shots rang out. Steve's shoulder burst outwards, showering the wall with blood and he fell to the floor screaming. The brown wolf turned towards the shots and caught one in the side. It yelped and ran, bursting past Knowles and Carruthers disappearing into the garden. Steve followed closely, back in wolf form, trailing blood from a wound above its right fore-leg.

Jones walked into the house, gun aimed into the kitchen. "Who fucking wants some then?"

Alex snarled at Knowles. "Another time." He turned into a wolf and ran out through the back door.

"I have never been so glad to see you," Knowles said.

"We should go," Jones said.

"Yep, police on the way," Carruthers said.

Jones looked grim. "This place is fucked up, we ain't never coming back."

He helped Carruthers carry Knowles to the car then checked that Stadler and the woman were still in the boot. Stadler was out cold and the woman still dead. *As it should be.* He got in the driver's seat as sirens became audible in the distance.

"Fucking Devon," he said and gunned the engine.

7

Katie woke suddenly. She lay in bed unmoving for a moment. *What was that noise?* It had sounded like a big bang with some popping noises after it. *Gunfire?*

In Huntleigh? Don't be ridiculous.

She felt the empty side of the bed and started to cry. It felt like she'd been crying non-stop for days now. Was it really only this morning that things had been normal? Her eyes were itching, bloodshot and raw. *Where are you Jack? What's happened to you?*

Josh was sleeping on his back and looked so peaceful. In the distance she could hear sirens and crossed to the window to have a look. A car pulled away from a couple of doors down, its tyres screeching on the tarmac. *Strange time of night to start a journey. In a hurry too, so I hope it's nothing bad.* A huge yawn escaped her lips and she suddenly realised how tired she was. She crawled back into bed, unconsciously avoiding Jack's side altogether. She fell asleep, despite the sirens getting louder and the flickering lights causing an eerie glow in the room.

8

Alex made them stop several miles into the woods around Huntleigh. He examined Steve's wounds and managed to stop the bleeding.

"You've got an exit wound," he explained, "so you'll be ok."

Steve grunted by way of reply. "Now what?"

"I want blood," Anton said.

Alex nodded. "We all do. They will pay for the deaths they caused tonight. I promise you."

"We nearly got killed there Alex," Steve said. "I'm hurt."

"I will track them down by myself if I have to," Anton growled at Steve.

Alex grinned. "You won't have to. We're going to get some help."

Part Two: Kent

Chapter 20

1

Knowles sat on the uncomfortable plastic chair and waited. His ankle itched underneath the bandage and he was hot to the point of sweating in his uniform. Rolling his walking stick back and forth in his hands, he knew he'd been lucky: it was a sprain and would be better in a couple of days. He could already put his weight on it and was hoping to run on it tomorrow.

Either side of him were two burly soldiers standing rigidly to attention. They were the only feature in the otherwise sparse room. Grey and bland walls lined the room; no artwork or photographs broke the monotony of the room. No windows either, so only harsh, artificial light lit the room. Two doors: one in to the meeting room and the other out to the main office area.

He had been waiting for almost half an hour – never a good sign. Everything should run precisely to time in the military. Who was in the room with Major Smith? It had to be some pretty big hitters. The presence of the armed guard gave that away.

It had been a hectic two days since their hurried return from Devon. The drug had kept Stadler unconscious for the whole journey, which had been a huge relief to all of them. As soon as they arrived on base, Stadler and the corpse had been whisked away. Knowles had had his ankle x-rayed and bandaged, whilst the others had their various cuts and bruises cleaned up.

Then, every question had been met with stony silence. They were ordered to stay on base. No phone calls allowed. The three were all put in the same barracks and a guard assigned to watch the door night and day. The barracks were big enough for eight soldiers, but they were left alone.

Until today, when Knowles had been summoned to meet with Major Smith. Nobody else, just him. *Another bad sign.* The door to the meeting room opened and a young man beckoned him forward.

"Sergeant, this way please."

Knowles stood with the help of the cane and walked into the room. He tried to hide the limp and not use the cane. *Never a good idea to show weakness.* It was a long thin room, dominated by a wooden table. Chairs lined either side of the table and three were occupied. Smith sat at the head of the table and on his left was a Captain who Knowles didn't recognise. On his right was Colonel James, the man in charge of the whole Battalion. Knowles felt his stomach and sphincter tighten. All the officers were reading a pile of papers. The young man sat next to a laptop and seemed to merge with the nondescript background. *Just a desk jockey then.*

Knowles saluted as smartly as he could. Smith gestured to a chair and Knowles sat, stretching his leg in front of him. The three officers all stopped reading as one, as if some secret code had been given.

"Sergeant Knowles," Smith said, far too loudly for the confines of the room. "This is a hell of a report."

"Yes sir."

"We have a problem," Smith said, tapping the papers. He steepled his fingers under his chin and looked at Knowles with a curious half smile on his lips.

"Yes sir?"

"You have left a hell of a mess here, sergeant," Colonel James said, his voice deep with each word clearly enunciated.

"Yes sir," Knowles said, trying to stay calm.

The three officers looked at each other, but their expressions were too hard to read.

"Sir, permission to speak freely."

"Granted, Knowles, you are not on trial here."

Feels like it. "Sir, my report can be verified by my team. Corporal Meyers is covered with spider bites. You have the corpse of one of the spiders because Corporal Carruthers thought very quickly in a difficult situation. We were woefully unprepared. The spiders alone are an unprecedented find."

The long drive back had let them all fill in the various events they had been involved in. Disbelief hadn't been an option, as much as they might have wanted it. Carruthers' knowledge of spiders and wolves would, under any other circumstances led to much piss-taking. Instead, it had been invaluable. The last thing he wanted now was to have grief from some Ruperts.

"You have Jack Stadler on base," he continued. "He's alive despite being shot over thirty times. Jonesey shot him at point blank range. Go to the house and look at the bodies. I understand things did not go smoothly, but it was pretty fucked up." That earned him a glare from Smith.

"We have," the unknown man said. "We have cleaned up the mess you left and have calmed the local police down. They are understandably upset that one of their own is missing. Everyone is, for now, buying the animal story. The true body count has been brought down. The dead wolves helped with the pack theory. We even arranged for the other car to be collected."

"Who are you?" Knowles demanded.

"Knowles!" Smith said. The other man held up a hand.

"It's ok, David. I am Captain Daniel Starky." He stressed the rank and held Knowles' gaze.

"Never heard of you."

"Watch your tongue, Knowles," Smith said.

Knowles nodded. *Great, so why are you here?*

"Wait a minute, you said wolf bodies."

"Yes?"

"They were humans, well, like Stadler."

"Do you have evidence for that?"

"No, but-"

"No, but what?"

"They stayed as wolves when they died. I thought-"

"Stop thinking Knowles. This would appear to be different to the stories."

Knowles didn't need to ask *what* stories.

"As far as the outside world goes, you were never in Devon," Starky said.

Realisation began to dawn on Knowles.

"The truth of this matter must never come to light. You and your team are to tell no-one what happened to you."

"I understand, sir."

"You must ensure that this is fully understood. We will court martial anyone who talks of this."

Knowles nodded more vigorously. James cleared his throat.

"We thank you and your team for your work in this matter Sergeant Knowles. You will be granted extra leave in a place of your choosing."

"Sir," Knowles paused. "One of my men died, sir. What do I tell his family?"

"Nothing." James looked genuinely surprised. "Corporal Scarlet was back in Afghanistan on a top secret mission. He died serving his country. His family has already been informed."

Knowles nodded again. *So that was how it was going to be.*

"You will need to fully debrief our team here," Smith said. "You and your men have information that could be vital to the safety of this country. We have a team working on Stadler at the moment. Another team is analysing the bone fragments you retrieved from the cave. You will work closely with them for as long as it takes for us to understand the nature of our enemy."

"Yes sir, but-"

"Dismissed, Sergeant."

"Sir, Stadler is not our enemy. He has no idea what is happening to him."

Starky had picked up his pen, but he put it down with a thud. "We intend to find out exactly what makes Mr Stadler tick."

"I said dismissed!" Smith barked.

Knowles stood awkwardly and turned to open the door. Smith called out as he gripped the handle.

"Sergeant, I am sorry, but Harrison Meyers died this morning. The venom proved too powerful and he died due to multiple organ failure."

2

Knowles drank from the bottle, relishing the taste of the cold beer as it slipped down his throat. He didn't say a word until the bottle was empty and Carruthers passed him a new one.

"Meyers is dead."

Carruthers and Jones didn't say anything. They were sat in their barracks. Their food was brought by unspeaking soldiers and things cleared away by the same men. Mobile phones had been confiscated. They only had beer because Jones bribed one of the unspeaking men.

"To Meyers," Knowles said, raising his bottle. They clinked glasses. "And Scarlet."

"What did he die of?" Jones asked.

"If you'd seen him, you wouldn't need to ask that," Carruthers said. "Those spiders-" he didn't finish the sentence, but shuddered instead.

"We are on a silence order," Knowles said. "They've invented a story to cover Scarlet's death and will now, I assume, do the same for Meyers. No-one is to know what we've been through."

"My ex?" Jones asked.

"No-one."

Carruthers shook his head. "The police were on their way to that house. They must have got there ten minutes max after we left. They'd have seen the bodies, the wolves."

"The police will be told to shut up, evidence buried or explained. Remember, everyone thinks its wild animals down there. Body of a wolf found, case closed."

"Yeah, but that's a wolf that can turn into a human," Jones said.

"They won't ever get to examine that corpse though will they? The Ruperts will make sure of that." Knowles drained his second bottle. He opened a third without pausing. "Also, those dead wolves stayed as wolves. They didn't change back."

"What else did they say?"

"We're to debrief the team looking into this. We are to offer them every assistance as they attempt to find out the nature of our enemy." Knowles sighed. "We're not leaving this base any time soon."

He felt numb inside, though the beer was helping. Scarlet. Meyers. Jesus. Both had served with honour in Afghanistan and the Gulf. Both had been lifers. Scarlet in since sixteen, Meyers eighteen. Knowles had known them both for years. Fought alongside them in some pretty rough circumstances. How could an op in Devon – Devon! - go so wrong?

He had seen enough men die to know that it wasn't his fault. He shouldn't blame himself, but he couldn't help it. *We were unprepared. A jolly, that was what the op had felt like, one big jolly. Giant deadly spiders. People who could turn into wolves. All very fucked up.*

He would not be unprepared next time he came face to face with the wolves.

3

Jack lay on his side staring at the same patch of wall he'd been looking at for a couple of hours. The paint was flaking slightly and it played tricks on his eyes. He kept seeing Katie or Josh or sometimes both.

No one answered his questions. They pushed food through a hatch in the door and ordered him to put the plates back on the other side of the hatch when he was done. He had a shower that was a basic nozzle and curtain – it reminded him of wet rooms that surfers often had in their houses. The toilet was clean, but that was all he could say about it.

One of the walls was dominated by a large mirror. Given the lack of privacy in the room, he surmised that the mirror was really a one way window. He had been in the room for nearly three days, or at least that was his best guess by counting meal times. He had stopped shouting after the first day.

Katie would be going apeshit.

His mind wouldn't let him rest despite how exhausted he was. He kept thinking of his family. Josh with his perfect face, thin mop of dark hair and the way he slept with his head tilted back at that unnatural angle that looked so painful. Katie with her thick dark hair. Sometimes he pictured her with hair up, other times down. Sometimes, and most worryingly, he couldn't make out her features at all. Her smell would come to him, her favourite perfume overwhelming his senses, making him sob.

Mostly, he remembered her look of horror as he turned into that *thing*.

4

Knowles watched Stadler lying on his side. Tears were running down Stadler's face, but he didn't move to wipe them away. Four of them stood in the narrow hallway by the observation room. Carruthers and Jones were also there and the doctor made four. She was a small woman, pretty, but her body was well hidden by her fatigues. *Pity*.

"He hasn't moved for hours," she said. Her badge identified her as Claire Biddlestone.

"Has he-" Jones paused, "y'know."

"No," Claire smiled. "No change at all."

"Has anyone spoken to him?" Knowles asked. He had Stadler's file under his arm, complete with pictures of the baby. *Josh*. He thought about the miscarriage that had been the first nail in the coffin of his marriage. *What would it be like to have a kid and not see it?*

Claire shook her head. "Orders. He is to be in solitary."

"Why?" Carruthers said.

"So he doesn't fucking eat anyone?" Jones said.

"He's not like that." Knowles put the folder on the thin desk in front of him. He deliberately left it open on the pictures of Josh and Katie Stadler.

"Come on Pete, we saw him eat that woman."

"It wasn't him, it was the wolf."

"But he *is* the wolf," Carruthers said.

"We don't know how much control he has. Look at him. Does he look like a killer?"

"West didn't look like a killer, Knowles, or Brady. You know better than to go on looks."

"Did you see the others?" Knowles said to Jones. "It was like they wanted him to like them. You seen dogs approach each other, right? The way they are submissive to each other?"

"Yeah, and then they take a right good sniff of each other's arses." Jones grinned at Claire. She didn't return it.

"That's exactly the way that woman was with him."

"Until he bit her head off."

Knowles shook his head and gave up. *He's different. The others enjoyed the killing. Stadler didn't.*

They watched Stadler for a few more moments. He stood up and walked over to the mirror. Claire made a note on a pad in front of her.

"We have to document every movement he makes," she said.

"10:30 a.m., took a shit," Jones said.

Stadler raised his nose and sniffed the air. He looked exactly like a dog getting a scent.

"Well, would you look at that," Carruthers said. "Can he smell us?"

"I doubt it. This is a pretty thick wall."

Carruthers didn't look convinced.

"They have nearly finished the report on the dead woman," Claire said. "Briefing is at 1500."

"We'll be there," Knowles said. "When can I talk to Stadler?"

Claire shrugged. "When the CO says you can, until then he's on his own."

5

Jack stood and walked to the mirror. He could – *what?* He pressed his face up against the glass and cupped his hands around his eyes. He couldn't see anything, obviously but he was sure they were there, watching him.

He knew the smell. *Familiar smell. The man who had drugged Ginny and the other two. The ones who had put him in the boot of the car.* Mixed in with that was another smell, another that he recognised, but it was impossible.

He turned away from the mirror and lay back on the bed. The same questions started bouncing around his head again.

Where am I?
Where's Katie?
Who are these people?
Can I be cured?

He closed his eyes and started to cry again.

Chapter 21

1

"We have finished the autopsy of the dead woman," Starky said, opening the folder in front of him. Everyone around the table opened identical manila folders. "I don't think I need to elaborate on how she died." There was nervous laughter around the table, from all except Knowles and his team. "There are several interesting things about her though."

Knowles was flanked by Carruthers and Jones. Claire Biddlestone sat next to Jones, her hair pulled back into a bun, emphasising her cheekbones. Knowles forced himself to look at the photographs in the file. She had been a beautiful woman. *What a way to go.* He turned the page over and came face to face with Katie Stadler. *Great.*

Next to Claire sat a young soldier who was clearly there just to take minutes of the meeting. Starky was next to him and Smith sat at the head of the table. *The colonel has gone then, nothing more to see.* He could keep clear now until something significant happened and then come in and take the credit.

"Firstly," Starky continued, "the amount of force to bite through the neck muscles and spinal column is immense. You would need something sharp to even begin to penetrate and the range of bite would be larger than just about every land animal alive today." He looked at Knowles. "Certainly bigger than anything alive in Britain."

"I saw it and so did Corporal Jones." He sounded defensive, and hated himself for it. Jones was sitting next to him and he nodded. Both Jones and Carruthers were under orders not to speak. Knowles was only to answer for them. They were there to offer advice only. Bollocks, Jones had said and so far, Knowles had to agree with him. Knowles had insisted they attend, pointing out to Smith that they might remember different things.

"Well, certainly the skin damage around the neck wound is consistent with a bite. It also had begun necrotizing before the patient died."

"Necrotizing?" Major Smith said.

"The skin dies, and it starts to destroy itself, like with a flesh eating bacteria."

"Jesus," Knowles said, earning himself a glare from the Major.

"You are quite right Sergeant Knowles," Starky said. "The bacteria that can cause this condition are present in every human mouth, but it is still thankfully rare. It can be found in young men following a weekend. You see, they punch someone in the mouth, the uh, punchee's teeth break the skin. If untended, it can become quite a problem." Starky beamed at the group, an inane grin that made him look like an idiot. He seemed to realise this, and continued. "What is impressive here is the speed with which it acted. Necrotizing should take several hours, if not days as a minimum."

Silence greeted his comments. Knowles swallowed hard. *This is worse than we thought.*

"The woman was also completely healthy in every other regard."

"No diseases?"

"No sir."

"So why did she change into a wolf? How could she *do* that?" Knowles was almost shouting.

"Enough Sergeant," Smith said. "Captain Starky, please explain. This woman was a wolf thing, yes or no?"

"Our witnesses are reliable, sir," Starky said, flashing his inane smile at Knowles and Jones.

Damn right we are, Knowles thought.

"Yes they are," Smith said.

"I cannot explain it sir. There was nothing in her blood or tissue samples to explain *how* she could change."

"Magic," Jones muttered. Starky glared at him, then nodded agreement.

"You might be right there." Silence descended again.

"Anything else?" Smith said.

"We have no idea who she is. There is no record of her anywhere in any of our medical records."

"Have you tried international?"

Starky nodded. "We have been in touch with the usual agencies, but have heard nothing yet. I could hurry them up."

"Do it."

2

Smith cleared his throat and everyone fell silent. "Sergeant Knowles, perhaps you would like to tell us all what you and your team saw."

"Sir, it is all in the report."

"Indulge me, Sergeant."

Knowles looked at the folder in front of him. Katie Stadler was still looking at him from the photograph. She was clutching Josh to her chest whilst looking straight at the camera. It was a weird shot, she should have been unaware that the photograph was being taken. Now, as he looked, her gaze became accusatory: *you have my husband. This boy needs a father.*

He ran through the op quickly, but without skipping any of the details of what had happened in Barnstaple. The complete scene of terror in Boutport Street; the dead, including the police; Jones and him emptying entire clips into the large wolf and bundling the corpse into their car.

"We realised Jack – uh, Stadler – was still alive on the journey back to Huntleigh."

"Why did you think Stadler was alive?" Smith interrupted.

"He was banging on the boot of our car."

"The woman was still dead?"

"She, uh, didn't have a head, sir."

He saw Starky suppress a grin. It wasn't a good idea to laugh at a Major. Smith had a face like thunder.

"You said you and Corporal Jones emptied mags into the wolf. Your words, Sergeant. Did you miss?"

"No sir."

"But he was alive?" Smith said. "I need to know what we're up against here."

"Sir, we believe that he healed and pushed the bullets back out of his body. We found bullets in the boot of our car."

Jones was nodding.

"So why does one wolf die and the other doesn't?"

"I don't know, sir." Knowles spread his hands and again looked each person in the eye. *They don't know either.*

The awkward silence descended again. Smith looked at Starky: "We need to know more. The patient has not changed since we have had him, correct?"

"Yes, sir."

"Then we need to know why. What triggers the change?"

"Well," Starky said, "from the reports, we can rule out the full moon. The night of the first attack was a full moon, but there has not been one since. That part of this would appear to be legend."

"All legends have a basis in truth," Carruthers said. Smith glared at him. "Permission to speak, sir," he added belatedly.

"Granted, but keep it pertinent."

"Fear might be a factor in his changing sir – he might not be able to control it. When I placed the bugs in the Stadler household, he saw me. I was chased by him as a wolf – he changed and I didn't realise it." Carruthers was going red, but continued. "I probably wouldn't have believed it anyway. His next change was when we think he was assaulted on his way home from the pub."

Starky nodded. "I agree. Each of the changes, bar the one in the hospital, came following a period of intense anxiety or fear."

"Hospitals are not the most calming of places," Smith said.

"Sir, we can try to put Stadler under stress and see if he changes."

"Do it," Smith said, and though his voice hadn't changed, he was clearly giving an order. "Tomorrow."

"Yes, sir."

"Sir," Knowles said. "The woman and her, uh, friends, all changed at will."

"Can Stadler do that?" Smith demanded.

"Not that we've seen sir," Knowles said.

"Well why not?" He looked at Starky. "Get your team ready. I want that man tested for every possible thing you can. I want to know if he can force himself to change. If so, I want to know how. I want to know what is in him that makes him do that, and I want to know if he can control it. Gentlemen, and lady," he added with a nod at Claire, "there is far too much about this that we don't know. We must find out what we can."

Knowles knew what was coming next.

"Then I want to know if we can use it."

They all looked at their folders, no-one quite sure how to answer that.

"How is the analysis of the bones going?" Smith said next.

"Slowly, sir. It takes time," Starky said.

"Hurry it up. Stadler was normal until he fell on them."

Knowles looked at the photo of Katie Stadler again, and thought about her standing in the doorway of that pub. Wind in her hair, with the glow of a new mum. Pregnancy was supposed to make women glow, but Knowles preferred the look of new mothers. Something about the pride and love just appealed to him. His mind wandered to miscarriages again and he forced himself to concentrate.

"We have a specialist team from the Natural History Museum looking at them," Starky said. "They have no clue what animal it could be and all have signed the OSA."

"Those bones are the key to what happened to Stadler," Smith said. "If we can control him, then maybe we can make our soldiers better with whatever is in those bones."

Starky looked at his notes and the others stared at Smith.

"Sir, you can't-" Carruthers began.

"You will not speak again, soldier," Smith bellowed. "That man, a civilian, bested two of you easily and survived being shot – on two separate occasions. His friends caused the death of the experienced, and capable Scarlet and very nearly beat you three as well. He is fast and strong. Tell me," he paused and smiled at Carruthers the way a father smiles at a child he's just finished scolding, "you couldn't have used that in Afghanistan."

Chapter 22

1

Jack woke at the sudden noise. He had dozed after the last meal. That made it four days according to his meal counting. Potatoes and a chicken pie. He had devoured it – boredom was making him very hungry. *Sleeping a lot, eating a lot, nothing else to do. I would kill for a book to read, or a guitar.* The thought instantly made him feel guilty. The tally of dead was high now. He had to control himself; learn what was happening to him. Help the soldiers. Maybe *that* would lead to redemption.

A high pitched whine engulfed the room. He leapt off the bed and spun around on the spot, looking for the speakers. None were obvious. The sound increased in pitch and his ears started to hurt. He fell to the floor with his hands clasped over them and started to scream.

2

"Increase it again," Smith said. Despite the obvious distress of Stadler, there was no emotion in his voice.

Claire looked at the dial and turned it fractionally to the right. A dial on amplifier turned to 40 MHz. Whatever Stadler was hearing he didn't like, and it was well outside the range of human hearing.

She felt a knot of anxiety in her stomach. This didn't feel right: it was more like torture. She nearly felt sorry for him, then remembered those that had died – some at his hands. In the room, Stadler fell to his knees, hands over his ears.

Claire continued to watch, eyes moving from the dial to the room as if she were watching a high quality tennis match. Stadler was now screaming with pain, his whole body convulsing. Fur was bursting out along his arms and his limbs seemed to be lengthening.

"Sir!" she said, mouth opening. She'd read Knowles' report; she hadn't really believed it though, not really. *Some kind of group delusion.*

Smith nodded. "This is what we were waiting for. Open the door."

Waiting outside, Knowles and others were waiting with weapons primed. The plan was to see if the wolf would take the opportunity to escape. Once outside, it would be shot or sedated. The evidence they had so far suggested that it wouldn't matter which.

Claire pressed a button and watched the door to Stadler's cell swing open.

3

The wolf had taken hold. There was nothing he could do. It seemed to burst through him and into the room. It roared and started to jump around, getting caught in the blankets from the bed. Finally it broke free and shredded the blankets with its teeth. Next the toilet was knocked off its stand, the cistern breaking with a loud bang. Water poured out of the wreckage.

The wolf lapped at the water for a moment then continued its rampage. The bed was upturned and the mattress got the same treatment as the blankets. Feathers from the quilt filled the air.

It stopped suddenly. The noise had gone. It sniffed the air, turning slowly. A door was open to its left. Fresh air, pine mixed with fresh mown grass, engulfed it. A stronger scent came with it, more familiar and nearer. The wolf looked at the mirror and padded over to it. It sniffed again, its breathing leaving twin v's of condensation, then walked away.

It turned and charged at the mirror.

4

"Sir!" Claire shouted as the wolf leapt. They both jumped back against the wall as it hit the glass with a dull thud. The whole of the glass shook violently. The wolf padded away again, then ran at the mirror. It hit again, harder this time.

"Magnificent," Smith said in a whisper that failed to disguise the awe in his voice.

"We should leave," Claire said as the wolf charged for a third time.

"Nonsense, that's reinforced glass," Smith said, just as a crack appeared down the centre of the glass. They both shrank back from the glass.

"It knows we're here," Smith said, a look of fascination on his face.

"I can see that sir, but it is going to break that glass and I don't want to be in here when it does."

"Sound the alarm," Smith said. The wolf hit the glass again and the crack spread with an audible screech, smaller spider web lines spreading in all directions. He watched as the wolf went to the other side of the room before starting its charge. He felt himself grinning as it leapt at the glass. "Do you know what this means?"

"Sir, we need to go." Claire hit the alarm and a klaxon sounded in the distance as if it were a million miles away. She squeezed past the Major and opened the door. A short corridor led to another thick door. Outside would be the courtyard and armed men. They would be running towards them now. Claire turned back to Smith.

"It's still able to think, to *reason,*" Smith said.

The glass shattered and the wolf flew through, landing on Smith. He screamed and held his hands over his face. The wolf growled. Claire screamed and it looked up at her. She turned and ran. Adrenaline coursed through her, making her run faster than she ever had before. The grey paint on the walls was a blur as she sprinted down the corridor. Sunlight flooded in where the outside door was propped open. The bright sunshine blinded her momentarily but she managed to kick the crude block of wood holding the door open. It crashed shut behind her, but she stumbled, landing hard in the courtyard. She tried to get up, but couldn't, panic making her limbs operate independently of her thoughts. *I'm like a horse on ice.* She ended up on her back, shuffling backwards away from the door.

The wolf slammed into the door, splintering it so that it hung off its hinges. It stopped, sniffing the air and then lowered its head. Yellow eyes watched her all the time, saliva dripping from its immense jaw.

It bit her head off. Claire was still screaming as she crawled backwards. *It bit her FUCKING head off!* Out of the corner of her eyes, she saw men running towards her, all carrying guns. Even as she saw them, her heart sank. She knew and they knew.

They would not reach her in time.

5

Knowles was sprinting across the courtyard, Browning in his hand when he saw the doctor come flying out of the containment hut. *First day without the cane. This is going to hurt like a bitch later.* He watched as she fell to the floor. She was screaming – an out of control, almost primal sound. She was about 100 metres away from him. *Be there in about 11 seconds, even with a crocked ankle. Too long.* He raised the gun and looked through the sights, ready for what was coming through the door.

The door splintered with a crash and the wolf was *there* standing in the courtyard. Even though he was expecting it, it still turned his blood to ice. Several of the soldiers running next to him slowed down and a few stopped dead. Under different circumstances, the line of slack jawed soldiers would be comical. *But not today.*

It was almost two metres long and just under one and a half metres high. Its legs were short but powerful. Knowles could see muscles rippling even through the thick black fur that covered it. Long razor sharp teeth shone bright white in the sunlight and its jaw was huge. It walked slowly towards the fallen doctor, sniffing the air deeply.

Knowles stopped and took aim. His heart was hammering in his chest as he looked down the sights. He took a deep breath.

Don't miss.

6

Claire stopped screaming as the wolf sniffed her. It worked its way up her body, sniffing in exactly the same way as an exuberant dog. It stopped by her head and gazed into her eyes. The yellow eyes were watching her with interest, and she fought down revulsion. She turned her head to the side as it bent its snout to her cheek. Saliva dripped onto her turned cheek and she stifled a scream again. *Don't be sick. Oh God, our father in heaven, please help me.*

The wolf looked up suddenly and started to growl. Claire followed it gaze. Knowles was standing about twenty metres away his gun pointing straight at the wolf. The growl increased in volume and the threat was clear: *stay away.*

"Don't shoot!"

The voice came from the doorway. Smith was leaning against the door frame. His uniform was crumpled, shirt out and tie halfway down his chest. The medals were askew on his chest. His hair was unkempt, but he was unhurt.

"Sir?" Knowles shouted.

The wolf continued to growl.

"I want to see what it does."

Knowles swore loudly, but didn't drop his aim.

Shoot it, Knowles, please shoot it. The wolf sniffed at Claire again then stepped away from her, facing the approaching group of soldiers. It kept its head low and its bushy tail was between its legs, but its teeth remained bared.

"Move to me," Smith said, "slowly, no sudden movements."

She gritted her teeth: *I'm not stupid.* It took an exorbitant act of will to get her muscles to obey her. *Come on, no worse than that night with spotty Dave in college.* She slid away from the wolf, moving on her bottom as quietly as she could. *This is way worse.* When there were a few metres between her and the wolf she got to her feet and ran to Smith.

The wolf turned when it heard her run. It snarled at her and started to move.

"Take it down, Sergeant," Smith said as if he were ordering a pint in his local pub.

7

Knowles sat in the chair by the side of the bed and waited. Stadler was lying in the bed, although he had no choice in that matter: his ankles were shackled to the metal frame and straps lay across his chest and legs. He was covered in blankets, although they had only been put on him in the last five minutes. The cameras had recorded his healing until then.

He had shot Stadler twice in the side. It had been enough to put the wolf down this time, though he didn't know why. There had been gasps from the onlookers when the fur had slipped away to leave Stadler lying unconscious in the courtyard sun. A lot of people were now going to have to be briefed about what exactly they were guarding here. Smith had already transferred all staff who hadn't seen anything away. It took a little under an hour, but they were all gone. *We are seriously understaffed here now.*

They had moved Stadler to a single block adjacent to the original one. The set up was identical: a single room with a small access corridor and observation room. The observation room had been sealed shut once all surveillance equipment had been routed to transmit to the other block.

Two hours had passed and they were fully expecting Stadler to be awake. Knowles was alone in the room, but he was armed with a single hypo filled with the strongest sedative they had on base. Watching Jack sleep, Knowles felt something close to pity. Stadler was out of his depth: that was becoming clearer and clearer to Knowles.

Stadler opened his eyes and screamed. He tried to sit up but couldn't move. The shackles on his arms and legs ensured that.

"Try to relax," Knowles said as calmly as he could.

Stadler's eyes were wide with fright and he stared at Knowles.

"You."

Knowles nodded, "Me."

"Please, help me."

"That's the idea, Jack."

"How do you know my name?" Jack tried to look around the room again, but his head was held in place by another strap across his forehead.

"Don't try to move Jack. You are strapped down for my safety. There are people watching who will electrocute you if you make a wrong move. Clear?"

"I'm scared."

"I think I'm the one who should be scared, Jack."

Stadler slid his eyes over to look at Knowles. He saw the smile, but didn't return it.

"I didn't kill the soldier."

"No, Jack, you didn't. That's good."

"Who are you?"

"I am Sergeant Peter Knowles. You are in an army base in Kent. Nobody knows you are here."

Jack look stunned for a moment. "An army base? Why?"

"We need to know all about you and what you can do."

"What I can do?" Jack said. "You mean the wolf?"

Knowles nodded. "My superiors think you could be very useful to us."

"How?"

"Think, Jack," Knowles smiled. "You're a smart man – degree, teacher, blah, blah, blah – you think about how you could be useful to us."

Jack nodded. "I've killed people." His voice broke and his eyes filled with tears.

"We have evidence that you killed two people – a doctor and a Jane Doe."

Jack's face drained of all colour. "Four people. It's-" he gulped, "-*I've-* killed four people."

"What do you remember?"

Silence descended on the room. Jack looked at the ceiling again, tears rolling down his cheeks. His breathing started to get more ragged, speeding up and increasing in volume.

Knowles stood up quickly, hand on his gun. The door was two metres away, but at that moment it might as well have been two hundred.

"Sit down, Mr Knowles," Jack said through quick breaths. "Nothing is going to happen."

Knowles kept his hand on his pistol grip, but sat down anyway. "Did you just control it?"

Jack laughed. "I don't know."

"What do you remember?" Knowles asked again.

"I was in the hospital, then on the beach. I think it might have been Croyde."

"Croyde?"

"It's a beach, Mr Knowles," Jack said. "It's about ten miles out of Barnstaple."

"Anything in between?"

"Well, there's Braunton and-"

"No, no." Knowles smiled. "Do you remember anything in between?"

"Sorry," Jack said. He paused for a moment. "I remember running."

-on all fours, wind whistling in his ears as he ran. The smell of the woods assaulting him from all sides: deer in the distance; scent of dogs and other animals; the smell of the sap from the trees and the cooking from the houses surrounding the woods. The iron taste of the blood in his mouth-

"I think I might be sick." He started to retch. Knowles quickly untied him and helped him sit up. He thrust a small bin under Jack's chin. The other man retched several times, but nothing came out.

"You ok?"

Jack nodded. "Thanks," he sniffed, "that's about the nicest thing anyone has done for me for days."

Knowles looked at the floor for a moment, embarrassed by the pathetic gratefulness in Jack's voice. "Can you tell me about it? What were you thinking about?"

"Running."

"Anything else?"

Jack nodded again. "Can you help me?" he asked, tears rolling down his cheeks once more.

"We're going to try," Knowles said. "As you said, you didn't kill the Major."

"He was a Major?" Jack asked. "My wife is here. Where is she? Can I see her?"

"Your wife?" *What the hell?*

"Yes. Where is she?" Jack started to look wildly around the room. "Please, I need to see my wife and child. I want to see Josh."

"They are not here," Knowles said.

"Please, Mr Knowles – Peter -" Jack pleaded.

"Katie and Josh aren't here."

Jack started to pull at the braces on his legs. He got one undone before Knowles had really registered what was happening.

"Jack, stop doing that," Knowles said, "now."

"I need to see my wife!" Jack yelled. "Now!"

He ripped one of the braces off the bed and fur started to sprout along his arms.

"Calm down Jack," Knowles stood, kicking his chair away at the same time. His hand went to his holster.

Jack's face was elongating, teeth lengthening. Knowles pulled the gun out and shot him with the tranquiliser dart. He watched as Jack flailed at the huge needle sticking out if his chest.

The door flew open and two soldiers ran in, guns in front of them. Claire ran in behind them. Jack roared at Knowles, fur appearing on his cheeks now. Knowles shot him again.

Jack suddenly went limp and crashed to the floor.

"Fuck," Knowles said, looking down at the naked man.

"You ok?" Claire checked Jack's pulse. "He's got a good strong pulse, and it's normal."

"We need a stronger dose in these guns," Knowles said when Claire stood up. He caught a whiff of her perfume, a subtle smell – almost undetectable.

"What's that?" he exaggerated the sniff.

"Its Elle," she said, blushing. "Giorgio Armani."

The two soldiers had relaxed when they saw Stadler on the floor and returned to their posts by the door.

"It's nice," Knowles said. He helped her lift Stadler back onto the bed and retie the straps.

"Never untie these unless you have someone in the room with you," Claire scolded as she tightened the last strap.

"He wasn't going to hurt me."

"You don't know that."

"Yeah I do. He doesn't want this, any of it."

Claire walked back to the door and paused in the doorway. "You need to be careful, Knowles."

"Yes Ma'am," Knowles said with a smile. "How long will he be out?"

"Rest of the day probably with those two doses."

"Fancy a coffee?"

"I'd love one."

Interlude: Devon

1

Katie woke at six am, as she had every day for the last week. Josh's cries were not loud but they were insistent, like the mewling of a cat. She lifted him out of the cot and he started to feed. Her eyes were heavy and she dozed, letting feelings of love for her baby overwhelm her.

He finished half an hour later and she changed his nappy, talking to him as she did. She explained everything to him, from wiping with cotton wool and water, drying with a small towel to putting the fresh nappy on. He smiled up at her throughout it all. The health visitor and midwife had said it would be weeks before he could smile and that what she thought was a smile was wind, but she didn't care. Josh was smiling for her, brightening her day, giving her the strength to carry on.

She dressed him in a stripy baby grow and carried him downstairs. Ginny came to say hello, sniffed at Josh and then curled up on her bed with a very heavy sigh. *Must take her for a walk today.* She had breakfast with him on her lap.

She ate tasteless cornflakes and drank bland tea. She ran a bath and got in with Josh. At some point she cried, but couldn't remember when. She dried and got dressed, spraying some perfume to make herself feel better.

It didn't work.

2

She tried to ignore the stares of the people in the shop, but failed. Her cheeks were hot so she kept her gaze fixed firmly ahead, not making eye contact with anyone. On some faces was shock, but on most was that expression of sympathy you get from strangers who know you've been through a tragedy but whom it doesn't affect.

Josh gurgled and settled into his favourite position: head as close to her neck as possible. His eyes were open and he was staring up at her. He would sometimes look around the shop, wide-eyed with wonder, then return to cuddling into Katie.

The shop was packed, which was of course typical. Normally, at this time on a work day, you would be lucky to see two people in the place. Not today and not since that night. The locals were all there to buy the North Devon Journal, to get all the scandal featuring their very own village. Of course, now their own superstar – *widow, victim, freak* - was in the shop with them. Tongues would be wagging in the local tonight.

Katie put enough food to cook for the next couple of days in her basket and joined the end of the queue. Three people stood in front of her. It seemed to take a lifetime for them to be served. By the time she approached the till, four more were waiting behind her. She felt as though she had two heads.

"Hi Katie," Sue said from behind the till, "how are you today?"

The words were out automatically and Sue turned pale when she realised who she was talking to. "I mean-"

"I'm fine Sue," Katie said with a thin smile. She rested her hand on Josh's thin coating of hair. "Thanks for asking."

Sue quickly scanned the items and asked for money. "It's good to see you out and about."

"Yes," Katie said. "We have to eat, don't we, munchkin?"

"How's he doing?"

"Good, thanks. Sleeps like a baby."

Sue's mouth opened and closed in what would have been a great goldfish impression in different circumstances.

"That was a joke," Katie said.

Sue laughed, but too little, too late. "Sorry, it's just-"

"I know," Katie said, looking at the others in the shop. "My husband has gone. Life goes on."

She walked out of the shop and almost made it to the church before the tears came, yet again.

3

Katie sat on the sofa, clutching Josh to her despite the fact that he was fast asleep. She knew she should put him down; that she was creating problems for later, but she needed something to fill the emptiness inside her. The television had been on since she'd returned from the shop, but she couldn't remember turning it on, let alone what she had watched for the last two hours.

Her first outing had not gone well. She did not like to be stared at and she liked less being gossiped about. *Better get used to it, girl.* The main headline of the Journal had been "Village in shock following further deaths." Her copy had been waiting on the mat when she'd returned from the shop. The whole article was now seared inside her mind and bits of it flashed on the inside of her eyelids whenever she blinked.

-death toll of savage animal attacks mounts-

-amongst the dead are a policeman who had, ironically, moved from London to escape violence-

-local popular teacher, Jack Stadler, the final victim-

-tragically burned to death whilst attacking the vicious beast-

She had finally stopped crying. Her eyes were puffy and she felt that if she cried any more it would just be tiny salt crystal tumbling down her cheeks.

It was the last part of the story that she had most difficulty with. Jack had been in the street when he died – two doors away - and she'd been asleep. He had been alone, burning with that horrible wolf, when he drew his last breath.

What had he thought about? What had been his final coherent thought? Had he thought about her? Josh? What would Josh grow up to be? A teacher, like his father? A detective? An astronaut? A street cleaner? All things that Jack would now never see. The sense of loss was all powerful and tears came again. *Wrong again then –plenty more to come out.*

Detective Wilson had found Jack just outside Huntleigh when he had left her. He had turned round to bring Jack back to his family when – it was believed – they had seen the wolf attacking an unknown man. They had tried to rescue him, but Wilson had been killed. The wolf had attacked Jack, but he had managed to drag the wolf out to the garden where he found a gun and shot at the wolf.

The bullet had hit a gas canister. The resulting explosion had killed Jack and the wolf outright and the subsequent fire had consumed a large part of the house.

The unknown man had been a soldier on leave. A popular theory, reported by the Journal, was that the soldier – still unnamed – had just returned from Afghanistan and was looking to commit suicide. The gun was supposed to have been his, but the army were very tight lipped about how he had a gun with him. The army were not releasing the man's details as they wanted the man's memory and honour to remain intact in his family's eyes.

Jack and Wilson were being hailed as heroes by the press. They had stopped the mad wolf and now the streets of Huntleigh were safe. The death toll from Barnstaple only helped the impression that the men were heroes.

Jack. My Jack.

Katie had a big problem with the reported version of events. From her fractured memory of the hospital, she was sure that Jack had turned into the wolf.

That made her doubt her sanity.

Chapter 23

1

The sunlight was bright and warming in a way artificial light could only aspire to. Jack squinted and raised his hand to cover his eyes. It was his first time outside since arriving. *Well, first time in human form.*

Knowles was standing next to him, hand on the grip of his pistol. In front of Jack, two soldiers were backing away slowly, guns aimed right at him. He turned his head and saw two more watching from the flat roof of the building they were keeping him in. He knew from conversations with Knowles that these were Carruthers and Jones; he also recognised them from Huntleigh even though he had not spoken to them yet.

A woman came out of the building opposite. Apparently this identical building had been where they'd first kept him, until his break out attempt. Knowles smiled when he first saw her, then seemed to remember where he was and returned to his usual stern expression.

"Mr Stadler, my name is Claire Biddlestone," she said formally. "We've not actually met before, well not like this." She blushed. "You know what we're about to do?"

Jack scanned his surroundings. He was in a large concrete square. Four identical buildings lined one side of the square, with four more opposite. He had come out of the second building on one side. In the distance, about a half mile away, large trees bordered the entire plot. A single road lead away from the square and they were surrounded by open grass fields. Another set of buildings sat at the end of the road, and another road led to a gatehouse. Trees obscured the view from the outside. People might not even suspect there was an army base here.

"Call me Jack," he said with a coolness he did not feel. "Nice perfume. Elle?"

She ignored him. "Mr Stadler, you are aware of what we would like you to do?"

He nodded once.

"Remember, Jack," Knowles said, "we've got you covered, so nothing can go wrong."

"But it could."

"Trust us, Jack."

"I don't want to kill anyone."

"You won't." Knowles tapped the butt of his gun.

The gesture did not fill Jack with confidence. "Let's get it over with then."

Knowles nodded and he and Claire backed away. They disappeared into one of the corner buildings. The two soldiers remained, guns trained on Jack. Both were wearing armour plated versions of the suits dog handlers wore in police videos. They looked like heavily armed American football players. *Like that old board game. What was it called again?* The guns had two darts in each, and each dart would stop an elephant. Despite this he could smell their fear. *Yes, fear has a smell. It's like crack for people like me.*

Jack kicked his shoes off. No laces, which struck Jack as a bit pointless – from what he'd been told he wouldn't be able to kill himself anyway. He pulled the standard army issue t-shirt over his head and dropped the trousers. He folded both and put them in a neat pile next to him. Finally he pulled the boxer shorts off and placed them on top of the pile. *Why have I done that so neatly? Nice time to develop OCD.*

A breeze made him shiver, goose bumps rising on his arms. He turned on the spot, letting the cameras on the buildings get a good look at him. His hands covered his cock and balls and he was strangely relieved that the events of the last couple of weeks had left him in great shape. He actually had a six pack he hadn't paid for.

He stopped turning when the two soldiers came into view again and nodded at them once. "I'm ready," he said in a voice that suggested he wasn't.

Here we go.

2

The high pitched whine surprised him, even though he was expecting it. If anything, the anticipation made it louder when it started, like a phone ringing when you're sat right next to it. He immediately fell to the floor, hands over his ears and curled into a foetal ball, screaming.

"No! I've changed my mind!" Jack screamed. "Don't make me-"

The wolf burst out of him, snarling. Its dark coat seemed to absorb the sunlight, making it a cloud of darkness in the courtyard. Its yellow eyes seemed to glow, shining bright.

Two small red dots immediately played over the wolf's head as the soldiers took aim. Target locked.

The wolf stood its ground. It lowered its head and growled at the soldiers. Fur around its neck stood on end and its tail was between its legs. Suddenly it threw back its head and howled. The sound echoed around the square of buildings, the pitch changes making it seem as though many wolves were in the courtyard.

Both soldiers looked at each other, turned and ran.

3

Knowles was in the control room with Major Smith and Claire. He had ignored her admiring gasp when Stadler had removed his clothes, but his stomach had twisted all the same. She had gasped again when Jack had turned into the wolf. Lines of fur had run up his arms and legs before the wolf just *appeared*.

"It's like it burst out of him!" she said.

"It's as if he's some sort of shell and that's what's inside," Smith said.

"The world's worst Kinder surprise," Knowles muttered. Claire suppressed a grin and his stomach untwisted for a moment.

"It's magnificent," Smith said. On the screens, the wolf sank to its haunches and growled. They all flinched when it howled.

"Shit, don't run," Knowles said, as the two soldiers looked at each other. "Whatever you do, don't run." He reached over and switched the high frequency transmitter off. His hand hovered over the external tannoy, just as the two soldiers started to run.

The wolf gave chase.

4

It was like trying to run through treacle Adam Salmon would later explain. Try as hard as he could, he just couldn't get any acceleration. He would never tell anyone that his legs turned to jelly as soon as he saw the wolf. He watched in horror as his friend overtook him. The wolf hit him square in the back, knocking him to the ground.

"Stop!"

A voice boomed out from the tannoy system around the courtyard. The wolf looked around wildly, trying to track the source of the noise. Adam was face down in the dirt, hands across the back of his helmet like a rugby player at the bottom of a ruck. He had dropped his gun when he started running and he could see it six metres and a lifetime away.

"Jack. Stop."

The wolf howled then stepped back.

5

"Those two want shooting for running away," Jones said.

Carruthers bit back a laugh. "I'm up here and I want to run. There's no shame in it Jonesey."

"Maybe. But we're here to do a job." Jones looked down the sight of his rifle, red dot on the wolf's head, letting him know that his aim was true.

"Not yet," Carruthers said without taking his eyes off the courtyard below.

"When?" Jones snorted. "When he takes that lad's head off?"

"Not yet," Carruthers said again as Knowles' voice came over the tannoy. He couldn't help smiling as the wolf stepped off the fallen soldier. It stood close enough to be a worry, but it was just snarling.

"Jesus," Jones said. "Here doggy, doggy."

"It's a wolf, you idiot."

"Still getting trained though, in it? It'll be scratching at the door when it wants a shit next."

6

Adam stood up slowly, eyes on the wolf at all times. It sat on its haunches and licked its lips. The fur seemed to be receding back into its body, much like a film running backwards. Eventually, a naked man sat on the floor in front of him.

"Mr Stadler," Adam said, voice breaking.

"Blood Bowl," Jack started laughing. "The game is called Blood Bowl." His laugh was genuine for the first time in weeks. He clutched his stomach where it was cramping from the laughter.

It had worked. He had stopped the wolf.

Chapter 24

1

The first successful attempt came after three unsuccessful ones. Jack Stadler has been on the base for three weeks at the time of writing. We began to suspect that he could control the changes to the Wolf when he failed to attack Captain Biddlestone following his escape from the initial unit (see report JS27072014).

I suspect that Captain Biddlestone reminds Jack of his wife in some way. Shortly following the attempted escape, I interviewed Jack and he asked repeatedly to see his wife. The most likely explanation is that Katie and Claire share perfume, shower gel or shampoo, although we would have to investigate this initial supposition further.

The team explained to Jack that we would try to force the Wolf out of him and that he would then try to revert to human form. He agreed – I believe he still thinks we can cure him. Doctor Starky has not yet ruled this out (see report JS25072014) but he can find no evidence of the Wolf in Jack when he is human.

The first three attempts to get Jack to control the Wolf all ended in failure. Each of those attempts were internal and the destruction the Wolf caused was large, although not to human life. He had to be treated with a heavier dose of our tranquiliser each time, which suggests his immune system has an incredible adaptability rate. Further evidence of this is the healing that Jack can perform (see report JS25072014-A).

Jack did not give up at any point, despite his increasing discomfort with being turned into the Wolf. In fact, today he shouted "No, I've changed my mind, don't make me" as we turned the white noise on.

However, today was different. He tried to attack Private Salmon, but desisted when I called his name. He simply stopped when I asked him to. This is a very exciting development for obvious reasons. Doctor Starky is devising tests to see if Jack can control turning into the Wolf. The first of these tests is scheduled for tomorrow. I would prefer to continue investigating the control that Jack has when he is the Wolf.

My recommendations are:

Continue to develop Jack's ability to control his actions as the Wolf.
Develop stronger tranquilisers. We cannot afford to lose any men to the Wolf. I believe that Jack is traumatised by his memory of killing the civilians in Devon.
Katie Stadler should be brought to see him, with Josh Stadler. I believe that seeing his wife will help Jack's psychological recovery.

2

Knowles took a long sip of his beer and reread what he'd written. He went back through, changing 'Jack' to 'Mr Stadler', 'Katie' to 'Mrs Stadler' and 'Claire' to 'Captain Biddlestone' but left the capital on 'Wolf' then pressed Send. Smith and Starky were the two recipients, but who knew who they would forward it to?

When had he started to capitalise the Wolf? He wasn't sure, but they were all doing it now: every report featured the Wolf. You could even hear it in speech.

He knew they would ignore his recommendations. Starky was too keen to figure out how Jack could change: he wanted to be able to control the ability. Once they had that nailed, they could then try to develop it for use with front line troops. *All that speed and power would be useful, but at what cost to the men?*

He drank more beer and switched to looking at the internet. He wasn't searching for anything in particular, but read some film and music reviews. His mind kept coming back to Jack.

Katie should be here. He drained the bottle and got another, opening it and emptying half down his throat before he sat back down. *It would help Jack. And brighten the base up.* He grinned to himself. *Claire Biddlestone did that too.*

"You've got mail," Homer Simpson's voice informed him through his computer speaker. Knowles clicked on it and grimaced. *Well that was quick.*

3

Sergeant Knowles,
I have considered your recommendations. We are pushing ahead with phase two, as you are already aware. Stronger tranquiliser has already been developed: it will be circulated to all team members prior to the next test. Mrs Stadler believes

her husband is dead. There is no reason to bring emotion into this project. Mr Stadler needs to focus on what we require of him, not his wife and son. When he has given us all he can, we will re-evaluate the situation.

Captain Daniel Starky, M.D.

4

The last sentence chilled Knowles to the bone.

It had been less than thirty minutes since he had sent the email, so Starky had not spent much time considering his recommendations. *Just a grunt, making up the numbers.* He put the empty bottle on the table, ran his hands through his hair and made a decision. His rucksack was to hand and he filled it quickly.

He stepped out of his single room cabin and crossed the courtyard. One of the two soldiers on guard started to salute, but Knowles scowled at him. It was Salmon, the one who had run first.

"I'm a sergeant, you idiot." He opened the door to the room – *prison* –where they were holding Jack. They didn't search his bag: metal detectors would sound if he were to take a weapon into the room. He walked down the short corridor, swiped his card and opened the newly reinforced door.

Jack sat up when he entered.

"Sergeant Knowles."

Knowles pulled up a chair. "May I sit?"

Jack snorted and nodded. "To what do I owe the pleasure?"

Knowles paused for a second. *Now, that was a really good question.* "I just wanted to talk," he said, then grinned. "Like Bob Hoskins."

"Showing your age, Sergeant."

"Yeah." He looked around the room, even though he'd been in there dozens of times over the last few weeks. Fresh grey paint on the walls. Basic amenities. *He'd have better living conditions if he was a rat in lab 32.* "How you doing?"

"Do you really care?" Jack asked.

"Can I get you anything?"

"My wife. My child. My home. My fucking *life* back."

"You know I can't do that."

"Well, what *can* you do?"

"How about a beer?" Knowles opened the bag and held up two bottles of Sol. "You look like you could use one."

Jack shook his head in disbelief then smiled. "Do you have clearance for this?"

Knowles shook his head and returned the grin. "I'll probably get a bollocking when they review the tapes, but fuck it."

"They're not watching me now?"

"Yeah, but it's supposed to be me."

Jack laughed. "Abusing your power to bring me a beer. Sergeant, you just went up in my estimation."

"Call me Knowles, everyone else does."

"Not Peter?"

"I don't think my mother even calls me that anymore." Knowles opened the beers and handed one to Jack. "Called," he muttered quietly.

"You don't speak?"

That bloody hearing of his. "She died, three years ago."

"I'm sorry." Jack drank a tentative sip of his beer.

"Don't be. We hadn't spoken since I joined up."

"When did you join up?"

"I was 16."

They fell into an awkward silence, both sipping their beers.

"It's not the same without lime," Knowles said eventually.

"It's not the same as a proper beer, but I'm not complaining."

"Proper beer?"

Jack smiled. "Something like Exmoor Gold."

"Ah, real ale." Knowles returned the smile. "Doesn't that rot your guts though?"

"Yeah, god-awful wind." Jack looked around his small room. "Probably not too wise in here, eh?"

They both laughed, and a more comfortable silence fell between them.

"Am I allowed to drink?" Jack asked as he put the empty bottle on the floor. "It wasn't good last time I did."

"Probably not," Knowles said. "The docs will want to know how much control you have. Beer takes that away." He reached into the bag and passed Jack another bottle. "Fuck 'em."

Jack nodded. "Will they cure me?"

"I don't know," Knowles admitted. "If you can control it, then maybe you could live a normal life again."

"I don't think my life will ever be normal." Jack drank more beer to hide the break in his voice. "I just want to see my wife and child again. He'll be two months now and I've missed it all."

Knowles nodded. "We'll get you home, Jack, I give you my word."

"Do you break your word often, Knowles?"

"Never intentionally," Knowles grinned, "although my ex-wife might disagree with that."

Jack stood up and paced the room, drinking all the while. "I could use a stereo."

"Not a TV?"

"Never been a big fan of the box. All that reality shit and wideboy chefs telling me what to eat," Jack said.

"Yeah, it's a bit shit isn't it?"

"We seem to be a nation that worships fucking talentless idiots." Jack sat back on his bed. "But don't get me started on that. I've been known to rant, and getting angry is not good for me right now."

"Like the Hulk."

"Yep. I'm Bruce fucking Banner."

They both laughed again. "So, music?" Knowles asked.

"Music," Jack nodded. "I've never been able to handle silence you know? I have music with everything. If I'm not teaching, I play some tunes whilst I plan. It annoys the shit out of the English teacher next door to me. First thing I always did in the morning was put the stereo on. Used to annoy Katie too."

"What kind of music?" Knowles said, before Jack could dwell on Katie.

"Anything really, but you can't beat a bit of rock." Jack smiled. "I keep waiting to grow out of it, but nothing cheers me up more than a fantastic guitar riff played real loud."

"Same here," Knowles said. "In Afghanistan, I took my mp3 player everywhere. Green Day, Doves, Feeder, even a bit of Bon Jovi, but don't tell anyone. Kept me sane."

"Bon Jovi?"

"Yeah. Used to have long hair, before I joined up. That was a shock, all that being shaved."

"I saw them live once," Jack said. "They were good, but they played a few Beatles covers and I thought 'what's the point of that?'"

"Yeah?"

"I can't stand the fucking Beatles."

Knowles spat beer across the room as he laughed. "I thought it was just me."

"No," Jack said, grinning.

"Bon Jovi live? Bet it was a good show though?" When Jack nodded, he continued, "So what was your best concert?"

"Bruce Springsteen. Around '93. He played all his hits, and played for hours. It was sunny and there was plenty of beer. No massive light show, just him and his band. Fantastic."

Knowles nodded. "Good choice. I always wanted to see him, but never got round to it."

"Yours?"

"Easy. U2, on the Zoo TV tour. One hell of a show."

"Good choice."

"Bono gets a lot of flak, but he's got great presence."

Jack emptied his bottle and Knowles drained his. "I'm out. Sorry."

"No problem," Jack said. "Thank you for the beer. It's been a while – it's gone right to my head."

"Just don't get angry." Knowles stood and picked up the ruck sack. "Take it easy Jack."

"Knowles," Jack said, as the other man opened the door. "Thank you."

"Any time."

Chapter 25

1

Steve used the tree as cover from the rain. He leant against the bark and brushed water out of his hair. The rain came down hard for a couple of minutes. Shivering, he pulled his coat together.

He scanned the area around him. Trees lined a road that ran up through the park and the road swept up a long hill. In the distance, he could see the naval college buildings and off to his right, on the hill overlooking the whole park, was the famous Greenwich Observatory. Near the foot of the hill, Anton was leaning against another tree and it was hard to tell which was wider, the tree or Anton. Standing next to him was Alex.

This is not going to work.

The thought ran through his mind for the umpteenth time that day. They were due here any minute, if they were going to show. Steve fingered the gun in his pocket, but it didn't reassure him. *Guns only get you so far.*

Alex waved at him, beckoning him over. Steve swore, pulled his collar up and ran over to him. The grass squelched under his feet and water seeped into his trainers. One downside to this lifestyle was constantly having to steal new clothes. Sometimes, you just couldn't guarantee the quality.

"They're coming," Alex said. Steve looked up nervously, but couldn't see anyone. "Remember, I do the talking."

Alex pointed at the main gate as four men stepped through. They all walked with a clear gap between them and Steve was reminded briefly of Reservoir Dogs, the last film he'd seen as a human. All four were big men, on a par with Alex. One was bigger even than Anton and he had a scar running down the left hand side of his face.

Callum.

Steve swallowed hard. The four men spread out more when they reached the grass area in front of Alex. Behind them, more people were flooding into the park. *More of us.* He started to count. *At least fifty. No sixty, seventy maybe.* He gave up. *Jesus, they came.*

Alex smiled. "Callum."

"Alex," the bigger man nodded. "I thought I made it clear you shouldn't come back."

"Just passing through," Alex said, suddenly pale. "I have news."

"That you needed all of us for? I swear you will not leave this park if you are wasting my time."

The three other alphas all nodded. Steve clutched the butt of his gun, but left it in the pocket. *Good to have some surprises.* He wondered what the tribal tattoos on Callum's neck would look like when he changed.

"We have seen one of the Originals."

"Originals?" Callum snorted. "They died out centuries ago. You went to Berlin on that rumour didn't you?"

The alphas all started to bare their teeth. "You are wasting our time," one of them growled.

"It's true." Alex stood his ground. Callum stepped up to him and started to sniff.

"You don't smell afraid," he said, with a theatrical look at the other alphas.

"There is an Original here in Britain. We have to rescue him."

Steve risked a glance at Anton when Alex said that. The other man remained impassive. *Interesting. I wonder what he'll actually do when we catch up with Jack.*

"Wait a minute," Callum shook his head, then laughed. "Rescue? Why would an Original need rescuing from anyone?" The other alphas joined in the laughter.

Steve swallowed. *Here we go.*

"Because he doesn't know what he is," Alex said.

2

The pub was empty before they walked in and the solitary barman looked very surprised when they poured in through the doors. Various pack members segregated themselves by sitting at different tables in different parts of the pub. Steve and Anton stayed close to Alex.

Callum put a credit card on the bar. "Drinks. Until we leave."

The barman swiped the card, then picked up a phone. Callum's hand shot across the bar, long nails digging into the man's arm. The barman screeched.

"What are you doing?"

"Getting help," the barman replied. "Please, you're hurting me." His voice was very light and effeminate. Steve repressed a grin. *Greenwich Theatre pubs. Excellent.*

"No. Just you." Callum snarled. "We are locking the doors."

"Sir, I-"

Callum growled, baring his teeth, before letting the man's arm go. The barman was trembling as he nodded. "Just me." He set to work, tears obvious in the corners of his eyes. Callum had that effect on people.

Callum pulled Alex close to him. "Tell me more." They moved to sit at a table and the other alphas joined them.

"My boys," he gestured at Steve and Anton, "went to recruit, you know as standard when we get a new one."

Steve tuned him out. He remembered the smell of new recruits. That unmistakeable wolf tang in the air, tinged with something that wouldn't last long when they were recruited: cleanliness. He thought back to his first meeting with Jack, on the beach. Had he thought then that there was something different? Or was his memory telling him he *should* have?

"They saw him get shot?"

Alex nodded. "Then, we got a trace of him again. We followed the scent to a village and he was there – alive!" He looked round the table, eyes shining with excitement.

"People survive being shot all the time."

"Thirty times?"

Callum inclined his head slightly. One of his pack handed him a pint which he drank greedily.

"He was shot again," Alex continued, "before we could attack. They were ready for us when we did attack. Most of my pack died. We killed two of them but they escaped by burning us."

"Who the fuck are they?"

"I don't know." Alex accepted a drink from the same man. "They were prepared for us though."

Steve used his drink to halt a grunt in his throat.

"Something to say?" Callum looked at Steve.

Christ, he's got a mean stare. Steve's legs trembled as he returned the stare.

"Steve isn't convinced they knew that we were coming," Alex said.

"I wasn't talking to you," Callum said without taking his eyes off Steve.

"I think they were lucky," Steve began, "or we were unlucky. Those men just shot at us, but they were all scared. You could smell it."

Callum nodded. *Fear probably smells like strawberries in summer to him.* Steve had been told that you could smell fear when he first changed but he hadn't believed Alex then. *No, not then.*

"Also, there were no silver bullets or any of that shit."

Callum threw back his head and laughed. White teeth glinted sharply in his mouth. "I like you. This guy is good."

Steve felt himself relax as Alex threw him a warning look. "They got lucky," he repeated.

"So who are they?" Callum asked again.

"Steve has a theory," Alex said. He sighed heavily and shook his head.

Callum growled, his nose and mouth momentarily elongating, his teeth growing. "Don't make me tell you again," Callum said, when his mouth was normal again.

Jesus, he can change just part of him. Steve tried to gather his thoughts. *Only the Originals can do that. Or are supposed to be able to.*

"I think they might have been soldiers. They were tooled up and reacted well to seeing us change," Steve said. "They were trained."

"Have the Army found out about us?" Callum asked.

"Possibly," Alex said, snarling back at Callum. "But we should find the Original."

"His name was Jack," Steve said.

"You spoke to him?" Callum asked.

"Yes."

Silence around the table. Callum raised his eyebrows. "Well?"

"He seemed normal. We talked, and he smelled of a fresh kill."

"But you saw him get shot?"

"Me and him." Steve gestured to Anton leaning on the bar. "He killed Anton's woman."

"The Original did?"

Steve nodded. "Bit her head off." His voice croaked at the memory. Anton's face still held no trace of emotion, bar the single tear that rolled down his cheek. He made no effort to wipe it away. "Then he got shot by the soldiers."

"Thirty times?"

"We were running away, so I'm not sure." Steve looked down at the table. Admitting cowardice was not a good idea in this company. "But it was about that."

"You ran?" Callum laughed.

Steve looked him in the eye. "You weren't there. He bit her head off. Not ripped, not chewed through. He bit it off. He is huge. Bigger than anyone in this room. Do you understand?"

Callum hit him hard enough to knock him off his chair. Steve stayed on his knees for a moment, ears ringing. Alex stood, kicking the table over with a roar. He landed two punches on Callum before the big man reacted.

Callum grabbed Alex by the throat and lifted him off the floor with one hand. His pack started shouting and everyone else dropped any pretence of doing anything other than watching the group. Fights between alphas were usually short and brutal. Alex brought both his hands down in a chop on Callum's neck. He didn't even flinch or loosen his hold for a second.

"You forget so quickly Alex." Callum reached up with his other hand, turning it into a paw topped with long nails and sliced open Alex's neck. Blood geysered out of the wound, spraying Callum and the table with blood. Alex's eyes opened wide and he kicked his legs against Callum. The bigger man still didn't move until Alex's head rolled back and the blood stopped gushing out so quickly. It didn't take long. The pub was filled with the sound of shouting and jeering.

"And you shouldn't turn your back in a fight," Steve said, standing up and pressing his gun to Callum's temple. One of his pack stepped forward, but Anton smashed him in the face hard enough to knock him out cold. Anton then pulled his own gun out and waved it at Callum's pack. They stopped moving. The other packs waited, trying to see which pack would win and be the new dominant one.

"Put him down," Steve said with a calm he didn't feel. "Now."

Callum didn't look concerned at the gun to his neck. He dropped Alex into the spreading pool of his own blood. His eyes remained fixed on a point somewhere far away. Steve tried not to look at the body. *First part not gone to plan. Not a bad turn of events though.*

"What now?" Callum asked. He looked at Steve out of the corner of his eyes. His hand was raised slightly, telling his pack to just wait. Blood covered his face and he licked his lips, clearing a thin white path around his mouth.

"We need to work together to get the Original back," Steve said. "We need your help."

"You want us to work together?"

"Yes."

"Despite what I just did?"

Steve shrugged. "His time was past. He got our bitches killed."

"Put the gun down and I won't kill you."

"I'll put the gun down, so I don't kill *you*." Steve did not feel the confidence he forced into his voice. "We need your help. The Original is real. It could be like the stories we were told." It was a gamble, reminding Callum of their shared past; the one that had ended with so much violence.

"Legends, nothing more," Callum said. He righted the table and sat down. The tension in the room eased a little. The smaller packs started talking amongst themselves again. At some point during the exchange, the barman had fainted, so two of the pack had jumped the bar and were helping themselves to drinks. It would be messy on the streets of Greenwich that night.

"*We* are legends," Steve said.

Callum nodded. "If he is an Original, what does that mean?"

"I don't know," Steve said, "but I have a theory." He sat down and put the gun back in his pocket.

"Go on."

"He doesn't know what he is – maybe he needs someone to help him."

They all contemplated that for a moment. Callum nodded his big head again.

"We will help you, but on one condition." He looked at Steve. "Next time you point a gun at me, you'd better pull the trigger. You understand?"

Steve nodded. *And I will.*

3

"We will help you find the Original," Callum said, after a brief conference with the other alphas and his pack. "But we will not take orders from you. You are not in charge."

Steve nodded. "Thank you."

"When we find the Original, if he will not accept what he is, then we will kill him."

"Agreed."

Steve glanced up at Anton, who was leaning on the bar watching the group with keen eyes. The other packs were all watching too: some had climbed onto tables to get a better view of the alpha group. Callum was after an angle here, but what was it? He would only help Steve if there was something in it for him. Did he think he could control the Original? Use it to unite the packs?

"How do we execute it?" One of the other alphas asked, "Aren't they immortal?"

"We cut its body to pieces and keep the limbs and head separate from the body." Callum smiled as he said the words. He raised his glass and everyone in the pub raised a glass towards him. "To the Originals!"

The shout threatened to raise the roof. Steve crossed to Anton and clinked his glass.

"Why?" Anton whispered to Steve. "Why cut it to pieces?"

"What do you know about Originals?"

"Not much. I never really believed all that." This was the most Anton had spoken since Lucy had died.

"Let's go outside."

They pushed their way through the packs and stepped into daylight. The rain had finally stopped and the sun was shining. Steve squinted and held up his hand to shield his eyes. The street was deserted, as if the pub was now giving off a bad vibe and people were staying clear.

"What do you know?" Steve asked.

"The Originals made us. They ate some humans and we were the result. It all happened years ago and they died out suddenly."

Steve nodded. "That's a very brief version." He looked up and down the street. The gates to Greenwich Park lay on his right. *In a few weeks it will be summer and these streets will be packed with tourists. With an Original at our head, we could come back and feast.* "Basically, it was back when humans were first walking around. A loooong time ago. They were getting more populous than the Wolves."

"Populous?"

Jesus. Steve groaned to himself. "There were a lot more of them. The Originals were being pushed off their land, some of them were hunted by the humans. Obviously, the Originals were pretty scary to the humans and so they tried to wipe them all out."

"Ok," Anton said, "so the Originals started to fight back."

"Yep, and they started to win. They can't be killed, see?"

Anton nodded. "Like the guy that we saw?"

"You got it. So, the humans were fighting an enemy they couldn't ever beat. Must've upset them a little. They tried everything: fire, drowning, chopping things off."

"How come drowning didn't work?"

"It did. Until you got the body out of the water, then it healed itself. They noticed that limbs stayed gone, so they started to cut heads off and keep them separate from the body. Usually, they decapitated the wolf, then burnt the head. It worked."

"When did we come along?"

"Who knows? Maybe a hunting party didn't quite all get killed by the Originals and we were made. Maybe it was deliberate: an attempt by either side to make peace by creating a hybrid." Steve paused. "Half and half."

"That what you think?"

Steve paused. "No. I think we're an accident."

"I like the thought of peace," Anton said after a long pause. "We wouldn't have to hide then."

He's turned into Tolstoy. "Yeah."

"What happened to the Originals?"

"No-one knows for sure. There was never that many of them. Immortal, see? No need to have thousands of them. They just died out. Maybe two, three thousand years ago, humans finally won. Look, how come you don't know this?"

"Nobody ever told me before."

Or you didn't ask. Big and dumb. What a combination. "But now it looks like an Original has been found."

"How?"

"I don't know. Maybe he hid himself amongst men and did such a good job he forgot what he was."

"We will find him."

"Yes," Steve said. "We will. All those packs working together, we could find anyone. It'll take time, but we will find him."

"Good."

Something about the way Anton said that gave Steve pause.

"Anton?"

"When we find him, I will kill him."

Interlude: Devon

1

Katie pushed Josh in his pram as Ginny padded along by their sides. It was good to be out, sun on her face, cool breeze in her hair. Josh was fast asleep, head at a much more comfortable looking angle than in those first few weeks. He was so big now and getting heavier. His hair was thickening, hiding the god-awful cradle cap.

She was exhausted. He woke every three hours, regular as clockwork. Most nights she would just be drifting off to sleep when he woke again. His cries were louder now and seemed to echo around the empty house. It wouldn't be long before he would sleep for longer, or at least that's what the midwife told her on her visits. Karen always agreed. *I just need to sleep. Please let me sleep.*

However, when she did sleep, it was not much of a comfort for her. Her dreams were dark things full of snarling mouths, dripping saliva and sharp teeth. Last night she had dreamt that a wolf was inside her and eating itself out of her womb. The creature that finally emerged from her ruined midriff was Jack. He had been smiling, blood all around his mouth – *her blood* – and he had said, "Nice starter." Then he'd picked Josh out of the crib and eaten him whole.

She had not been able to get back to sleep after that.

2

She had no real idea where she going until she stopped outside John and Karen's house. Their house was nearly four hundred years old and was one of the few left in the village to still have thatch on the roof. Once she had been jealous of their house, but now worrying about things like houses seemed so insignificant. It was a lifetime ago.

She was about to knock when the door opened. Karen was smiling at her, but it was a smile that didn't reach her eyes. They were full of sadness.

"Don't even think about not coming in," she said, opening the door wide.

Katie wrestled the pram over the step into the house. Despite banging it on the frame several times, Josh remained asleep. She tucked a blanket over him and then went into Karen's living room.

John was lying on the sofa watching News 24, but switched the TV off with the remote when she came in. He crushed her with a hug then sat back down. Karen went to the kitchen and made tea without asking.

"No work today?" Katie asked.

"No," John shook his head. "Best thing about being your own boss – the lads are taking care of everything today. I get a long weekend." John had started a building supplies business two years ago and it was doing a roaring trade – mostly because John was the cheapest for miles, literally.

"How's Josh doing?"

"Great."

"Is he sleeping?"

"Pretty much all the time now," Katie smiled. "He had a wobble a couple of weeks ago where he kept waking, but he pretty much goes from about ten to about six." *Why are you lying to your friends?*

"That's fantastic." John grinned. "Ours were buggers for sleeping."

Karen came in with a tray holding three steaming mugs of tea and a biscuit barrel.

"I heard the bit about sleeping," Karen said. "You're really lucky."

She put her hand to her mouth, eyes wide with panic. "Oh God, I didn't thin-"

"It's ok," Katie said, a tired smile coming to her face. "I *am* lucky he's such a good sleeper."

"How are you doing?" John asked.

"Mostly fine," she said after a pause. "Then, you know, I see something that reminds me of him. Something random. The other day an Audi TT went past us and I cried for hours."

"Christ, he loved those cars." John grinned again. "The convertible."

"It's been nearly three months, can you believe that?" Katie said. "They've nearly finished rebuilding that house that caught fire. What happens when someone moves in? That's where my husband died. Will I take Josh there in a couple of years and say this is where Daddy died? It's in my *fucking* street."

"Maybe it will help you move on," Karen said.

"I don't *want* to move on," Katie replied. "I don't want to forget him. I want Josh to grow up with a Dad. Teach him about women, how to drink. Play rugby."

"Yeah, not footie," John said. "Jack would've hated that."

"Wouldn't he just?" she smiled. "I got a letter this morning."

John and Karen both put their mugs down and watched her carefully.

"It's from the Teachers' Pension Agency. I get a lump sum from them."

"How much?" John asked. He could tell it wasn't good news.

"£107, 940."

"Jesus."

"Yeah. It's a lot of money, but I don't want it. I want him."

3

She stayed for another hour, as Josh woke and needed a feed. They drank more tea and made small talk, all of which left her cold. She really wasn't interested in how people were doing or what party was happening when. She knew that she had cared once, but *that* Katie was missing at the moment. Maybe she would return in time, but right now the only person important in her life was Josh. Nothing bad was going to happen to him; she would move mountains to guarantee it.

She had been thinking about her dreams (*memories?*) about the wolf and had made the decision before opening the letter from the TPA. She hadn't said anything to John and Karen: she'd had enough of their pity without causing even more concern, even if it was well meant.

She knocked on the door and waited. Josh gurgled so she lifted him out of the pram and clutched him close. He nuzzled into her neck and went back to sleep.

Frank opened the door and nodded sadly when he recognised her. "Katie. Come in."

"Thanks, Frank."

They sat in a living room that was totally characterless despite being at least as old as John and Karen's. Furniture that had seen better days cluttered the room and Katie sat in a chair that looked like a good clean would make it fall to pieces.

"Cup o'tea?" Frank offered. "Beer?" He looked awkward for a second. "I don't 'ave no wine."

Katie smiled and shook her head. "Tea would be great, thanks Frank."

He busied himself getting the drinks ready and Katie looked around the room. Old photographs lined the walls, many depicting Frank and his wife in fields and country shows. Katie peered closer at one of them and saw Frank holding a baby and grinning broadly from ear to ear. It was an expression she had not seen on his face since they'd moved to the village.

"My son," Frank said, making her jump. She lowered Josh into his pram and he remained asleep.

"He's a very handsome boy," Katie said, taking the proffered cup of tea by holding on to the saucer. "How old is he now?"

"'e died," Frank said.

"Oh, I'm sorry," Katie said, hand covering her mouth. *Shit.*

"Not your fault." Frank sat on the sofa and waved Katie into a chair. "Now you sure about this, girl?"

"Yes, I'm sure. I've got the money."

Frank gave her a look as if he could see right into the depths of her soul. She stared back, refusing to blink. Satisfied, he nodded once, a short sharp bob of the head. For a moment he looked like a chicken.

"Well, drink your tea up then and let's go 'ave a look at it."

He waited until she finished and put the cup on the sideboard. Pale rings on the wood matched the size of the saucer perfectly. She looked at Josh, sleeping in his pram.

"Am I ok to leave him here?"

"Ain't no-one gonna come get 'im," Frank said. "Will 'e stay asleep?"

"Probably."

"Well, let's get on then."

He led her through a surprisingly neat kitchen and out into the field beyond the house. Stones crunched underfoot as they crossed to his barn. He took a huge ring of keys out of his pocket and flipped them round, looking for the right one.

"Bloody keys," he muttered.

"I suppose you can remember when you didn't need keys round here."

"Yep. Before all them bloody incomers." Frank found the key and opened the padlock with a practised flick of the wrist. He caught the expression on Katie's face. "You're all so bloody serious."

Despite herself, Katie started to giggle. Before long, they were both laughing. When the laughter died to be replaced by uncomfortable silence, Frank opened the door and they entered the barn.

He flicked the lights on, and they hummed into life. The inside of the barn had been turned into a shooting gallery. Bales of hay lined the sides and marked the start of the line. Targets plastered the walls at the other end. He opened a cupboard with another key and took out a long wooden box.

He put it on the floor and prised the clasps open, then he lifted the long dark object out.

"This is a Bettinsoli o'er an' under shotgun. 12 gauge. A damn fine gun. You shoot anything within fifty yards, provided you 'it it, t'ain't gettin' up again."

He could have been speaking Chinese for all that Katie understood.

"Couple o'things about shotguns now. To load, you break it open, like this." He clicked the gun open, exposing the two barrels. "An' the shot goes in." He slid two cartridges into the gun, then clicked the barrels shut. "Firm, don't force it."

She nodded.

"Never leave it loaded," Frank said. "Law says shot should be kept in a separate, locked container."

"Seems sensible."

"Yep. Remember to keep the gun unloaded."

"You already said that."

"I know. Worth saying it twice, girl. 'Specially as you've got a little one who'll be movin' round before you know it."

"Ok."

"Nobody ever got killed by an empty gun." He offered her the gun. "Wan' a go?"

She took it and raised it to her shoulder. She aimed down the barrel.

"Now, shotguns are slow. Aim in front of your target, not at it."

"If it's moving?"

"Well, yeah." Frank pointed at the end of the barrel. "Here's your sights. Squeeze the trigger and keep the butt of the gun firm against your shoulder."

She pulled the trigger. The bang was deafening and the gun pounded back into her shoulder. Later, she would have a bruise there. One of the targets shredded as the shot tore into it.

"Good shot, girl," Frank said.

She barely heard him over the ringing in her ears. The ruined target had surprised her: she did not want to picture what the gun would do to a human at close range.

"That's it basically," Frank said. He popped the gun open, ejecting the spent cartridge and removing the unused one. "Questions?"

She shook her head. "How much?"

"This gun is about £700 new, but I've had it a while." Frank returned the gun to its case and sealed it. "I'll gi' it you for £200."

"£200," Katie said, her mouth dropping open. "The advert said four."

Frank chewed his bottom lip. "I know. You look like you could use a bit of help."

"I'm not a charity Frank."

He held up a calming hand. "I'm no' tryin' to offend girl. You a neighbour. I'm trying to help." He looked even more awkward than usual for a second. "Las' time I saw your Jack, I weren't good to 'im. Trying to make amends is all."

"Do I need a license?"

"Depend on who you're gonna tell," Frank said. "£50 gets you one for five years."

"Cash ok?"

"Aye."

As Katie counted out the notes, she thought about the feeling of power when she had held the shotgun. She had felt a thrill that she wouldn't have dreamed of having a few months ago.

Now if the wolf ever came back, she would be prepared.

Chapter 26

1

"What the hell is he doing?" Smith demanded.

Claire watched him go red in the face. "He's playing his guitar, sir."

"I can see he's playing guitar," Smith said. "Where the hell did he get a guitar?"

"I'm not sure," Claire lied and went back to recording things on the clipboard. The hourly surveillance logs were getting really tedious now. Page after page of Jack sitting practising guitar, reading a book, listening to his mp3 player. He had not turned into the Wolf for over a week.

"Tell Sergeant Knowles I want to see him in my office, as soon as he's on duty."

"Yes sir."

Smith walked out, slamming the door as he went. In the room, Jack looked up for a second at the sound, then resumed playing. On the pad she wrote:

12:57 showed signs of advanced hearing again. Looked up at the sound of a door being slammed even through the sound proofing. Jack's hearing is more and more acute even in human form.

She put the pen down and watched the man again. He was playing an old Green Day song over and over, tentatively singing the words. Every now and then he would stop, swear to himself and start again. *Not a bad singing voice, just not a good one either. At least the strumming has improved over the last week.* She didn't want to know how Knowles had got the instrument through security.

She smiled at the thought of Knowles. Her first impression had him down as just another squaddie prick, but the last few weeks had shown a different side to him. He was looking after Jack very well, regardless of what Smith thought. She thought that the guitar, books and music were helping keep Jack on side. *They are keeping him calm. Keeping the Wolf from the door.*

There was a light tap on the door and Knowles came in. Jack glanced briefly up at the sound of the tap. Knowles grinned at her.

"He heard that?" he whispered.

"And that," she said in a normal voice, pointing through the one-way mirror. Jack had put his guitar down and was looking expectantly at the door.

"Christ," Knowles said.

"Major Smith wants to see you."

"Yeah, I guessed that was coming." Knowles grimaced. "He finally decided to come down here huh?"

"He turned up about twenty minutes ago, unannounced." She smiled, patting Knowles' arm gently. "Didn't have time to get Jack to put all his toys away."

"Well, I'll just say hello, then I'll go see him," Knowles said.

He walked into the short corridor and opened the security door that led into Jack's room. The key card beeped as the door opened. The armed guard saluted as he entered, which made Knowles roll his eyes. "For fuck's sake," he said and shut the door behind him, keeping the guard looking bemused in the corridor. He was going to see one of the most dangerous men in Britain and all he could think about was the warm spot on his arm where Claire had touched him.

2

"You gave him a guitar?"

"Yes, sir." Knowles stood smartly to attention. He fixed his gaze past Smith's shoulder on a patch of wall where the paint was flaking slightly.

"Who authorised that?"

"Sir?"

"Who told you to give the prisoner a guitar to play?"

"Sir, I was not aware he was a prisoner. I thought he was helping us."

"Don't treat me like a fool, Knowles," Smith snarled. "Mr Stadler is now the property of the government, at Her Majesty's leisure, until we can figure out what to do with him."

"Sir, yes, sir."

"So who authorised you? Was it Starky?"

"No sir. I did it myself sir."

Smith sighed, flexing his fingers under his chin. "I'm not paying you to think, Sergeant."

"No, sir!"

"You have given the prisoner a guitar, a book and an iPod," Smith said, looking at his notes before he said the last word.

Idiot. It's not an iPod. Knowles elected not to say anything.

"We are not running a fucking summer camp!"

Knowles flinched at the raised voice, even though he'd been expecting it.

"I know that sir, but permission to explain myself sir."

Smith slumped back in his chair. "Make it good, Knowles."

"Sir, Jack, Mr Stadler-" He caught the expression on Smith's face. "- the prisoner was becoming more difficult. He is a civilian, sir, we need to treat him as a human being. This isn't Guantanamo."

"We do not know that he's human. He is very dangerous."

"Sir, he can control the Wolf," Knowles said, trying not to get angry. "We have not seen it in over a week."

"And?"

"I think the music is helping him stay calm sir. It gives him something to focus on other than when he's going to see his wife again."

Smith tapped his fingers on the desk. "What does Starky think?"

"I don't know sir."

"Where is Captain Starky now?"

"Sir, I think the team analysing the bones we found are close to finishing their study. He has gone to hurry them."

"Does Starky know about the guitar and other things?"

"I cannot comment on what the Captain does or does not know, sir."

"You are on thin ice here, Sergeant. I will expect Captain Starky to be fully debriefed on his return. If necessary, we will remove the items."

"Sir, in my opinion-"

"Sergeant. My crown versus your stripes. Think carefully before finishing that sentence."

"Yes, sir."

"Dismissed."

3

Knowles stepped back into sunlight, and broke into a grin. He strode across the courtyard, heading for the small building. As he went, he heard a dog barking in the distance. It was joined by another bark, then another.

Knowles slowed, then stopped. He scanned the tree line and spotted the two base dogs and their handlers walking the perimeter. The barks were coming from the other side of the base. Without knowing exactly why, he put his hand on the butt of his gun.

Somebody grabbed him from behind. He spun quickly, moving into a combat stance.

"Easy!" Carruthers laughed.

"You idiot," Knowles said. He spun to look at the tree line again.

"What's up with you?" Carruthers said. "Fallen out with your boyfriend?"

"Grow up," Knowles said.

"Come on, Knowles, I'm just kidding," Carruthers followed Knowles' gaze. "What's up?"

"Probably nothing," Knowles said. "Just heard dogs barking."

Carruthers pantomimed listening hard. "Can't hear anything."

The barking had stopped. *Had it been there in the first place?*

"You know Jonesey is worried about you?"

"Why?" Knowles still hadn't shifted his gaze from the tree line.

"You are spending way too much time with the guy who got our mates killed."

Knowles finally looked at him. "Jack didn't kill Meyers or Scarlet."

"No," Carruthers said, "but if it hadn't been for *Stadler*, we wouldn't have been there would we?"

Knowles shook his head. "He is a good person. He's trying to control it."

Carruthers tutted. "Now you sound like someone defending an addict."

"Look, Jack is a good man, who has had something happen to him. We don't know what that is – and it looks more and more like-" Knowles shook his head again. "I don't know. Can you explain what's happened to him?"

"All I know is that there's a trail of bodies where there didn't need to be."

"It's not his fault."

"No?" Carruthers eyes opened wide. "Whose then?"

Knowles sighed and ran a hand through his hair. "I don't know. Those other guys killed Scarlet and a bunch of mutant spiders did for Meyers."

"They weren't guys."

"Those other wolves then."

"Listen to yourself. 'Those other wolves'! Like it's normal."

Knowles started walking again. "Right now, it's *our* normal. Like getting shot at. You deal with it, or it's game over."

"Remember which side you are on," Carruthers called after him. Knowles spun on the spot and strode to Carruthers, squaring up to him.

"Remember who you are talking to," he spat.

"Remember which side you are on, *sergeant*."

They stood toe to toe for a second then Knowles turned away and went into the observation booth. Carruthers watched him slam the door and exhaled slowly. *That could have gone better.* He looked at the tree line that Knowles had been studying. The branches swayed in the breeze, making it look windier than it was. Something had definitely spooked Knowles, but what? He'd heard dogs barking, but really? Knowles was made of sterner stuff. Carruthers headed for the barracks, but then changed his mind and went to the armoury. Wouldn't hurt to have a bit more practice, and maybe sign out an extra gun.

Just in case.

4

Slamming the door accomplished nothing; it didn't even make him feel better. The guard on the inner door raised his arm in a half-hearted salute. Knowles glared at him.

"I'm still a fucking sergeant, you numpty."

"Sorry, sergeant."

"Don't ever fucking salute like that anyway, you little shit. Get lazy, get fucking dead," Knowles prodded the soldier in his chest. He was looking up at the man, the irony of which wasn't lost on Knowles.

"Yes sergeant."

Knowles swiped his card and entered the secure room, slamming the door again. Claire jumped, spilling her tea on her lap. She leapt up, brushing at the top of her legs. She grabbed a paper towel from behind her and started soaking up the liquid.

"Shit," Knowles said, "sorry."

"Bad day?"

"I've been on duty for about twenty minutes and have been chewed out twice."

"Twice?"

"Yeah, once by my so called mate."

"Oh." She sat back down and gestured to the other chair in the room. "Wanna vent?"

Knowles looked through the one-way mirror. Jack was lying on his side on the bed, earphones in.

"He can't hear us over that racket," Claire smiled.

"Hey, I gave him all the music on that player."

"I rest my case."

It took him a moment to realise she was joking and then he sat.

"Its Carruthers and Jonesey," he said eventually. "They seem to be against me."

"You're their Sergeant, not their mate."

"I know, but we've served together for years. We were all the same rank once."

"Ah, that's your problem then, isn't it?" She nodded, and he imagined her hair tussling around her face. It was pulled back in a tight ponytail at the moment: the so called Essex face lift.

"It's not been a problem before."

She leaned forward on the chair, her face scant inches away from his. He could smell the subtle perfume again and he felt his face going red.

"Peter," she paused, "have you ever lost anyone in your squad before?"

"Yes," he answered, without pausing, "in Ghanners."

"You were in Afghanistan?"

"Yeah, two tours, about eighteen months in total. It's pretty fucked up, far more than they let on over here."

"I know."

"You've been?"

"I did a medic support tour for six months. Got back about three months ago." She smiled at him. "We were there at the same time."

"We were based in Sangin in Helmand."

"I was at Gerishk." She patted his knee. "I heard Sangin was bad."

He nodded slowly. "Yeah. Pretty bad." *Understatement of the fucking year.*

"So, how did you get assigned this one?"

"I'm not sure really. My unit hadn't been back long and we were offered a job watching a civilian for a month. Seemed like a piece of piss really."

Claire smiled again, her eyes sparkling. "Well, no-one knew."

"I'm beginning to doubt that."

"I saw the initial report," Claire said. "His blood threw up an anomaly that couldn't be explained. Discreet observation was recommended – it seemed the right call at the time."

"I have no idea what you are talking about."

Claire looked bemused for a second. "Jack fell into a cave and emerged without a scratch on him. The unit here has been scanning hospitals for a while now, looking for anything that might be extraordinary: super fitness, healing, that kind of thing."

"Jesus."

"Well, him too, but so far no joy."

Knowles burst out laughing and she beamed at him.

"They are looking for supermen right?"

"Or women," Claire said, glancing in at Jack again. "Anything that can give us the edge on the battlefield."

"So with Jack, why just observation? What he can do is pretty incredible."

"We had no idea what he could do. Starky wanted him brought in immediately, but he was overruled." Claire sighed. "It seems taking British citizens off the streets clandestinely is a bad idea."

"Starky is a twat," Knowles said without thought.

It was Claire's turn to laugh. "Yes, he is. But I never said that. Look, sleeping like a baby."

She pointed in at Jack, who had rolled onto his back. His mouth was open and eyes closed. She flicked the inner speakers on, and they both smirked as Jack's snoring filled the room.

"He wants to see his kid," Knowles said, his voice low.

"That's not going to happen," Claire said.

"Ever?"

Claire turned away from him. "I doubt that Jack will ever be free again."

"Starky?"

She nodded. "I think he wants to vivisect him."

"But-"

At that point, Jack sat bolt upright. "They're coming!" He screamed. Knowles jumped and was momentarily embarrassed until he realised Claire had also started. They exchanged a nervous look. "They've found me! They're coming for me." Then he lay back down and went straight back to sleep.

"Has he ever done that before?" Knowles asked.

"No," Claire said. "Bad dream?"

"Maybe," Knowles said, but he had a sick feeling in his stomach. *They're coming.*

5

Anton stood on his two legs and relished the breeze on his skin. He reached into his bag and pulled out a mobile phone. Around him, three others were changing back, fur disappearing to become skin.

Once the initial excitement had died down – and what a racket that had been – they had followed the trail back to their camp. They had been in the forest for only two days, but had gone the wrong way on the first day. If they had turned left, then they would have found him sooner.

No matter. He will soon be with us and then I will kill him.

Searches were happening all over the South East, from as far along as Dorchester, South to Southampton and across into Essex. The groups were in daily contact with each other and each had military targets as a focus.

Anton ignored the buzz of expectation from his team. He had nothing in common with them. They were in awe of the Original without even meeting him, but Anton felt nothing but disgust.

He knew Steve had a plan. Like Steve, it was simple. Anton would kill the Original, then Steve would kill Anton whilst he was tired after the fight. Steve would be a hero: the person who killed the godslayer. Steve was unaware that Anton knew this and equally unaware of the contempt Anton felt for him. *No matter. Steve's plan has many flaws, too many what ifs, like Alex dying. No-one had seen that coming. Callum, too, what did Steve intend for him?* Anton did not care about the plan.

The Original will not defeat me. He was not concerned about what would happen after that.

He pressed speed dial one, then waited until it clicked into answer phone.

"We've found him," Anton said. "Group four."

He returned the phone to the bag. "It's done," he told the others. "Get rest. Tomorrow will be busy."

Chapter 27

1

Jones stood when Knowles entered the barracks. He threw his book onto the bunk and stared at his old friend, arms crossed. Carruthers stayed in his seat watching the two men, his face a study of impassivity.

"I hear you're worried about me," Knowles said. He remained standing by the door. He felt weary: he'd been on watch most of the night, filling in those stupid forms for Starky. Now he had a pissed off Jones to deal with. It was just past midnight.

Jones snorted. "Not worried, sergeant."

"Cut the shit."

Jones exchanged a look with Carruthers. "Not worried, Knowles, I'm fucking furious."

"Why?" Knowles gave Carruthers a quick look. His eyes were darting between the two men. *Good. He hasn't chosen a side, not yet.*

"I watch you get all pally with that fucker. He killed our friends." Jones opened his arms, gesturing at the empty beds. "*Our* friends."

"He didn't kill them."

"Not directly. Those other *things* that are like him did." Jones took a step forward, fists clenched.

"The other *things-*" Knowles spat the word, matching Jones' intonation, "-are not like him at all. Jack is just a guy in the wrong place-"

"Don't even think about finishing that fucking sentence!"

Knowles paused. *So that was how it was going to be.* "Carruthers, did you just hear Jones threaten his superior officer?"

"I didn't hear a thing."

"Good."

Jones stepped forward, fist already swinging. Knowles stepped into the blow, catching the other man's arm and swinging his knee up into Jones' groin. Jones grunted, doubling over in agony. Knowles brought his knee up again, smashing it into Jones' nose. Jones fell backwards, landing in a crumpled heap, with blood flowing from his nostrils down over his chin. His expression matched that of a kid who'd been thrown a surprise party. *He'd actually thought he was going to win. They think I'm going soft.*

"Carruthers, did you see what happened here?"

"Didn't see a thing, sergeant."

"Good." Knowles pulled up a chair and sat next to Carruthers. He waited until Jones got to his feet. "Well, that was stupid and pointless."

Jones sat heavily in his chair. "My fucking balls man. That was low."

"You were being a twat."

"You were," Carruthers agreed, "although I disagree with our esteemed colleagues' choice of vernacular." Knowles and Jones looked at him with frowns. "Words, lads, your choice of words." Before they knew what was happening, all three of them were laughing and the tension in the room dissipated.

Jones reached over and picked a towel from a radiator by his bunk. He pressed it to his nose for a second before pulling it away and examining the red stain.

"I'm bleeding."

"Do you feel better?" Knowles asked. They'd had the disagreement, time to move on. It was one of the reasons he really liked Jonesey.

"Yeah, nothing hurt but my pride," Jones said. He dabbed his nose again. "I'm sorry."

Knowles nodded. "Me too. I wish I'd said no to this assignment."

"Bit late for that," Carruthers said. "Besides, it looked good on paper didn't it?"

Knowles crossed to the fridge and came back with three beers. He gave the first one to Jones. "Claire just told me that the Ruperts had no idea what Jack could do."

"Do you believe her?" Carruthers took his beer.

Knowles shrugged. "Yeah. Why would she lie?"

"To make you feel better," Jones said. "Fuck, my nose won't stop bleeding."

He tilted his head back, and pressed harder on the bridge of his nose.

"Something just happened," Knowles said.

"Between you and her?" Carruthers asked. He seemed to give the matter genuine thought for a moment. "I would."

"No, it was Jack." Knowles stopped for a moment, trying to get his thoughts in order. "He was asleep, but he shouted out 'they're coming.'"

"And?" Jones asked.

"That's it. He said 'they're coming, they're coming for me' or something like that."

Carruthers made a big deal of slurping his beer. "So what? Bad dream is all."

Knowles shook his head. "No, this was worse than that."

"Now *you're* being a twat," Jones said, earning himself a pained look from Knowles.

"What if he knows something?" Knowles said. "What if those other wolves have found us?"

"So what?" Jones said. "We pretty much kicked their arses last time and we'll do it again. There can only be about two, maybe three of them left and we're on an army base now. Bring 'em on."

"Yeah, come here little doggy." Carruthers mimed a gun with his fingers and thumb. "Bang, bang."

"I wish I had your confidence," Knowles said. "What if we get bit? What if we end up like them?"

"What, faster? Fitter? Stronger?" Carruthers said. "Wouldn't be so bad."

Silence settled on them like a tight glove – uncomfortable for no real reason.

"Well, I know one thing," Jones said, putting his empty beer bottle down. "It ain't right: they're not normal and I would like to blow every last one of the fuckers away. For Scarlet and Meyers."

Carruthers nodded his big head. "But think, it won't be long before we're posted back there, I wouldn't mind having a little extra in the tank."

"Are you serious?" Jones asked. He looked at Knowles. "You too?"

"I don't know," Knowles said. "I can see the benefits of the, uh, power and speed, but, I don't know."

"You have to eat people," Jones said.

"Not if you can control it. Jack hasn't killed anyone for two months now, and I'm not sure he's ever eaten anyone."

"Well, that's reassuring." Jones couldn't keep the sarcasm from his voice. "Not for me, lads, I'd rather chop off me own bollocks."

"Let's hope it doesn't come to that." Knowles threw his empty beer bottle to Jones.

"Another?"

"Yeah, but then I've got to go," Knowles said.

"We keeping you up?" Carruthers got the beers and sat back down. "Or are you seeing someone a bit easier on the eye than Jonesey?"

"Hey!" Jones said, taking the bloody towel away from his nose. "I clean up good you know."

"Not as good as a certain doctor we all know."

"Leave it," Knowles said. "It's not like that."

"What's not?"

"She's not," Knowles said. "She's, uh, well, uh-"

"Fit?" Carruthers smirked. "Like I said, I would."

"Yeah," Jones said, "but there's not a lot you wouldn't."

Carruthers shrugged. "The ladies love me, not much I can do about it except share the love."

"I'm getting my head down. I've got a meeting first thing," Knowles said. "Starky's team have finished doing whatever the fuck they've been doing to the bones. You guys want in?"

2

The alarm was loud and obnoxious. The simple beeping sound grated more than a seventy minute rap album and he swore at it, before eventually reaching out a hand and slapping the top of the machine. It went silent.

His quarters were small and functional. Basic wardrobe, small chest of drawers and a shelf for any books. Two folders full of paperwork sat on the shelf, squashed between two speakers which looked like they would fall off the shelf in a stiff breeze. The speakers were attached to his laptop, enabling music to be played to help him get to sleep. He hadn't used headphones for a few weeks now. *Maybe I am getting soft.*

Knowles jumped out of bed and almost ran to the shower. The room was cold, but sunlight was coming through the thin curtains. He regretted the other two beers he'd been talked into after saying he was going to bed. His bathroom was just about big enough for the shower and toilet, but you could forget swinging a cat.

Or a medical captain.

He showered, thinking about Claire for a couple of minutes then got dressed in his uniform and stepped into the sunshine. He shivered; despite the sunshine, the day had not yet heated up. He jogged across the courtyard and banged on the door of the barracks.

Jones and Carruthers were up and dressed. Two other soldiers were in their bunks sleeping. *Must be on the late shift.* They'd moved in when Knowles had been assigned his own quarters a month ago.

"Let's go."

3

Knowles sat when he was told to. Jones and Carruthers sat either side of him. Jones showed no bruises from the night before, which was a relief because neither of them wanted to explain that. Starky had two men with him that Knowles had not seen before. Smith was the only other person in the room.

Outside the room was a solitary guard. Security had become more relaxed since Jack had got control over his changing. *Maybe too relaxed.*

"The invite to attend this meeting was for you only, Sergeant," Starky said with a sniff.

"I believe that these two men may have information that is pertinent to this meeting. Please remember that Carruthers saw the exact location of the bones in the cave; I did not."

"Let them stay, Daniel," Smith said in his public school baritone. "You will not discuss the outcome of this meeting with anyone. Understood?"

"Yes, sir!" Jones and Carruthers said at once.

"Then let's get on with it." Smith looked at Starky and opened his arms, inviting the doctor to speak.

"The analysis of the bones threw up some interesting ideas and theories," Starky began. "This is Doctors Jason Henson and Gethin

Shanklin. They are palaeontologists but both are also experts in folklore and myth."

"Hello," Henson said with a deep American twang. Shanklin just nodded. Henson opened a laptop lid, fiddled with the keyboard for a moment, then Shanklin pressed a button and the screen was projected on the wall behind them. Knowles hadn't even realised there was a projector in the room. He noticed a tiny box sitting next to the laptop. *Jesus, that's small. It could fit in my hand.*

"The spider was extremely unusual. I have not seen anything like it before. That is incredible."

"We are not interested in the spider," Smith said.

"I am," Knowles said, "those spiders killed a man." Smith glared at him.

"Killed?" Henson said.

"Carry on with your report, Doctor."

Henson glanced at Shanklin, cleared his throat and continued. "I have shared the spider with a colleague of mine. Arachnids are not my area of expertise."

"Who gave you clearance for that?" Smith demanded.

"I did," Starky said, and from the expression on Smith's face, he would regret it later.

"My colleague will be in touch with Captain Starky regarding the spider."

"Make sure your colleague understands the sensitive nature of this," Smith said.

"Ok," Henson said. He tried to smile at the room, the corners of his mouth moving up and down like waves on a beach.

"We have managed to reconstruct a partial skeleton from the bones you have given us, and the results are interesting to say the least. You seem to have discovered a *Canis Dirus*, or more commonly a direwolf. What's exciting about this is that these bones have been carbon dated at approximately four thousand years old."

Henson beamed at the room. Nobody returned the smile. Smith looked blankly at the scientist.

"They are thought to have been extinct from about ten thousand years ago," Carruthers said.

"Exactly." Henson overcame his surprise and focused his huge grin on Carruthers.

"Way to go, Google," Jones muttered.

"Direwolves were common in the Pleistocene age. They hunted in packs and to date, most of the skeletons, indeed most of what we know about them, come from the tar pits of California. They are much larger than normal wolves, as I'm sure you are aware."

"Let's assume that we are not all as informed as Carruthers," Smith said.

"Yes, yes, of course." Henson nodded at Shanklin, who clicked the mouse button on the laptop. The skeleton zoomed into view, along with a picture of a very mean looking wolf.

"It has quite a small head, but extremely large teeth. Many believe that the teeth were used to crush bones, and indeed many of the fossils recovered in California do bear out that idea. Unfortunately your skeleton is missing its head, so we cannot ascertain anything about that. It also has very short legs, but they would have been very powerful. They would have to carry a lot of weight after all."

"It's all wrong," Jones said.

"Excuse me?"

"Your picture. That wolf is far too small. Double its size and you might be on to something."

Smith glared at him.

"That is the other thing that is exciting about this find. This is the largest direwolf that we have ever found. Indeed, it is so large, that it might even be a new species, one that we knew nothing about until you found it. May I ask where you discovered this magnificent specimen?"

"You may not." Smith stood, pushing his chair back. All the soldiers stood immediately, snapping smartly to attention. Shanklin looked surprised.

"Major," Henson began.

"Gentlemen, thank you for your time, it has been very much appreciated," Smith said. "Sergeant Knowles will escort you to your car."

4

Knowles escorted the two doctors across the courtyard and around to the back of the barracks. A very tired looking Ford Focus sat next to a jeep. Shanklin unlocked the car and Henson jumped straight into the passenger seat. Shanklin sighed and clicked the boot open. He put the laptop bag into the boot and closed it with a bang.

"You guys pay well," he muttered in a thick Welsh accent.

"Yes," Knowles said.

"But at a price. We can't talk about this?"

Knowles shook his head.

"He's not very happy about that."

Knowles shrugged. "I don't suppose he is. Listen, the guys that found the bones, they said that there was a carving of a man with horns. The devil right? Like a warning?"

Shanklin smiled. "Maybe, but probably not. The devil, as we would perhaps draw it, is a recent thing, maybe only a couple of thousand years old." He paused and Knowles had a glimpse of his intellect working. "More likely Cernunnos, or the Green Man. He was the old Celtic or Pagan god of nature. He was probably carved there to protect the site, a kind of 'return this body to nature' thing."

"Okay," Knowles said. *Carruthers was right.*

"You still won't tell me where you found them?"

Knowles smiled. "No, classified - sorry. You'll have to let your mate down gently."

"No matter, he's a total knob anyway." Shanklin stuck out his hand and Knowles shook it. "See you, Sergeant."

He climbed into the car and they drove off down the long drive towards the gatehouse. Knowles chuckled to himself as he watched the car go. As it approached the gates, he turned and walked back towards the meeting room. The sun felt warm on his face. No clouds in the sky and no breeze to speak of. It was a perfectly still day. Knowles smiled again and then re-entered the building.

He hadn't noticed that there were no birds singing.

5

Knowles sat back down. A plastic cup of water was on the table in front of him. He took a sip, glancing round the room. Everyone had water but there was no sign of who had delivered it. Starky opened a green manila folder and took out a large stack of papers. He passed them around the table.

"There are not enough copies," he said, with a pointed look at Jones and Carruthers.

Knowles picked his copy up. Its title was "Analysis of the physiology of Jack Stadler." Starky's name was in bold underneath and below that in a much smaller print was Claire's name. A stamp "EYES ONLY" lay diagonally across the title page.

"Proper James Bond stuff this." Jones muttered, leaning in to read Knowles' copy.

"Gentlemen, following on from the analysis of the bones, we have concluded our investigation of Stadler's physiological make up." Starky paused long enough to have a sip of water. "There are several remarkable things about his physical condition. Firstly, to all intents and purposes, Stadler is a human being. He looks like one, he acts like one and every test we can do confirms that he is, well, *normal*. He has a slightly elevated blood pressure compared to his records from his GP. This could easily be explained by stress."

Knowles and Carruthers exchanged a look that said: *Stress? No shit, Sherlock*.

"He is very calm. He seems to have accepted his lot and has so far co-operated fully with all tests that we have had to do."

"He is trying to get us to let him go," Knowles said.

"I am not trying to explain my findings, Sergeant, I am merely presenting them as facts."

"But his motives have to be important, surely?" Knowles said. "He wants nothing more than to see his wife and child again."

"Once again, I am presenting facts, not speculation."

"As I said in my email to you, Jack wants to go back to his normal life. He wants to see Katie and Josh. He has asked repeatedly for them to be brought here."

"And as *I* said to *you*, Mrs Stadler believes her husband to be dead. Until we know more, that is a very convenient state of affairs."

"What's this about, Knowles?" Smith said. "Let the man finish his report. Are you too close to this?"

"Sir?"

"You like Stadler?"

"Yes, sir, I do."

"Do I need to relieve you of duty? Is your friendship clouding your professional judgement?"

"No sir," Knowles said. "I don't think we should lose sight of the fact that he is a civilian with a family. What about his rights?"

"He lost them when he killed at least two people," Smith said. He stared unblinking at Knowles for a second. Knowles knew the conversation was over. "Continue, Daniel."

Round one to Starky, Knowles thought glumly.

"Stadler appears to be able to turn into a Wolf at will. As we've just heard, and from descriptions from witnesses and the unit on the ground, it appears that he turns into a direwolf – a species of wolf that has been extinct for thousands of years."

Starky smiled at the group. "The fascinating part of all this is that Mr Stadler has learnt how to control this-" he grunted, looking at the ceiling as if searching for the right word- "*ability* in a very short space of time."

"We don't know how much control he has," Knowles pointed out.

"Correct, Sergeant, but the point is that he has already gained some control. I suspect in time that he will gain full control over the ability and that he may even be able to part change."

"Is *that* a fact?" Knowles asked. He earned a scowl from Starky. *Round two, undecided.*

"What do you mean part change?" Smith asked.

"I think that he will be able to change specific parts of his body at a time. For example, change just his legs if he wants to be able to run faster."

Knowles conjured up a mental image of Jack on all fours running at them with drool hanging out of his smiling mouth. He shuddered, despite the absurdity of the image.

"That is excellent news, Captain," Smith said with a broad grin.

"Yes sir," Starky said. "If I am right, then this becomes a viable programmer for battlefield use."

Knowles felt his stomach constrict. He knew what was coming next.

"We move to phase two, tomorrow," Smith said, collecting his papers together and tapping them on the desk. "I want to see Stadler part changing by the end of the month."

"Yes sir."

Knowles banged his fist on the table.

"Careful, Sergeant," Smith said, an edge in his voice that none of them had heard before.

"Sir, he's a civilian. You cannot send him in to battle."

"Who said anything about that?" Starky said with a smirk. "I want him to part change here. Once he can do that, then we move to stage three: battlefield tests."

"Jesus Christ," Jones whistled through his teeth. "Sir, this is crazy. You're going to turn soldiers into those things?"

"You were told not to speak," Smith said.

Jones shook his head anger clear in his eyes and the tight lines around his mouth. "I've seen these things up close and I want no part of it. It's unnatural."

"That's what Oppenheimer said," Carruthers said. "I have become Death."

"Stop being so melodramatic," Smith barked. "Another word from your men, Knowles, and you will all be ejected from this meeting. Is that understood?"

"Yes sir." Knowles glanced at his friends. *Sort it out.*

Starky cleared his throat, "Sir, this is, of course, all hypothetical at the moment."

"Explain," Smith said. His face said that he had enough.

"We first became aware of Stadler because of an anomaly in his blood report."

"Yes."

Starky looked at his notes. "Stadler made a spectacular recovery from a fall. He claims to have fallen into a deep cave – one that your unit had to abseil into – and he didn't have a mark on him."

"Cut to the chase, Captain."

"Yes sir. Mr Stadler's blood was analysed as part of the Super-human program. It showed traces of a mutation in his DNA. We now know that the mutation was part wolf – we only discovered that retroactively. Knowing he could change into a wolf let us know where to look so to speak."

"I think we all know this Captain, what's your point?"

"The anomaly has gone."

The room fell silent.

"I don't understand Captain. The man had something wonky in his blood and now he hasn't?"

"Yes, sir." Starky paused, drinking the last water from his cup.

"So, what?" Smith said. "He's healed? He can't change anymore?"

"No, sir. I believe that he has totally absorbed whatever it was. It is now part of him. It might manifest when he has changed, but at the moment he is totally human."

"I don't understand," Knowles said. "What does that mean?"

"It means we can't cure him, Sergeant."

6

A heavy silence greeted his last comment. Starky looked at each man in turn.

"Let me be clear here gentlemen: if we can replicate what happened to Mr Stadler - and there is no guarantee that we can – we almost certainly will not be able to reverse the process."

Knowles drummed his fingers on the table. "If you cannot reverse the process, then you can't expect people to sign up for this, surely?"

"Yes we can," Starky said, with a glance at Smith.

"Sergeant, the details of our volunteer programme is way beyond your pay grade," Smith said.

"Sir-"

"No, Knowles, there is no discussion of this," Smith said. "Subject closed."

Knowles ran his hand through his hair. "Yes sir."

"Continue, Captain."

Not Daniel anymore. Smith has heard things he doesn't like. Knowles allowed himself a smirk.

"We looked back through Stadler's notes and have interviewed him at length. It appears that he lied to the hospital about his fall." Starky was watching Knowles like a hawk, looking for any sign of discontent.

"He claims that he landed on one of the bigger bones – we believe it was part of the rib cage – and it went straight through him. He said that it was 'like a spear'." Starky made the quotation marks with his hands.

"That's impossible," Smith said.

"We have already seen evidence of his rapid healing. It seems that this might have been the incident that started it."

"He's a lucky man if it did," Smith said.

"Lucky?" Jones said. "I'd rather have died than be turned into some sort of monster."

Smith stood without a word. He yanked open the door to the corridor and yelled at the soldier on guard, "Eject these men and bar them from returning to this building."

"Yes sir." The man looked worried, but entered the room with his rifle ready.

Smith turned to look at Knowles, Carruthers and Jones. "You were warned. Sergeant, I will speak with you later. Leave now."

"What did I do?" Carruthers grumbled under his breath as they all stood. The young guard saluted smartly as they all walked out. He closed the door behind them.

"Well done," Knowles said as they entered sunlight in the courtyard.

"His definition of lucky needs work," Jones said.

"I agree," Carruthers said, "if Stadler had died in that fall, we'd still have Scarlet and Meyers with us."

"They are going to cut him open, see what makes him tick," Knowles said, throwing his arms up in exasperation.

"Who cares?" Jones said. "Let them kill him."

"For fuck's sake, Jonesey. He's just a civvy."

Carruthers was ignoring them both. He was staring down the long drive to the gatehouse. "What's that?"

They turned to look at what he was pointing at. All the colour drained from Jones' face and he felt like he was standing on stilts.

"Shit," Knowles said. "Run!"

Chapter 28

1

Steve parked the car across the entrance to the base. Anton had a map on his lap which they were both stabbing. Steve got out of the car and slammed the door, hard. He had showered, cut his hair, shaved and was wearing a suit without a tie. The idea was to look like a stock broker on holiday. *At my age, I'd have to be a boss.* Anton was harder to disguise due to his bulk, but a suit had improved his appearance.

"Fucking idiot!" he yelled. "You don't have a fucking clue where we are do you?"

Anton climbed out just as a guard ran over to them. The other one stayed in the booth, watching. *Damn.*

"Gentlemen, can I help you?" the soldier was holding his gun across his body: ready, but not threatening, not yet. Behind him, a dark blue Ford Focus was coming slowly down the drive. The gate was down, and it was manual so the other guard would have to leave the gatehouse to raise it.

Perfect. Steve turned to the guard. "My idiot of a partner is trying to get us to Fosten Green, but we seem to be lost. Can you help us? Where are we?"

"Where's your map?" the soldier asked.

Anton reached into the car and pulled out the map. The soldier moved to look at it, spreading it on the bonnet of the car. Anton had placed it so that the soldier had his back to Steve. The soldier started pointing out landmarks and roads on the map. Anton nodded along with him.

Steve looked over his shoulder and almost on cue the other guard left the gatehouse. The guard started to raise the barrier, just as the Focus came closer. Steve snarled and changed. The suit ripped apart, the sound of the cloth tearing alerting both guards to the fact that something was wrong. *Too late. Much too late.* The wolf covered the ground quickly, leaping onto the guard before he raised his rifle. Steve ripped his throat out as they landed and then bounded onto the car.

Anton drove a fist into the first guard's face, breaking both his nose and cheekbone in one go. Then he raked his fingernails across the man's cheek, pulling the flesh away and leaving red muscle glistening in the sun. Anton licked the blood, smearing it round his mouth. He grinned at the soldier.

"Tasty."

The man started to scream.

The car careered into the post that supported the barrier and the bonnet crumpled. Steve leapt clear. A man tried to get out of the passenger side, but he forgot about the seatbelt which gave Steve all the time he needed. His jaws closed around the man's arm.

2

Shanklin looked in horror as Henson's arm turned into a bloody mess. The air bag exploded in his face, dazing and deafening him momentarily. The wolf – *shit, that's a wolf, a real live wolf in Kent* - was still ripping the flesh off Henson's arm, chunks disappearing into its wide mouth. Henson was emitting a sound somewhere between a scream and a moan.

"Help me!"

"Fuck you!" Shanklin yelled. He put the car into reverse and hit the accelerator as hard as he could. There was a horrible ripping sound, and something warm splashed across his face and chest. Henson fell back against him, seatbelt in tatters across his chest. His left arm was missing.

Shanklin started to shout – pure animal rage. The world had become dim, like he was looking out of a long tunnel. Deep inside he felt remorse for Henson: they had worked together for a few years now and whilst he was obnoxious and arrogant, he didn't deserve to be ripped to shreds by a wolf. *Nobody deserves that.* Henson had already lost a lot of blood. He was pale and trembling all over. His eyes were closed and Shanklin thought for a moment that the man was already dead. *Can't be dead and trembling, you idiot.*

Shanklin spun the wheel, but the car was going too fast. It tipped on its wheels and they flipped over. The roof crunched inwards and Henson was thrown clear. Shanklin reached for his seat belt clip, but it wouldn't release. He tried to buck against it, but it was no use: he was stuck.

With his whole world upside down, Shanklin tried to think about what to do next. He couldn't focus on anything, his mind whirling with the impossibilities of what he was witnessing. The windscreen had smashed open, a spider web of cracks leading to the hole that Henson had created when he flew out of the car.

Shanklin could see him now, lying on the grass, blood still pouring out of the hole in his shoulder where his arm was supposed to be. Beyond that, he could see the ruined block that the gate barrier had sat on. Padding towards him was a wolf. It was carrying something in its mouth.

"Oh, God, no!" Shanklin started to scream.

The wolf stopped by Henson and started to eat. Behind it, the other man was walking towards him. *There had been two men when we drove up,* he thought. Behind the strolling man, a combination of people and wolves were pouring through the gates. The wolves padded along besides the humans.

That's not right. Those wolves should be terrified.

He tried not to think about the fact that there weren't any wild wolves in Britain. He tried not to think about the mess that was being made of Henson's body. He tried not to think about the arm the wolf had just dropped. He tried not to think about the plain fact that these were clearly his last moments alive.

3

Knowles didn't actually move after he yelled "Run!" He couldn't quite believe what he was seeing. The blue Ford Focus that the palaeontologists had been in was lying on its roof near to the gatehouse. Even at this distance, he could tell it was smashed beyond repair.

Flooding across the field, pouring down the drive, came a mixture of wolves and humans. The humans were walking with purpose. At their head was an enormous man, who had his shirt open displaying an impressive set of abs. Next to him was a man that he recognised.

It was the one who had spoken in the house in Huntleigh. One of *them*.

A wolf in man's clothing.

They've found me. Knowles felt sick to his stomach. Jack had known and tried to warn them, even in his sleep. Had he smelt them? Heard them maybe? There was just so much about Jack that they didn't understand.

Carruthers and Jones were also staring. They had to move *now*, or they would be in serious trouble.

"Jonesey, get the Major. Carruthers, get the toys. Get as many as you can." Knowles looked at the bigger man. "NOW!"

His shout woke them up. Both men sprinted in opposite directions. Jones ripped the door open after swiping his card. Carruthers was running hard to their barracks.

The tide of bodies was coming closer – they were less than five hundred metres away. *About thirty seconds at most.*

He started to run towards the block where Jack was.

And Claire.

4

"Stop!" The guard who had just thrown him out looked none too pleased to see him return so soon. He lowered his gun to his waist, clearly pointing it at Jones without really wanting to.

"We're in the shit, mate," Jonesey said. "Wolves. Tons of them."

The soldier turned white.

"Keep your gun on that door. Shoot anyone who comes through it who isn't wearing green."

"Yes sir." The soldier's voice was shaky, like a teenager going through puberty. Jones didn't bother to correct him on the rank. *Probably a good idea to let him think someone is in charge.*

He burst into the meeting room. Smith and Starky looked up from the documents they were studying.

"Jones!" Smith got as far as saying.

"Sir. Wolves. Hundreds of them," Jones said, without a salute. "We're in trouble."

Starky stood, knocking the manila folder onto the floor. Jones caught a glimpse of Katie Stadler's face on a sheet of paper then it hit the ground.

"Are you armed?" Smith barked.

"No, sir," Jones said. "Google, uh, Carruthers is getting some weapons now, but we have to move."

"We are safe in here," Starky said. "There is only one door in and out. Private Wallace could hold them off until help arrives."

"Agreed." Smith said. "Has someone raised an alarm?"

"Not yet." Jones said. "I think Sergeant Knowles has gone to do that."

"What about Stadler?" Smith asked.

"Don't know, sir."

"Shit."

"Yes sir."

Starky delved into his bag and pulled out a Sig. "Fifteen rounds," he said with a grim smile.

You might want to keep four of those. Jones didn't vocalise that last thought.

5

Carruthers opened his foot locker and pulled out his Browning and a 12 bore shotgun. At the far end of the barracks lay the gun cabinet. He smashed the lock with the shotgun and the door swung open. He picked up two rifles, known to the team as SA80's even though they were officially GPMG 7.62mm rifles, and slung them over his back. He grunted under the weight and ran back to the door.

He stepped into the courtyard, and could see that the first of the wolves were less than 100 metres away. He dropped the two SA80s, raised the machine gun and fired a burst into the oncoming wolves.

Two at the front yelped, falling back in a shower of red. The next three stopped and scattered. Those following slowed right down. He fired again, taking a further two out. Then he scooped up the two rifles and ran straight for the building that Jones had gone into.

He yelled as he jumped at the door. It was shut tight and he bounced off it. "Open up!" he screamed. Behind him, he heard the wolves approaching. He could almost feel their breath on his neck. Dropping all the guns except the shotgun, he turned quickly. A wolf jumped at him as he spun. He fired once, hitting it full in the chest. Blood splashed onto him as the wolf landed in a bloody heap next to him. He banged on the door again with his foot.

"It's Carruthers! Open the door!"

Humans were now arriving at the edge of the courtyard. The biggest one of all was pointing at him, and the other humans all laughed. Three seemed to shrug off their skin, wolves bursting out of them. *That's got to hurt.* They joined the rest of the wolves, forming a large pack. At a conservative guess there were twenty wolves approaching him.

He pumped the action on the shotgun and raised it to his shoulder. "Come on then!" he screamed and started shooting into the crowd of oncoming wolves. His pulse was sky high, his heart hammering in his chest. Even in Afghanistan, he had not felt this afraid. There, you knew what you were dealing with. He fired, pumped, fired again, and each time another wolf went down. No need to aim, the wolves were so tightly packed that he couldn't miss.

Each time, another wolf took their place.

Carruthers dropped the shotgun and picked up the SA80. *Should have picked up some grenades. Thirty rounds; make them count.*

6

Knowles ran into the observation booth, ignoring the guard outside. Claire looked up and smiled. She started to write in the pad again, sipping her coffee as she wrote.

"We need to go. Now," Knowles said. She was so calm, so unaware of the trouble brewing a scant ten metres away. Through the observation window, Jack was pacing the room, his brow creased. "How long has he been doing that?"

"Five minutes or so," she said. "What's up?"

"We have about a hundred wolves bearing down on us, right now. We have to get out of here. Are you armed?"

"What?"

"Are you armed?"

Her mouth dropped open. "Wolves."

Jack started banging on the one way. Knowles nodded.

"We need to go."

She stood up, spilling the coffee. She started to gather the papers from the desk. Knowles grabbed her arm.

"Leave them, it's not important."

"All my notes."

"We don't have time, Claire. We need to go. *Now.*"

Jack was still banging on the window, shouting.

"What about him?" Claire asked.

"He comes with us."

He opened the door to the short corridor. For the first time, the young soldier didn't salute him.

"It's Salmon, isn't it?" Knowles asked.

"Adam, sir," The soldier tried to hide his surprise but failed.

"Outside that door," Knowles pointed at the security door to the outside, "is a pack of hungry wolves. They want what we have in that room. They will not get him and we are all there is to stop that happening. Do you understand?"

"Yes sir." Salmon stood a little taller in his uniform. *Good man.*

"You fired your weapon in action?"

"No, sir."

"I'm a sergeant, mate, try to remember that. You can call me Knowles." Knowles smiled at him. "You will today. Remember your training." Knowles opened the door to Jack's room with a swipe of his card. *Never guarantee they will live.*

Jack came to the door as soon as it opened.

"They're here."

"No shit, Jack," Knowles said. "There's a lot of them. How many of your kind are there?"

"I don't know," Jack moaned. "I don't know anything. Three months ago, my *kind* read the Guardian."

"Fuck," Knowles said. "Why do they want you?"

"I don't know," Jack shouted. "I just want to go home!"

He sounded like a petulant teenager. Knowles turned back to the door. Claire was watching them. In her hand was a Browning.

"How many bullets have you got?"

"Thirty," she said.

"When was the last time you fired that?"

"In Ghanners. On the range."

Knowles nodded. When they'd talked about her service, he'd assumed she'd been in the field. *Great. Two soldiers with no active service to speak of and a civvy. We're really in the shit.* He opened the gun cupboard in the corridor and took out one of the dart guns. It was preloaded with ten tranquiliser darts. *Better than nothing.*

"Ok, we're going to open that door, and cross the courtyard to the meeting room. Major Smith and Captain Starky are in there. If anything with more legs than us gets in the way we are going to put it down. Everybody ready?"

In turn, they each nodded. Knowles was quietly grateful that Jack hadn't asked for a gun. He walked to the end of the corridor and looked back over his shoulder. He mouthed *one, two, three*.

On three, he opened the door.

7

The door opened and a voice shouted, "In here, now!"

Carruthers fired a burst into the courtyard, but didn't stop to check if any more wolves had been killed. He scooped up the rifles and leapt through the open door. Jones slammed it shut behind Carruthers. A soldier had his gun trained on them.

"Point that elsewhere," Carruthers growled. "We need to barricade this door."

"What about Knowles?"

Carruthers shook his head. "There's too many of them. He won't be able to get to us."

Jones turned even paler. *Not Knowles too. Shit.*

Something thumped into the door. The three soldiers backed away quickly, even though the door held firm. They continued edging backwards until they reached the meeting room.

"We need to barricade the door," Smith said.

"Yes sir!" Jones said. He and Carruthers upended a table and pushed it back into the corridor, resting it against the door frame. They put another on its side and pushed it into the open doorway, legs into the room. Then they knelt up against the table, an SA80 each trained down the hallway.

Smith nodded, satisfied with their work. He was holding the 12-bore whilst Starky had his Browning. The young soldier had his rifle and was standing to the side of the room.

"What's your name private?" Smith asked. He hadn't paid any attention to the rank throughout this whole operation. They were beneath him, but now his life was in the hands of someone barely old enough to shave. For the first time, he regretted ordering the reduction to skeleton staff.

"Private Wallace, sir, 422 -"

"Well, Wallace, your job is to back up those two. If either of them falls, you are to take their place. If they have a stoppage or run low on ammo you are to give up your own."

"Yes sir."

"Stick with us, son, and we'll get you through this alive."

Jones and Carruthers exchanged glances, but neither said anything. They returned their gazes to the door. Another loud bang.

"How long till they figure out it's reinforced steel?" Jones muttered.

"Not long," Carruthers said.

He was right.

8

Steve looked around the courtyard with amazement. Some of the pack were dragging the dead away, piling the bodies in the middle of the space. Many of the wolves were now back in human form. The naked ones were smeared in blood: that of their colleagues and the dead humans. There hadn't been many soldiers, which judging by the number of dead was a good thing. *Far too many of us dead to get this far.*

Callum stood in front of the hut that the soldier had disappeared into. He was surrounded by his pack. One of them was throwing himself at the door, but it wasn't budging.

Steve sniffed the air. There were too many scents distracting him. The air was full of the stench of death and something else. The scent of the Original. He couldn't pinpoint it; it appeared to be everywhere at once.

"Stop," Callum commanded. The man throwing himself at the door turned to his leader. "We will not get them out that way. Search the other huts, find me some weapons."

He strode towards Steve. "They are holding something important in that hut."

"Yes," Steve said. "Maybe in some of the other huts too."

Callum nodded. "I will make them suffer for hurting our clan."

Clan. Jesus. Is that what he thinks we are?

9

Knowles stared into the courtyard. Hundreds of people were looking at the hut opposite him. Some were dragging bodies into a pile in the centre of the courtyard. Many of them were naked and covered in blood. He shut the door, quietly but quickly and deadlocked it.

"Change of plan," he said. "Back into Jack's room. Quick."

Had he been seen? He didn't think so, but it paid to be careful. They entered Jack's room and he closed the door, swiping his card to lock it.

"The courtyard is swamped. There's hundreds of them," he said. *Don't sugar coat it.*

"What are we going to do?" Salmon asked.

"Not panic," Knowles said. "The door is reinforced steel. The inner door is also reinforced. They're not getting in in a hurry. We just need to hole up and wait."

"Wait?" Jack said. "For what?"

"You're on an army base, Jack. People will notice what's going on."

"Then what?"

"They send the cavalry."

"How long?"

"Jack, for fuck's sake," Knowles said, "just let me think." *And stop asking so many questions.*

Claire caught his eye for a second. It was a long second, but it was enough. She knew he was bluffing, hoping for the best.

Bottom line, there are more wolves than we have bullets.

10

"Callum," one of the wolves said. "There are two locked buildings."

He gestured at the one that the soldier had disappeared into a few minutes before, and another that was roughly opposite it.

"The Original must be in one of them."

"His name is Jack," Steve said. Anton stood next to him. *Almost like we're equals now.*

"Which one?" Anton said.

"Does it matter? They have lost. We will have the Original soon and they will all be dead." Callum said. "Anything else?"

"We found some grenades." The wolf smiled. "And a grenade launcher. I think it's a 40 mm."

Callum smiled for the first time that day.

11

Jones watched the door. The banging had stopped and silence hung heavy in the room. *Like a tomb*. The reinforced door was doing a good job of blocking out all the sound from outside.

"Do you think they've gone?"

Carruthers shook his head. "Not until they've got what they came for."

"Well, that's Jack. Fuck him, give him up I say."

"Do you really think they'll let us live after that?"

Jones shrugged. "It's a chance I'll take."

"Can it, you two," Smith barked. "Alarms will be going off at HQ now. The birds will be flying soon."

Jones tried a few calculations. Depending on when the alarms went off, they could have support here in a few minutes… or hours. The wolves would find a way in soon. *Got to hope that the alarm has already gone off.*

Carruthers asked the question: "Is the alarm automatic?"

"Yes. A beacon sends a signal every 30 minutes. It has to be set by whoever is in the observation booth. If it isn't set, a fire support team is dispatched from Salisbury immediately. We set it up in case Stadler proved to be a-"

The door exploded. It flew off its hinges, ricocheting down the corridor until it hit the table that Jones and Carruthers were hiding behind. Splinters from the other table flew through the air, like miniature daggers. Wallace caught several splinters in his face, falling back as blood poured out of the wounds. The ruined door smashed into the table pushing it, Jones and Carruthers back into the room.

Wolves poured in through the opening. One leapt and cleared the barricade, jumping between Jones and Carruthers. It bit into Wallace's arm before Starky shot it in the side of the head. Wallace clutched his bleeding arm, screaming. Starky kicked the wolf carcass up against the wall and shot it again.

Carruthers had kept a vice like grip on his gun and he stood, opening up with the SA80. He roared as he did so, the sound combining with the gunfire and yelps to create a cacophony of noise.

Jones could see his gun lying just out of reach. *Must have dropped it when the fucking door hit me.* He rolled onto his knees and scooped up the gun. He held the gun against his shoulder and shot short controlled bursts into the mass of wolves.

No other wolf got close to the room. Bodies lay strewn along the corridor. Blood dripped from every conceivable surface. The lights had blown, so sunlight shone only halfway up the corridor. The room still had lights behind them, showing too much of the carnage for comfort.

Jones and Carruthers high fived. "Kicked their fucking arses again!" Jones shouted.

A grenade rolled into the room.

"Grenades! Out! Out! Out!" Smith roared. "Take cover!"

Carruthers and Jones leapt the barrier of the door and table. Something crunched under Carruthers boot, but he didn't stop to look. Jones slipped on the blood and fell to his knees. He put his hand out to stop the fall and it went straight into the ruined chest of a wolf. He looked at his hand in disgust and screamed.

"Come on Jonesey!" Carruthers pulled him up as Smith and Starky jumped the barricade. Wallace watched them go. Starky paused, looking back at him.

"Move!"

Wallace fell forwards, covering the grenade with his body. Another grenade popped past their heads and landed next to him. Starky swore and ran on, leaving Smith behind. The grenade under Wallace exploded first, igniting the one next to it. Bits of Wallace showered the walls and ceiling. The blast lifted Smith off his feet and carried him into Starky. Both men fell forward into the courtyard.

Carruthers and Jones were standing still, arms above their heads. Blood ran down Jones' arm making his shirt appear black. He looked on the verge of vomiting. Their guns were being picked up by two naked men. A huge man was grinning at them. In his hands was a grenade launcher. Behind them, more men were running into the building. Carruthers recognised the two men who picked up the SA80's, and knew they were in trouble.

12

Steve liked the weight of the gun in his hands. *This will help later.*

"Where is the Original?" Callum asked.

"I've no idea what you're talking about." The man had an accent straight out of a world war two RAF film. He stood up, dusting himself off.

"You in charge?"

"Yes. Major Smith, British Army. Who are you?"

Callum grinned and laughed, a false sound echoing around the courtyard. "I am Callum."

"Are *you* in charge?" Smith said in the same clipped tones. If he was scared, he was hiding it well.

"Yes," Callum said. No-one argued, despite there being several other alphas within earshot. Steve smirked to himself. *Does having a grenade launcher make you the boss?*

"I suggest you take your men-" Smith caught sight of the female wolves, "-uh, people and leave whilst you can."

"Why?" That same humourless laugh.

"Our support teams are en-route. When they arrive, you will be executed with extreme prejudice."

"We overran your base easily enough. We fear nobody."

"Then you will die here," Smith said. "I could help you survive this."

"*You?* Help *me?*" For the first time, Callum's laugh was genuine. "Give me the Original."

"I have no idea what you're talking about."

Callum moved so quickly that it was a blur. His head became a wolf's and his arm turned into a big paw. He swiped Carruthers across the face, drawing blood. Carruthers instinctively turned his head from the blow and Callum pounced on his exposed neck. He bit deep, tearing out Carruthers' muscles and arteries. Blood spurted from the sudden wound, coating both Callum and Jones with gore. Carruthers had enough time to cry out before he fell to the floor, a pool of blood spreading around him like oil on water.

Callum stepped back in front of Smith. His head and arm returned to normal. "Any ideas now?"

13

Smith blanched. Starky sank to his knees and started moaning. "God help me, please, oh God. Please don't kill me."

Pathetic. Jones was not going down without a fight. He leapt forward, drawing his fist back with a shout.

Steve stepped in and caught Jones' arm as it came forward, stopping the punch in its tracks. He twisted the soldier's arm, hearing it snap before kicking his legs away. Jones fell to the floor, screaming and clutching his arm.

"Don't," he said, deliberately making eye contact.

Jones looked at Steve and felt his will to fight disappear. There were just too many of them. If he carried on, then he would be dead next. Red hot lances of agony coursed up his arm, making him feel sick. Carruthers' corpse lay next to him. His eyes were open, looking at Jones without seeing. Jones remembered the times they had spent together, the battles they'd fought, the laughs they'd shared.

You will pay for this. Somehow. You will fucking pay.

14

Knowles had switched on the external cameras in the observation booth. He saw Carruthers die and impotent rage filled him. *Scarlet. Meyers. Carruthers. Jesus Christ, they will kill us all.* Jones was clearly in agony, with his arm hanging at an angle that was just plain wrong, and *they* were laughing at him. Smith stood to one side with grim expressions on his face, whilst Starky was kneeling on the ground, clearly sobbing.

He watched as Smith pointed at the building they were in. The big man looked straight at the camera and waved. Knowles couldn't blame the Major for giving them up: it was carnage out there. He didn't think he'd ever seen anything worse. Afghanistan, with guys missing limbs or worse, even that didn't seem so bad now. For the first time, Knowles wished he was back there, rather than here. *What the hell do we do now?* Knowles switched the camera off and went back into Jack's room.

Salmon was watching everything, but not talking at all. *Good.* Knowles didn't have the time to deal with frightened, green soldiers. Claire was talking to Jack, but he couldn't hear what she was saying.

"We're about to have company," he said.

"A company of wolves," Jack said, without humour. Knowles glared at him.

Claire checked her weapon, again, and nodded at Knowles. "Numbers?"

"Not sure yet, but they've got Smith, Starky and Jonesey in the courtyard."

"What about Carruthers?" she asked.

He shook his head. She swore. Then: "You okay?"

Knowles shook his head again. He had to get a grip. Friends and colleagues had died before: it was a fact of life he had become very used to on his tours, but this was different. *Nobody is supposed to die on home soil. What now? Think, for God's sake, or we will all die today.*

"Sir?" Salmon asked. "My friend."

"I didn't see anyone else," Knowles said with a frown. Salmon nodded once and tightened his grip on his rifle. Knowles knew better than to say something crass like *they might all be alright.*

"We should barricade the door," Claire said. She was very pale.

"They have a grenade launcher," Knowles said. "Not much point."

"What's your plan?"

He didn't have a clue, then he saw the controls for the tannoy system.

15

Callum looked straight at the camera on the roof of the single storey building and waved.

Cocky bastard. Steve watched the soldier with the broken arm. He was the one that had shot them in Devon. *The one that had shot me.* He was hungry and it would be easy, but he'd been told no. His moment would come. *Just be patient.*

"Hey big man."

The voice was coming from the tannoy.

"He's in here. You can have him but you let them go and come get him by yourself."

Callum shook his head.

"No-one else needs to die here today," the voice said.

Callum shook his head again.

"Come in by yourself and we can talk."

Steve touched Callum's arm. "Do it. You can take a bunch of toy soldiers."

Callum laughed. "I know that."

"We don't know if they really do have an alarm. Maybe we should be quick."

"We can just blow the door off again."

"And risk hurting Jack? The Original?"

"He would heal."

"Yes, but he might not take too kindly to getting hurt."

Callum mused that point, then nodded. "If I'm not back out in five minutes, you make sure they suffer."

"They will. I give you my word."

Callum handed him the grenade launcher and walked towards the building.

16

Knowles opened the door to let Callum in. He kept his body shielded behind the door. At the end of the corridor, both Salmon and Claire had their rifles aimed straight at Callum.

Callum stepped into the corridor. "I am unarmed," he said.

Knowles pulled him forward and spun. Simultaneously, he kicked the door shut and pressed the barrel of his weapon against the back of Callum's head. With his free hand, he entered the code to deadlock the door. "Don't even fucking *think* about changing."

"I give you *my* word," Callum said.

"That the same word you gave to Carruthers before you ripped his throat out?"

"I had to demonstrate my power and the futility of your situation."

"More of our troops will be here soon. Our situation is pretty fucking far from futile, and you just gave yourself up pretty easy."

"I want to see the Original," Callum said. "Now."

"Why do you call him that?"

"The Original?"

"Yes. What the fuck is an Original?"

Callum sneered at him. "You know nothing."

Knowles laughed, but it was a hollow sound. "You've got some bottle. No wrong moves, because I *will* kill you. I asked you a question."

"You cannot hope to understand."

"Try me."

"He is my God."

Callum walked down the corridor, with Knowles keeping the gun pressed tight to his neck. Claire moved into the room first, her weapon also trained on Callum. Salmon went in next and they took up positions in the corners of the room. Claire had her back against the shower curtain.

Jack stood by his bed. He was trying to stand straight, with his chest out. As an attempt to look dangerous, it failed.

Callum sank to one knee as soon as he saw Jack. "It is true, then."

Jack felt himself going red. He looked at Claire and Knowles in turn, but they were both frowning. The kneeling man kept his head bowed, even though three guns pointed at him. "Get up."

Callum remained on one knee. He raised his head to look Jack in the eye. "Are you going to lead us to overthrow the humans?"

Now the colour drained from his cheeks and he felt weak. His legs were trembling but he forced himself to stand strong. "Please, what is your name?"

"I am Callum. I have formed this Clan to free you. They are my gift to you."

"Well, Callum, get up," Jack said. He waited until the man stood and then wished he hadn't. Callum was at least a foot taller than him and twice as wide. Tribal tattoos lined both side of his neck and his arms were sleeves of ink. He was finding it hard not to be intimidated.

"Give the word, and I will slaughter these people now." Callum pointed at the others in turn.

"No," Jack said. "These people are not your enemy. No-one here is."

Callum looked confused. "But-"

"No, Callum. Now, tell me what I am."

"You don't know?"

"I don't know anything."

"How…" Callum struggled to get his words out. ".. can you not know?"

"What happened to me was an accident," Jack said. "This was not meant to be."

"But you are an Original."

"I still don't know what that means," Jack said.

Callum still wore the confused look of a child who had just been told there was no Father Christmas. "You must."

"Well, I don't." Jack looked in exasperation at Knowles.

"Why don't you tell us what that means?" Knowles said, giving Callum a nudge with the barrel of his gun.

"The Originals came first. They were the ones that created us."

"Were they humans who could change?"

Callum's confused expression deepened. "No, they were the Originals."

"Well, that's cleared that up then," Knowles said. "You said he was a God."

"They came first. They are all powerful."

"A God?" Jack laughed. "You think I'm a God? You did this because you want to worship me?" His eyes flicked to the door. "It's far too late for any of that."

17

The wolves all turned as one at the sound. A soft *thump, thump* that got very loud, very quickly. Two dots in the sky increased in size until two Westland WAH-64 Apache helicopters came over the tree line. The wolves didn't even have enough time to panic, not enough time to register the danger. Hellfire missiles and 70 mm rounds poured out of the first helicopter and thumped into the courtyard.

Two buildings exploded and the wolves scattered. Mounds of earth and bodies flew into the air and limbs and rubble rained down. Then both helicopters opened fire with their chain guns. Tracer bullets flew across the scattered hordes of wolves, cutting through them efficiently.

The air was filled with screams as the wolves were sliced apart. Limbs were blown off bodies; people were blown away from their limbs. A man in front of Steve had his head blown apart and his body quivered as if unaware he was already dead. *Get inside; we're fish in a barrel here.*

Steve made for the open building that the soldiers had abandoned, Anton close behind, unable to dispel the strains of 'Ride of the Valkyries' from his mind. Explosions rocked the courtyard, incinerating anyone within range. Bullets ripped bodies apart in seconds. Wolves and people ran in every direction. Most were cut to pieces. The sound of the guns eclipsed all other noise in the courtyard, almost a purring noise as bullets raked across flesh. Explosions punctuated the symphony and screams provided the coda. Some had nearly made it to the tree line, but the rest were being slaughtered.

They ran into the building, bouncing off the wall as they entered the narrow corridor. Two more wolves tried to follow, but didn't make it as far as the doorway. The inner room was carnage. Blood and flesh decorated the walls like some sort of Dali inspired wallpaper. They stood facing each other, hands on thighs, panting.

"He took too long," Steve gasped.

"We need to get out of here," Anton said, a touch of panic in his voice. *Never heard that before.*

"Any suggestions as to how we actually do that?" Steve said. He looked around the room and saw bits of paper lying in the corner. Natural curiosity got the better of him. He picked up the blood splattered paper, amazed that it was intact amongst the carnage.

"No."

Steve smiled. "We wait for the helicopters to pass over again. They'll come in to land soon after that, then we leg it. We need to be long gone before the reinforcements arrive."

"That's a shit plan."

"You got a better one?"

"It's too exposed out there."

"No. The helicopters are it. That's all. There are no ground troops, not yet anyway. When the helicopters finish a pass, we run."

"What if you're wrong?"

"Then it's Butch and Sundance and we won't worry about it for long."

"I want to kill him."

"I want to live."

Anton shrugged. "Where are we going to run to? They will hunt us down for this."

Steve smiled and held up one of the pieces of paper. "Stadler has a wife."

18

They heard the rockets explode and the clatter of machine guns. The building shook but held firm. *Don't need wolf hearing to know the helicopters have arrived.* Knowles grinned at Callum. All talk of Gods and Originals ended.

"Yes!" Salmon shouted, punching the air.

"Calm down," Knowles said, turning to the young man. "We're not out of the woods yet." *That's the best sound I've heard all day.* He turned his grin to Claire and she returned the smile. Her eyes lit up as she stared at him. *You and me. Oh yes.*

Callum moved. With a roar he pushed his head back, connecting with Knowles' nose. It cracked and blood pulsed onto his tunic. Callum spun, lifting his arm and punching Knowles on the chin. Knowles' feet left the floor; he dropped his gun and crashed back into Salmon. They both fell to the ground and Salmon grunted as the air was forced out of his lungs.

Callum leapt towards them but Knowles rolled clear. Callum's mouth changed as he jumped, his nose and mouth extending, becoming wolf like. Salmon was still trying to regain his breath as Callum landed on him. He bit down on Salmon's neck and there was another sickening crunch. Blood oozed out of the wound as Salmon tried to shout. He pressed his hands to the wound but it was a futile gesture.

Claire screamed. Callum turned, his eyes bright yellow and gore dribbling down his chin. She fired three times. Two bullets went wild, smacking into the wall behind Knowles, making him duck. Callum roared as the third bullet tore into his changing leg. He jumped before she had a chance to aim and fire again. The impact sent the gun flying out of her hands as he landed on her chest and bit down on her face. He bit and bit until flaps of skin broke off and her face was a red mess of blood and exposed muscle.

Jack stood still, his face white with shock. The entire fight had lasted less than ten seconds. He had ducked when Claire started shooting and now sat with his knees drawn up to his chest.

Callum stood and turned to face Jack. His face started to return to normal and he was grinning. "Join us, Jack, and I'll teach you how to do that."

Knowles shot him in the head at point blank range. Callum teetered for a moment, then collapsed, lying next to Claire, his head by her feet. They looked like a bizarre yin-yang symbol. Knowles shot him again and again and again until the gun clicked empty. Each bullet tore into Callum, destroying his head and chest, reducing them to a mass of torn flesh and gore.

Knowles sank to his knees looking at Claire. She wasn't moving. One of her eye sockets had broken and the eye was hanging out. He would never forget how she looked at that moment. However many times he tried to remember the look she'd given him mere seconds before, her face always morphed to the pulpy mess before him now. Her good eye was open, pupil wide and staring.

19

The first hellfire rocket exploded scant feet away from Jones. He was knocked off his feet and landed on Carruthers' corpse. He got up quickly and took in the situation with the calm of an experienced combat veteran. *Need cover. Now.*

Starky knelt next to him, covered in blood. He brushed fragments of flesh off his shoulder and looked at the pieces on the floor.

"Smith," he said.

"Run!" Jones screamed. He dragged Starky to his feet and pushed him forward. The Captain staggered, and Jones felt his heart sink. Starky recovered his footing and started to run towards the barracks. Jones felt relief wash over him and ran after the man, cradling his arm against his stomach. The pain had subsided to a dull throb as adrenaline took over. Wolves and humans were streaming around the courtyard, panic evident in their cries. Nobody tried to stop them, and Jones took full advantage by ignoring the wolves too.

They reached the cover of the corner building, opposite where Jack was being held. The helicopters had finished their first pass. Jones stopped, leaning against the building for support. Starky leant next to him. A gun lay on the floor next to them, a Browning pistol. Jones picked it up and grinned. *First bit of luck today. Might still get out of this.*

"The cavalry!" Starky said.

"Yeah, but they're just shooting everybody," Jones muttered. "We're not in the clear yet."

A wolf leapt at them, taking Starky down with its weight. It tried to bite him, but Jones put his gun behind its ear and shot once. Its head exploded showering Starky with fresh gore. Jones didn't think he'd mind.

"Did it get you?" Jones had to ask twice. The noise from the rotors was getting louder again.

Starky was checking himself like a man having an epileptic fit. "No," he said.

"Good," Jones nodded. "We need to get to somewhere safer than this."

"We can get into the building where Stadler is."

Jones shook his head. "Those helicopters are shooting everything. The buildings will be next."

"Don't be ridiculous! They are here to save us."

Bullets started to tear up the courtyard again, pumping into the ground and bodies. Mortar, bricks and glass flew out of one of the buildings. Many of the wolves fled for the trees and the helicopters screamed after them. Hellfire rockets blew the tree line to shreds, turning trees into a deadly inferno. Screams of burning wolves filled the air, clearly audible even over the Apache engines.

"Come on!" Starky shouted. He pulled at Jones and they ran around the corner, heading for Stadler's cell. A wolf hit Starky from behind, pushing him to the floor. Starky grunted as he landed, all air forced out of his lungs. The wolf bit at the back of his head. A chunk of Starky's skull and brain came out with the bite, dripping out of its mouth as it chewed.

Jones didn't have time to react as a second wolf swept his legs from under him. He crashed to the floor, dropping the Browning. The wolf bit into his leg, ripping through the fabric and muscle. Jones screamed as hot pain coursed up his leg. He felt an initial flood of warmth as the blood streamed out of his leg. Bone shone through the gore and tattered muscle and Jones knew he would not be able to walk again.

Fur ran back into the wolf and a man stood grinning at Jones. The other wolf had finished feasting on Starky and padded over to stand next to the one who had bit him. Jones felt cold inside as he recognised the man.

"Now," Steve said, his face inches from Jones', "you get to be like us."

He laughed, and a wolf burst out of him again and he was gone, heading in the opposite direction to the helicopters. A piece of paper he had been holding fluttered to the ground.

Jones punched the floor and screamed at the sky. The helicopters engine noise was getting louder again. The courtyard was empty now, except for the dying and already dead. *So* close. No sign of Knowles. From where he lay, he could see Starky. His face was intact, an expression of surprise etched onto his features. Even at the angle he lay, Jones knew that the back of the man's head was missing.

He scanned the courtyard, eyes coming to rest on a wolf lying only a couple of metres away. The wolf was whimpering, it's big brown eyes full of pain. It had lost its rear legs and a large ugly piece of shrapnel stuck out of its belly. As Jones watched, the wolf's breathing slowed, then stopped. *There's a man in there, stuck as a wolf forever.* Jones dragged himself to where he'd dropped the gun.

He put the gun under his chin and pulled the trigger without a moment's hesitation.

20

Knowles stood after several minutes had passed. His face was dirty, a combination of mud and blood but underneath it was still pale. Tears had created streaks in the dirt and his eyes were red rimmed. Claire's Browning was in his right hand, but he couldn't remember picking it up. He walked to Jack, stepping over the bodies. He didn't even look at Salmon's body. The man's head was at an unnatural angle, caused by the gaping hole in his neck. *So young.*

"We should go," Knowles said.

Jack was sitting on the floor with his back to the wall. His head was resting on his knees and blood was beginning to pool around his army issue boots. He looked up, with similar eyes to Knowles.

"Where? They will find me again," Jack said.

"I'm going," Knowles said. "You coming or are you going to sit there and feel sorry for yourself?"

Jack opened his mouth to complain, but ended up saying nothing. Instead he stood, unsteady on his feet for a second, and nodded at Knowles. "Let's get help."

"Well, my plan is just to get the hell away from here, then worry about what to do next."

"I'm sorry about-" Jack began.

Knowles whirled to face Jack. "Don't say her name. Just fucking don't."

Jack recoiled as Knowles turned back to the corridor. He was inching down it, Browning held in two hands in front of him. No sound came from the courtyard. Knowles exited the building first, scanning the courtyard with his gun.

Nothing was moving. The courtyard was like the floor of an abattoir. Bodies, limbs and chunks of red coated gore lay scattered, occasionally separated by craters. One of the small buildings was on fire, two others were ruined husks. The barracks seemed intact, although it was pock-marked with bullet holes. Naked human bodies and wolves spread before him like a carpet from Hell. Amongst the bodies, on the opposite side of the courtyard to where he stood, Knowles could see two uniforms.

Jones.

Starky.

Seeing the bodies was like a hammer blow to his gut. *Where the hell is Smith?* The courtyard was a mess. It seemed that not an inch of the area had been spared the gore. *Smith is here somewhere, mixed in with this lot.* The helicopters had been indiscriminate and wanton in their destruction. *Who gave this order?*

Knowles crossed the courtyard and reached Starky's corpse first. Whilst he had not seen eye to eye with the man, he would not have wished death on him. His skull looked like it had been licked clean. He looked at Jones next, and sank to the floor. The way he was holding the gun, the way his head was angled. *Oh, Jonesey, what did you do?*

Scarlet. Meyers. Carruthers. Jones.

It was an op in Devon – how exactly had this happened? He heard a crunch behind him, and spun, raising the weapon. Jack held his hands up, face pale.

"Motherfuckers," Knowles spat, aiming the gun at the spot between Jack's eyes. "He was right. None of this would have happened if it hadn't been for you."

Jack stared at the ground, hoping that by avoiding eye contact, Knowles' would calm down. He didn't speak as Knowles continued to rage.

"We went to Afghanistan. Iraq. They were my *friends*. What the fuck happened here? What the fuck are *you*, Jack, you piece of shit? Are you better than them? Better than my friends? Claire, you bastard, why the fuck did they kill her? She, she-"

Knowles stopped as a sob escaped his lips. He lowered the gun, but kept both hands wrapped around it. His finger had not moved from the trigger.

Jack continued to look at the ground, afraid to make eye contact. A piece of paper fluttered in the breeze and landed on Jones. Amongst all the destruction, the solitary piece looked wrong: pristine white but with four red smudges on the back. *Fingerprints. Someone has held that and thrown it away.* The paper flipped over and he saw the thumb print on the other side. He picked it up.

In the distance came the steady *thump thump* of the helicopters returning. Knowles turned the other body over, regarded Starky's horrified expression for a second then reached down and closed the dead man's eyes.

Knowles watched the helicopters approaching. They were slowing down, looking to land. "Don't move Jack, and put your hands up."

"Knowles." Jack's voice was too quiet over the increasing volume of the helicopters. He spoke again, louder this time.

"Shut up, Jack, just shut the fuck up." Knowles stood and started waving at the helicopters.

"Knowles!" Jack screamed.

Knowles turned to glare at him, raising the gun again. "Put your fucking hands up, I said."

Jack held up the piece of paper. "It's my address."

"Jack-"

"Why is it out here?" Jack's eyes were wild, full of desperation. "They know."

"What the fuck are you talking about?"

"They know where Katie and Josh are."

Chapter 29

1

"You're being a little paranoid," Knowles said.

"No," Jack insisted. "They know. This is the only piece of paper out here."

"Look at the mess. Anyone could have brought that out. Hell, the wind could've blown it out."

"I don't know," Jack said. "Maybe. But I'm worried, Knowles. Please. You have to help."

Knowles lowered the gun but his finger remained on the trigger. He was about to say more but the engine noise from the helicopters stopped him. Dust flew into the air as the helicopters started to land. Knowles turned, shielding his eyes to watch.

Soldiers jumped out of the helicopters, weapons ready. A perimeter rapidly formed and the helicopters took off again, circling the base. One of the soldiers stepped forward, weapon trained on Knowles with a tiny red dot in line with his heart, showing that his aim was true. Knowles raised his hands and glared at Jack until he did the same.

"Who is in charge?" the soldier demanded.

"Me, I guess," Knowles said. "Everyone else is either dead or missing."

"And you are?"

Knowles rattled off his name and number. The soldier repeated the info back into a radio then waited. Jack felt cold sweat drip down his back and he felt sick to the pit of his stomach. *Katie. Josh.* Every time he blinked he saw huge teeth biting down onto a tiny vulnerable neck.

"What happened here, Sergeant?"

"I'm going to need ID and clearance before I tell you that, mate."

2

It was all taking too long. Jack sat against one of the few intact buildings. Someone had given him a cup of tea, but it had gone cold before he thought to take a sip. He threw it away. The sick feeling in his stomach was getting worse. Knowles was deep in conversation with two men who had arrived in the second wave of helicopters. He seemed calmer now, the professional soldier taking over.

About half an hour after the helicopters had first turned up, three more had arrived. These had been chunkier, troop carrying machines. All three had held more troops than Jack had thought possible and now the base was crawling with men. The original two helicopters were out of sight now, scouring the landscape for any sign of the wolves.

Adrenaline had worn off ages ago leaving him weary, but Jack had lost all sense of time. It was getting dark, slowly but surely, which meant that if someone had started driving to Devon, they would probably be there by now.

Knowles saluted the two men, then came over to Jack.

"It's not every day you meet a general," he said. "They want you in custody."

"Custody? Knowles, please, Katie's in trouble."

"I told them that," Knowles said. "I also told them that you knew the wolves were coming here before we did. They're quite interested in that."

"Fuck them all Knowles, my wife is in trouble!" He only realised how loud he'd shouted when the General looked over at him. "You gave me your word. You said you'd get me home. Remember?"

Knowles nodded. "I did. I've got us a ride."

3

Stealing the car was easy. Steve and Anton had retrieved their clothes from the woods, ignoring the scent of other former clan members. They had stayed under cover of the trees when they heard helicopters overhead. Once fully dressed, they had started to hitch hike. Anton killed the first driver that stopped and they took the car. Driving to Devon took a long time, especially as they had stopped twice to change drivers and once to steal a different car.

Now, he sat in the dark in the garden of the house where Katie Stadler lived. He hadn't moved for nearly an hour, all his attention on the house. A light was on – he could see the faint glow through the kitchen window, although the kitchen itself was dark. The light was coming from under the door to what he presumed was the living room. They had a simple plan: wait for her to go to bed, more surprise that way, then kill her.

Or at least that had been the plan. Katie Stadler was a lot prettier than her picture made out. *Could have a bit of fun first. Maybe create a new mate. Could do with a pretty bitch to go with my new status as leader of this pack.* A tiny pack granted, bit *his* pack all the same.

Oh yes.

4

Steve didn't register the downstairs light going off at first. The darkness in the garden was absolute, but his eyes were so good that he took a moment to realise the golden glow had gone. An upstairs light snapped on.

It's time.

Steve stood up and walked slowly to the back door.

The dog started barking.

5

Katie climbed the stairs with heavy legs. Every limb felt lined with lead and her head sagged on her neck, causing her to stoop. *Please sleep through tonight.* She put the sleeping Josh into his cot. He gurgled once and she held her breath, afraid to move. He didn't make another sound. She relaxed and sank to the bed.

Even though she knew it was a mistake, she put her head on the pillow and closed her eyes. Her mind started whirling with all the things she hadn't done that day. *When did you last do the hoovering? The dishes from breakfast are still on the side. Ginny hasn't had a walk today.*

On cue, Ginny started barking and her eyes snapped back open.

Don't wake him. Please, Ginny, shut up! Bloody dog. She didn't stop barking; if anything her barks were getting louder and louder. That meant only one thing: someone was at the door.

6

Steve kicked the back door as hard as he could, and felt his leg change as he connected with the wood. The door burst off its hinges, flying across the kitchen. *Cool.* He grinned. *So Callum's not the only one who can do that now.* His pride in his own achievement passed quickly as a dog leapt at him.

He caught it in mid-air, snapped its neck and tossed it aside, like a child throwing away an old toy. The dog yelped once, then was still. He heard a crash from the front of the house and knew that Anton was in.

He ran through the kitchen and dining room and met Anton at the bottom of the stairs. Anton was in wolf form already, so Steve stripped off quickly and changed – completely this time.

Both wolves growled at the same time and started up the stairs.

7

The helicopter ride was fast. The ground blurred beneath them. Jack clung onto his harness, knuckles white. His hands and feet were bound tightly, wrists in handcuffs and legs in manacles. A thick chain ran between the bindings of both. Five men sat around him, three opposite all holding guns and two next to him holding pistols. Jack knew the handguns were loaded with the tranquiliser dart from the base.

Knowles sat next to the pilot and wasn't talking to Jack. He had shown the team an aerial view of the house and pointed out various locations around it. Jack hadn't listened, but he knew that they were tactical positions to cover the whole house. Then he had spoken to the pilot, giving him a grid reference. Knowles did not speak again for the rest of the journey.

Suddenly the engines changed pitch and the world outside tipped onto its side. Vertigo came and went as the helicopter started to descend. It was very quiet, some sort of stealth mode, Jack assumed. They landed in a field, and Jack realised that it was the field he had first woken in all those weeks ago. *Frank's field, where I ate his sheep.*

As the wheels hit the grass, they all heard it, loud and clear in the still night.

A shotgun blast.

8

Katie heard Ginny's awful yelping noise and knew they'd come back.

The wolves are here.

Josh was still asleep as she crossed to the wardrobe and opened the doors. She took out the shotgun and went to the door. She opened it a crack and saw two wolves moving on the stairs.

A low growl came from the front one and the threat it contained seemed to be a physical presence between them. Its teeth were very white in the dark and its eyes shone a terrifying yellow.

She raised the shotgun to her shoulder, holding it tight the way Frank had shown her, and fired once. The wolf's head erupted in a mess of dark blood and white bone. A thicker mass of flesh splattered onto the wall behind it.

Its brains. I just blew its brains out.

The other one paused for only a second. It opened its mouth wider and snarled. She aimed and fired again, but it jumped forward. The shot spread into the wall, plaster exploded showering the hall with dust. Katie screamed and slammed the bedroom door shut.

She scuttled backward across the bedroom floor until her back hit the cot. Josh suddenly cried out, making her jump. She lifted him out of the cot and sank back to the floor, tears streaming down her face. *The cartridges are downstairs. Why did I leave the cartridges downstairs?*

She held the shotgun like a club in one hand and her son in the other.

The wolf nudged the door open with its nose.

9

The helicopter had only just touched the ground when the men moved. They jumped out, spreading out around the machine with weapons ready. Knowles leapt out into the middle of the semicircle they had created.

"Move now, tactical positions, go." Two men stood and sprinted across the field, heading for the gate barely visible in the gloom. "You," Knowles pointed at two of the men, one with a rifle, the other with a pistol, "watch him."

Knowles started to run across the field, heading to the neighbour's lower hedge. Another shotgun blast ricocheted around the buildings. Jack snapped his harness in standing up so quickly. He jumped out of the helicopter, as the two men turned to face him. It had not yet been a full second since Knowles had spoken and Jack caught them by surprise. He swung his chained hands and caught the first man in the side of his head. The man grunted and staggered into his colleague. Jack's limbs changed and the chains shattered as the Wolf burst out of him.

"Holy fuck," said the pilot. The two men Jack had pushed stared open mouthed, weapons dangling impotently by their sides. The Wolf sprinted past Knowles and leapt at the thick hedge leading to the Stadlers' house. It left a large hole in its wake, but did not break his stride. "Get after it!" Knowles roared. He looked back at his men, seeing their expressions and swearing. *I am the only person alive who has seen that happen before.*

Knowles jumped through the hole, followed closely by one of the rifleman. He sprinted towards the house, seeing the Wolf push itself through the back door. *This is bad, really bad.*

10

The Wolf was instantly assailed by familiar scents. Images of a woman and a baby filled its mind. Happy scenes, mostly filled with the woman smiling at it. One memory overrode all others: a baby boy gurgling. Other smells hit it then, still familiar, but these were wolf scents. The Wolf snarled and ran through the house, following the trail.

11

A wolf was nosing open the bedroom door. Katie could see its snout and teeth, could see the eyes full of hate. She pushed herself further into the corner of the bedroom, trying to force herself into the walls themselves. Josh was clutched tight to her breast, wailing a plaintive cry. She tried to shield him but knew it was futile. Tears streamed down her face as she tried to quieten him.

The wolf snarled before opening its mouth and roaring. Suddenly another wolf hit it from behind. They skidded across the bedroom floor, smashing into the chest of drawers next to Katie. The new wolf was enormous, nearly double the size of the first, and there was something horribly, deadly familiar about it.

She screamed as the wolves fought. They rolled into the cot, crushing it and sending pieces of wood flying through the air. Katie felt splinters embed themselves in her face, which galvanised her into action. She ran for the door as the larger wolf rolled the other onto its back. She heard bones cracking, and a cry of pain.

Ginny had once impaled herself on a stick by jumping into a pool of muddy water. Her cries then were similar to these. She heard more whimpers and cries, followed by a large crack and then silence.

At the bottom of the stairs was a man with a gun. He was yelling at her.

She turned back to the wolves. The larger wolf had bitten through most of the neck of the other. It sat on its haunches, holding the dead wolf limply, like a dog with a rabbit.

The large wolf didn't move. She stared at it, looking straight into its eyes. Josh had stopped crying and was also staring at the wolf with wide eyes. He gurgled, a noise she had always associated with a laugh. The wolf dropped the corpse and padded over to her. It sniffed her, huge muzzle filling her vision.

She didn't acknowledge the man behind her with the gun; she couldn't take her eyes off the wolf. Memories of the hospital filled her mind. It seemed to be staring at her. Its head angled to one side and its gaze shifted. She realised it was now looking at Josh. She hugged him tighter to her, but he craned his head round to return the wolf's stare. His mouth was open in a perfect O. The wolf's head shifted again until it was staring at her. She started to shake and silent tears coursed down her face.

"Mrs Stadler," the man with the gun said. "I'm Sergeant Knowles, British Army. Please don't move."

The wolf snarled when the man spoke. Its teeth bared, saliva dripping from its enormous mouth. It looked at Katie again, then Josh and back to Knowles.

"Don't do anything stupid," Knowles said, but now Katie didn't know who he was talking to.

The wolf was looking around the room again. Its gaze settled on the corpse, Josh and Knowles in turn. Katie looked into its eyes again, unable to move. The wolf raised its head and unleashed a plaintive whine.

"Jack-" Knowles said, and winced.

"Jack?" Katie said, a touch of hysteria in her voice.

In two large bounds, the wolf jumped on the bed and then leapt at the window. It shattered, glass raining out into the street beyond. Knowles heard the familiar *pop* of rifles being fired and heard the wolf yelp.

He ran to the window, weapon ready but the wolf was nowhere to be seen.

"Shit," he said. *Now what am I going to do?*

Epilogue

The Wolf ran and ran. Pain throbbed in its side where the bullets had hit, but even that was already fading. It felt strength and power coursing through its limbs and it pushed on faster and faster. A deer broke from undergrowth and fled, terror clear in her scent. The Wolf ignored her. For now it wanted to just run and run until it could run no more.

Maybe then it would forget that it had once been a man.

Acknowledgments

Any novel is not written by just one person. The words might be, but the effort required needs the help and support of other people. So my thanks go to:

Tinú – for unswerving faith and support. Excellent editorial advice, even if I didn't always listen.

Pat – for technical answers, and not laughing too hard at the army bits in the first draft.

Frank at www.gfivedesign.co.uk for the lovely cover and Rowan Kendall-Torry for the slightly spooky photo that Frank used. Keep clicking, buddy!

Tim at www.undiscoveredwriters.com for being the first person to show an interest in this novel and all the lovely people who bought the book when it was only available there.

Nikki, Tin and Dad for proof reading and finding all the errors. Any that remain are my fault because I didn't pay them enough. Actually, I didn't pay them…

Josh & Ethan – just for being.

Mum & Dad – without them, literally, none of this would be possible!

Finally, if you enjoyed this book, feel free to connect with me online via twitter @joshfishkins. Don't forget to tell all your friends/family/random people you meet in the street about it!

Printed in Great Britain
by Amazon.co.uk, Ltd.,
Marston Gate.